Searching for Arthur

The Return to Camelot Trilogy
Book One

DONNA HOSIE

DEDICATION

For Steve, Emily, Daniel and Joshua, who gave me time
to pursue my dream.

CONTENTS

ACKNOWLEDGMENTS

With thanks to Suzie Forbes and Victoria Marini, who gave their time to make this better.

I am indebted to Mike Weinstein for his super keen eyes and attention to detail.

To those friends and writers who follow my blog: Musings of a Penniless Writer.

And Harry!

Searching for Arthur was inspired by Roger Lancelyn Green's *King Arthur and his Knights of the Round Table*, and many of the characters featured in this novel are taken directly from the myths and legends laid down through the centuries by writers and poets such as Sir Thomas Malory, Charles Williams, Dryden and Tennyson. A few knights, such as Sir Talan and Sir David, are my own invention. I would, in particular, like to point readers to the epilogue of *King Arthur and his Knights of the Round Table*, which is titled *Avalon*. There is a legend told in Gwynedd, Wales that King Arthur and his Knights of the Round Table are simply sleeping, waiting for the day when they will awaken to bring glory to Britain once more.

I thought it was about time they woke up!

1 ARE YOU ARTHUR?

Mr. Rochester was jumping through the long grass. It made me laugh because he looked like one of those newborn tigers that you see on nature programmes. Mr. Rochester was a floppy-eared baby rabbit, honey-yellow with large white patches of downy fur on his paws and belly. My brother, Arthur, had given him to me for my seventeenth birthday, two months earlier, and I had fallen in love with him instantly.

Mr. Rochester *had* slept in my room in a box lined with towels. My first mistake was taking the towels that nobody ever used. Stupid me thought they were old ones for mopping up any old mess, but apparently they were "special ones" for guests.

What guests? We never lived anywhere long enough for people to update their address books and actually find us.

My second mistake was using Mr. Rochester as an excuse to not go to the school dance: an event that everyone, apart from me, was obsessing about.

"He's a baby. He needs me here." I knew my mother was standing behind me in the garden, but I was intent on watching Mr. Rochester. He was trying to catch an orange butterfly that was almost as big as he was.

"I am not arguing with you, Natasha," said my mother coolly. "You will go to the dance and that is the end of it."

"But I don't want to go."

"How do you expect to make friends if you don't even try, Natasha? Look at your brother. He has lots of friends and a girlfriend already."

"Arthur can go to the dance then."

"You're going and that is the end of it. Now put that rabbit back in the cage, wash your hands, and come and try on the dresses Net-A-Porter just delivered. Other girls would be overjoyed to have their parents spend so much money on these things."

"I'm not going to the dance." There was no point in shouting. Being louder didn't make my mother hear me any better.

Mr. Rochester stopped chasing the butterfly and stood upright, like a periscope. He looked like he wanted a cuddle, and so I scooped him up and buried my face into his downy tummy. I could hear my mother's clicking tongue over the chirping insects.

"I'm sorry little guy. I'll be back soon, I promise."

I hated - absolutely hated - putting Mr. Rochester in the chickenless chicken coop, but I needed to get my mother off my back for a while. As soon as she was over me using her *special* towels, then he would be back in my room where he would be safe.

I kissed his little nose and he nibbled my chin, but his large black eyes looked sad, almost teary, when I placed him on the hay in the coop.

My mother was waiting in the kitchen. She had already placed the antibacterial soap dispenser on the table.

"Why can't you be more like your brother?"

There. She had said the magic words. The ones

guaranteed to piss me off. The ones that could make me disappear. *Poof.* Gone.

I've always been good at running. It's a skill that was inherited. My parents – the Foreign Office diplomat and the housewife – were professionals. They'd been running for years, although Arthur and I never knew what they were running from most of the time. It could have been job postings, terrorists, or even ghosts.

I liked to blame the entity, because the reality was they were probably trying to run from me.

My father refers to any disagreement that takes place as *an exchanging of words.* We can't use the term *fight* or *argument* because that would be too confrontational, and nothing gets tackled head on in this family.

Not really. Not anymore.

So, not for the first time in this wretched place, I was retreating. Running from my mother and her voice and then the silence that follows which is worse.

We lived on the edge of a forest. Perfect for escaping. Running through it though was difficult, even in sneakers, and being handicapped by stupid tears didn't help. The ground was uneven with fallen branches and ditches of decomposing vegetation.

I was not going to a stupid dance. I hated dancing. I hated my new school even more.

I could hear whispers as I ran. When I was ten years old, my parents forced me to see a child psychiatrist because I suffered nightmares about ghosts and being haunted. The psych told me that ghost stories were way worse than the reality of death because it was the fear of the unknown that was terrifying. It was one of the few things that she said that actually made sense. I do remember she smelt of cabbage and coffee. That was all I took away for 200 bucks an hour, but as I wasn't

3

paying, I didn't care.

But now the ghosts were back. They were trying to trap me amongst the trees instead of in my past. Creaking boughs were reaching down like thick arms; their spiny fingers clawing at my clothes, my hair, my soul.

I wanted to carry on running away from my mother and dancing and designer dresses, but sharp twigs had invaded my socks and scratched my skin. I noticed one tree that had long exposed roots snaking away from the trunk, like ribbons of tagliatelle. It looked like a good a place as any to sit down. I thought if I stretched back against the bark and closed my eyes, I would be able to fool myself into thinking I wasn't being haunted anymore.

The ground started rumbling the second I slotted in between the roots. I could feel the vibrations through my legs. It was like sitting on top of a washing machine. I knew the rumbling wasn't an earthquake because nothing above the earth was swaying except me.

The twigs in my socks could stay there. I wanted to start running again, and my sixth sense was telling me to get the hell out of there.

But my legs weren't quick enough, not this time. The leaves and dirt started to crumble away beneath my feet. I didn't have time to grab hold of anything as gravity claimed me, and I fell down, down, down through the thick, snaking roots.

The ghosts I had heard whispering became real.

He had no eyes. That was what I noticed first. He had a moustache as well. Not a moustache like Hitler's. This ghost had a long thin moustache that blended into his beard, like an anorexic Father Christmas. His hair was fine, almost dusty, like the mane on a white stallion. If I had touched it, it would have crumbled. His whole body would have disintegrated into ash, and the strands of his hair would have flown away on the wind as if they were never there.

But he *was* there. And there were others too. I counted at least six bodies in the darkness, all lying in state, too exhausted and old to move.

Waiting. Biding their time.

Because they were solid, I wasn't scared. Not for the first few seconds anyway. It's hard to be frightened of something that is so ancient the air itself becomes powerful enough to destroy it. For a brief moment I thought it was a game, a bizarre enactment. So why were the strange people in their strange clothes underground and not out in the open?

Then I heard a guttural noise, like the moaning you would expect from someone who had forgotten how to speak. I went back to the eyes, or rather the gaping black holes in his heavily creased face.

"Are you Arthur?"

The ancient soul groaned out the words as if he was in pain. Dazed and disorientated, I said nothing at first. My forehead had connected with something solid. It was cold stone, like roughly textured pumice used to scrape dead skin off your heels when you have a pedicure.

"Are you Arthur?" he groaned again. The sound echoed around the earth-made sepulchre, magnifying as it bounced off the dirt in deep waves.

My next thought: why did he want my brother?

The thought after that: I'm in a hole with a person with no eyes.

That was when the screaming started.

I knew from the throbbing pain in my head that I was conscious. Then I noticed the blood on my hands. With my feet, legs and hands failing to coordinate, I scrambled in the dirt on my arse and threw myself into the curved lumpy wall of the pit.

I was in a grave. I started screaming again.

"Are you Arthur?"

The ancient man still hadn't moved from his sentry position in front of the other prostrate figures. This wasn't a game or bizarre enactment. Between two cadaverous hands he clutched a sword, which was pointing down into the powdery earth.

Yet he looked frail, fragile. I doubted he had the strength to pick up the sword, let alone strike me down with it. Then another voice spoke. It was familiar. It was mine.

Do you think it has super-human strength? it asked.

"I don't know," I whispered back, still afraid the un-seeing man was about to skewer me like a kebab.

Then presume it doesn't. Now look around. Is there a way out?

Orange coloured dust swirled in the claustrophobic space. I could see it through a thin shaft of light that had penetrated the roots of the tree that had swallowed me whole. The back of the tomb was dark, and I was in no hurry to find out what was there. An entire army of warriors could have been waiting to feast on my tender – slightly spotty – flesh for all I knew.

"Are you Arthur?"

For the fourth time, he spoke those words. But I noticed something different in his voice as he choked out the question. He wasn't demanding or even asking anymore. The ancient warrior was pleading.

Be careful how you answer, warned my inner voice. *You don't know whether he means your Arthur or someone completely different. Friend or foe right now is all that is keeping that sword from connecting with your neck. One swipe and your head will be getting an extreme close-up of your Converse All Stars.*

"I thought you said to presume it doesn't have super-human strength," I hissed back.

Why are you listening to me? replied my inner voice. *I'm not the crazy chick having a conversation with herself, fool.*

And with that, my inner voice abandoned me to my fate and certain decapitation.

Then the person shuffled forward. It was only one step, but it caused him enough pain to make his eyeless face grimace. The edge of his filthy cloak swept along the dirty ground like a brush, catching mounds of brown earth and the sun dried leaves that had fallen down with me.

"I'm not Arthur," I said quickly, pre-empting the question from the crumbling, blind watchman, "but he's up there, and he'll be coming for me, so you had better stay away or…or…he'll kick your ass," I added with brave optimism, pointing towards the shaft of sun.

He sighed long and slow, like the sound of air being released from a blow up mattress. How could anything exist in this world that was so old? Was he a zombie? He didn't look like a creature of the night. Why didn't I pay more attention during horror movies?

"He will come," sighed the warrior. The cracked edges of his thin mouth started to rise. It would have been optimistic to call it a smile, but it was an attempt. His entire being was now surrounded by light. I could see the dirt particles whizzing around him at electrifying speed. The dust had wings.

"Yeah, he *will* come," I shouted back. My voice was defiant in my head, but it came out as a squeak. "My brother isn't scared of anything or anyone, and when he realises I am missing, he will move heaven and earth to find me. Plus he's a third degree black belt in Taekwondo, and can break wood with his head."

This bold - and rather exaggerated - statement appeared to placate the ancient warrior. He took two steps away from me and went back into the shadows.

I seized my chance. I leapt to my feet, and with a running jump, I grabbed hold of the thickest tree roots I could see. Ignoring the stinging pain in my hands, I climbed up, kicking hard as I went.

With the grace of a bull elephant, I made it up and out into safety. The tree that had betrayed me earlier and sent me falling into the abyss, swayed in the autumn wind. Its creaking boughs were laughing.

I vomited over its trunk. Adrenaline was pumping through my veins like acid. I stumbled forward, tripping over everything that appeared in my path.

I would deal with the accusing silence from my mother with my own taciturnity. Right now, I needed to run back to our house. I needed to do my homework. I needed to feed Mr. Rochester.

I needed to put as much distance between myself and rotting zombies with swords as was humanly possible.

I fell through the trees, and rolled several feet into a ditch. It hadn't rained for weeks, and yet a thick sludgy layer of black mud lined the bottom. My skinny white jeans were no longer white. Looking like the stuff of nightmares, bloodied, battered and now filthy, I scrambled up the other side and into the road. I fell to my knees, and clawed at the loose gravel as I attempted to control my breathing. My heart was pounding against my ribcage.

Silence. Deathly silence surrounded me. My senses went into overdrive as I waited on my knees for the sound of the wood floor to snap, for the voice of the lost to ask once again, "Are you Arthur?"

But there was nothing, and that was just as unnerving. Complete silence isn't natural. Where were the birds? Where was the scratching and scuttling of forest animals? Why, for the first time in months, was I not being bitten to death by insects?

Then the growling started. It was low-pitched, but

distant, like a waking bear yawning in a cave.

Be sensible. You live in Britain now. There are no bears here.

"So you're back are you?" I snapped at my inner voice. "Thanks a million for running away back there."

I was the one who got you out, moron. Now calm down and listen.

The growling noise was getting closer. The road beneath my fingers and knees started to vibrate. There was only one thing on earth that could make that much noise and cause the ground to shake.

"Arthur," I cried, as I staggered to my feet and ran in the direction of the rumbling. Running really was *my* sport, and I was good at it. It didn't matter whether it was long distance, short distance, or the distance required to escape from zombies with no eyes – I could own it every time.

A battered white car, held together by long streaks of red rust and black masking tape, drew level and then stopped. The driver's door flew open, and out jumped a tall male with loping limbs that were way too long for his body. His sun-streaked blonde hair reached the back of his neck, and had been layered in such a way it looked as if a blind hairdresser had attacked him with blunt shears. A few freckles dotted his oval face, mostly grouped together around his suntanned nose, and his eyes were a blinding blue colour.

"What the…" swore Arthur.

"Warriors-old-men-with-swords!" I screamed in one continuous sentence as I fell into his arms. "I-fell-in-a-hole-a-grave-he-had-a-sword-thought-he-would-chop-my-head-off…"

"Titch, calm down," said my brother, pushing my filthy body away from his clean white t-shirt. He held onto my forearms while he scanned my injuries, making a *tutting* noise with his tongue - similar to our dear mother - as he shook his head.

"no-eyes-NO-EYES…"

"Titch, you know you are screeching so high only dogs can understand you now," said Arthur, slipping an arm around my waist. "Come on. I'll get you home and then we'll survey the damage once you're clean. You may need stitches in your head, you klutz."

It was only when Arthur mentioned it, that I realised the wet stuff dripping down my face wasn't sludgy mud. It was blood.

Arthur said later that was the moment I fainted.

I could feel hands on my ankles. I yelped in fear of the ghosts, and threw myself forward towards the blurred figure in my peripheral vision.

"Titch, Titch, it's alright," cried a familiar voice. "You're safe now."

A thin beam of light shone directly overhead. I became aware of the burning smell of bleach and antiseptic in my nostrils. Bile rose in my throat; I twitched dramatically.

"Do you think she's brain-damaged?" said another voice: a simpering high-pitched Welsh accent.

"SSSSSSSSSSSSSSSSS."

"Why is she hissing?" said the female.

"Because she's awake," replied Arthur, and I felt him slap my hand.

"Be nice," he whispered in my ear, "she's been really worried."

I couldn't believe that my brother had brought his girlfriend to my hospital bed. I could have been dying or worse, but no, even *then* Arthur would have needed a crowbar to part him from Slurpy Sammy. When she sees me, she starts kissing Arthur like he has turned into an ice cream. A big dollop of vanilla ice-cream. It's why I came up with the nickname, although I always shorten it to SS when my brother is around. I use the initials because I don't like to hurt Arthur's feelings. Her full name is Samantha Scholes-Morgan, although she likes to be called Sammy because she thinks it's cute.

Rabbits or hamsters called Sammy are cute. Slurpy Sammy with the hyphenated surname is one of the undead.

I knew I would have to open my eyes eventually. When I did, I saw that I was lying in a hospital bed with a drip in my arm.

"How's your head?" asked Arthur. He was wearing a different t-shirt from the one he had been wearing earlier.

"Still attached to my neck, I hope," I groaned. My throat was dry and sore.

"The docs will be back in a minute. They said you'll have to stay in tonight. You have concussion apparently." Arthur's fingers were now wrapped around my pinkie, squeezing it tightly.

Where was my mother? I wanted to know why she wasn't there. We had *exchanged words*, I know, but she wouldn't really stay home while I was hurt, while her kid was in the hospital? I mean, she's had the practice....No. That wasn't how it worked in our family anymore. I was still being punished.

So I didn't ask why she wasn't there. There was no point.

I glanced over towards Slurpy. She didn't look worried at all. She was helping herself to green grapes that had been left on a sliding tray at the bottom of the hospital bed. Her heavily made up eyes were glued to a ceiling mounted television set.

"I'm gonna get the docs," said Arthur. "They should at least know you're awake."

The second he was out of the room, Slurpy's eyes

left the television screen and fixed on me.

"You do it on purpose, don't you?" she said accusingly in her thick Welsh accent.

"I have no idea what you're talking about."

"Arthur was taking me shopping. He promised to buy me a ring."

"So what? Is the world suddenly expecting a ring shortage in the next 24 hours?"

"You do it on purpose, you little freak. Always wanting to be the centre of attention."

Slurpy had a special way of saying *freak*. All of her friends did; I heard it often enough. It was the Welsh accent that did it, with extra emphasis on the letter r which rolled off her tongue. It made the word last longer.

"You really are a total loser, Natasha. It's pathetic the way you cling to your brother. Why can't you hate him, like a normal sister? I would rather die than be near my brother – but then Arthur is too good to you, you attention seeking freak."

There was no point wasting oxygen in replying. If there was a competition to find Britain's Next Top Hermit, I would win hands down. I detested being the centre of anyone's attention, even my brother's.

"You know what they call you at school?" continued Slurpy viciously; she cackled like a witch.

I knew what they called me. It didn't bother me, despite the lump now forming in my throat.

Arthur walked back into the room. Slurpy went back to watching the television and shovelling grapes into her enormous mouth.

"Did you tell anyone about the person with no eyes?" I whispered, hoping beyond hope that he hadn't. "Or the grave, the hole I fell into?"

Arthur kept his lips tightly sealed but still spread them out into a knowing smirk-like smile.

"It's bad enough that I have the world's biggest klutz

for a little sister," he whispered back, "without everyone thinking she is also the biggest mental-case in the village as well."

"But you believe me?" I whimpered.

My brother smiled again, this time showing his perfectly straight – and very expensive – top teeth.

"Yeah, I believe you, Titch," he whispered, "but we know from experience that most people don't."

Five days later, Arthur was gone.

2 AVALON COTTAGE

The painkillers helped me sleep a little, but it wasn't restful. My head – which had required six stitches – throbbed continuously, and my scratched hands were stinging. Afraid of the dark, I left the lights on around my bed. A well-meaning nurse kept coming in to turn them down once I had dozed off. The slightest movement woke me, and that only meant I had to put the lights back on again.

This nurse and mouse game ended at daybreak, and by the time my mother and Arthur came back to collect me, I was beyond exhausted. If Arthur hadn't placed an arm around my back and gently nudged me forward, I would have slept where I stood.

They arrived in mother's car: a gleaming black BMW which smelt of leather and pine air freshener. I definitely saw her flinch when I climbed into the back seat. While she and Arthur had brought me a fresh change of clothes: black leggings and a long blue and white striped sweater, neither had thought to replace my Converse sneakers. They were still caked in mud and dirt and microscopic pieces of ancient flaking brains. All of which transferred onto the black carpet of the prized

BMW.

I hadn't told my mother the gruesome details of the previous day's adventure. I wasn't stupid. My mother believed what she wanted to hear, not necessarily the truth. So I told her I had fallen. The *exchange of words* that led to it remained the elephant in the hospital room that nobody wanted to mention.

Falling while running was the basic truth, and so I didn't feel too guilty.

At least I wasn't lying.

We arrived back at the cottage we had been renting for several months. It wasn't home, although Arthur called it that. I knew he was trying to cheer me up, but I really had had enough of being uprooted. I just didn't think it was normal to have lived in more houses than years I had been alive. I had just turned seventeen, and *Avalon Cottage*, with its little windows and overgrown garden, was the eighteenth place I had lived in. Even hermit crabs didn't change shells that often. My parents said the hotel in Bangkok or the serviced Government apartments in New York didn't count, but as my clothes were hanging in closets, and I was forced to attend school lessons, I thought they did.

Nobody, other than Arthur, understood how hard this was. It wasn't a matter of geography. My life had become a battle with words. In the US, you order fries and you get fries. In Britain, they are called chips. I get used to calling them chips, move back to the US, order chips and end up with what the British call crisps.

I couldn't even eat anymore without getting confused.

My father worked as a diplomat: Foreign Affairs. When people asked me what he did, I replied that he took up the crap that nobody else wanted to do. It was the only way I could explain the constant moving, the running, often with no notice.

It wouldn't matter anymore if there *was* notice. It wasn't as if I bothered to make friends. I would watch other girls at other schools, clinging like limpets to one another when it was their turn to leave. A small part of me was jealous at the attention, but once the tears had dried, those left behind carried on as normal. The person who had left was a ghostly imprint, a name on a Facebook page, but nothing more.

But I never forgot them, even if they never gave me a second thought. You can't forget those who have gone – no matter how hard you try.

Flowers from my father were on the kitchen table: red roses, at least thirty of them. I tried to be cool, but I know I smiled because my head thumped as my jaw muscles stretched.

"Your father will call later, Natasha," said my mother, placing her burnt orange Birkin handbag – an *I'm-sorry-I'm-never-there* present from my father – on the kitchen dresser. "I have a luncheon, but I can cancel if you want me to stay and look after you."

We looked at each other. It was my turn to play at diplomatic relations.

"I'll be okay, Arthur will be here."

If she had hugged me, I would have let her.

My mother nodded instead, and called out to my brother who had run upstairs in search of his cell phone. I didn't wait to hear what she intended to tell him. My hand was already sliding back the thick cast-iron bolt that secured the back door. I hadn't seen Mr. Rochester for over twenty four hours, and I was worried about him. I wanted to cuddle his little body. I wanted to let him know that it wouldn't be long before he could come back to where he was safe.

After being thrown out of the box in my bedroom,

Mr. Rochester was put at the bottom of the garden in a large two storey chicken coop. There *had* been chickens, but my mother got rid of them within a week of our arrival. My father was living in London, and we were all supposed to live there – for the third time in six years – but my mother had become paranoid about terrorists and she refused to live in the capital, or anywhere even remotely resembling civilisation. So my mother, Arthur and I all decamped to Wales and some unpronounceable village in the middle of nowhere.

Terrorists don't bother attacking nowhere you see.

Everything that my mother thought charming and quaint about *Avalon Cottage* soon started to drive her insane. The untamed garden, with its climbing roses and thick vines of ivy, was too much work to maintain. The small lead-latticed windows never let in the light. The gravel track that led to the house was chipping away every scrap of paint from the BMW, and pity any person who got her started about the plumbing, electrics and the fact there wasn't a decent manicurist this side of the English border.

Terrorists didn't come to nowhere, and neither did a decent hairdresser, apparently.

I wasn't entirely sure what my mother did with the chickens. We didn't eat them because we were all vegetarians. Me, through choice; Arthur, because he lived off peanut butter and jelly sandwiches; and my mother hadn't eaten in nine years.

Not since *it* happened.

I made my way into the garden. Overnight, small rings of wild mushrooms had dotted the long grass. Legends would say the fairies had been playing. A rotting trellis had fallen down beside one of the huge oak trees that stood in our garden. Several spiders had already made themselves at home in the diamond shaped holes. Silence had returned again, but as I walked past the trees, I heard whispers.

It's just your over-active imagination, said my inner voice. *The wind is blowing through the leaves, that's all.*

But the whispers grew louder. I stopped and looked behind me. The temperature had plummeted. My chest tightened; I could barely breathe. My heart was beating like a bass drum.

The whispers continued. They were low pitched, definitely male. The voices multiplied. There were dozens of them.

You've hit your head, and you are pumped with painkillers. Calm down. It's just the wind.

"Arrrrrrttttthhhhhuuuurrrrr."

The whispers echoed all around me, groaning in the boughs of the trees, the overgrown stems of grass. The elongated vowels filtered through the spider webs, causing them to shudder with fright.

I still hadn't reached the chicken coop and my baby rabbit. Out of sight, out of mind was my mother's mantra. Mr. Rochester was alone, hidden behind laurel and holly bushes. It wasn't right. He was only a baby.

It was so cold. The hairs on my arms rose like the dead. I felt them pushing up the thin fabric of my cotton sweater.

"Arrrrrrttttthhhhhuuuurrrrr."

Tears of terror were pooling in my eyelids. Sickened with shame, I turned and ran back to the house, slipping on the chipped stone steps as I fled. Arthur was already standing at the bottom of the narrow staircase, as I flew through the kitchen and into the hallway.

Screaming was becoming a habit.

"Titch, what the hell is the matter? Was that you calling my name?"

I was crying so hard, snot was running down my

face. Arthur didn't flinch. He just grabbed me and pulled me in, like he always did when I was in trouble.

"Calm down, Titch. Listen, do you need something to help you sleep?"

I knew what he meant and I shook my head, wiping my gloopy face over his t-shirt in the process.

"I heard voices again," I sobbed.

Arthur sighed.

"That's it. You're going to bed right now, Natasha."

"Don't *you* call me that," I sniffed, as he propelled me up the creaking stairs.

"Then do as you're told," warned my brother, stabbing me in the back with his fingers. "If I skip anymore school because of you, I'll be getting my qualifications when I'm thirty at this rate."

Avalon Cottage had three bedrooms: two decent sized rooms that you could actually fit a bed in, and then the box room which was mine. I would like to say that we at least drew straws for the rooms, but that would be a lie, and I don't lie anymore. Understandably, my mother took the largest room overlooking the front of the house, while Arthur – in a display of testosterone driven selfishness – stole the other bedroom. My box room – it must have been illegal to describe it as a bedroom – was squeezed in at the far end, next to Arthur's and opposite the bathroom. It was north facing, cold and damp, regardless of the weather.

Mrs. Pratchett, who ran the village shop, had taken great delight in telling me that three of the four seasons in the middle of nowhere were usually cold and damp.

I fell down onto my soft bed and curled my legs up. Arthur drew the curtains across my tiny little window, and pulled a patchwork blanket up over my knees.

"Sammy is coming over later," he whispered, "but I won't take her out until mum arrives back. Just yell if you need me, Titch."

"Arthur."

"What?"

"Can you go and check on Mr. Rochester?"

"Will do."

"And Arthur…"

"What now, Titch?"

"Take a poker from the fireplace with you, just in case."

Arthur laughed.

"Has Mr. Rochester gone rabid on us?"

"It's not Mr. Rochester you should be afraid of," I whispered. "The voices were calling your name. It's you they want."

My chilly, damp bedroom seemed even colder than usual.

"It was just the wind, Titch, plus the ridiculous amount of painkillers you've swallowed."

"You heard them, Arthur."

I heard him inhale because it was sharp: a short reflex sniff through his nose.

"I'll check on Mr. Rochester, and then bring you up some vegetable soup or something," he said. "Now don't get out of that bed. I don't care if a whole platoon of soldiers with swords starts marching up the garden. You stay put, do you understand?"

Boys don't scream like girls, yet Arthur's cry was so high, it could have been mistaken for one. He stopped me from running further than the fallen trellis, and once I knew why I was grateful. My heart would have broken into a thousand pieces if I had seen him.

The police blamed the attack on a group of local feral kids, but I knew they were wrong. The local animal shelter said my baby rabbit was probably gutted with a large knife, but I only saw the pointed end of a sword.

One that I had seen before.

We buried my beautiful baby rabbit far away from *Avalon Cottage*. Arthur, Slurpy and I walked for hours to find a pretty little spot where we could bury him. Arthur wanted to dig a hole near a clear blue stream, but I couldn't bear the thought of Mr. Rochester lying forever near water. It wasn't safe, and Arthur, of all people, should have known that. So instead we put Mr. Rochester to rest in a shoe box, containing fresh straw and chocolate drops, underneath some wild roses. I didn't want Slurpy there, but as I had no friends, I had no choice. Mr. Rochester deserved more than just me and Arthur at his funeral.

Two days later, and Arthur knocked on my bedroom door. He had soup.

"I need to tell you something, Titch."

I sat up and put the book I hadn't been reading on my bedside table. My fingers nudged the only photo of Mr. Rochester that I had. I had been holding the camera, so I wasn't even in it – Arthur was.

Twisting his fingers around the cup of soup, Arthur sat on the edge of my bed. He looked really tense; he was chewing on his tongue, and his blue eyes were fixed firmly on floating bits of carrot.

"What is it?"

"It's about Mr. Rochester."

I sat up a little straighter. "What is it?"

"You aren't going to like it. Mum and dad don't even want me to tell you."

That just made me want to hear whatever it was even more. I wasn't a child.

"What is it, Arthur?"

Arthur was gulping. He knew what to say, he just didn't know how to say it.

"There's a reason I put Mr. Rochester in the box, Titch. I didn't want you to see him."

Of course I hadn't wanted to see him. He had been

sliced open. My baby had been gutted and...no, even thinking about it made me want to puke. Why was Arthur doing this to me?

"Whoever killed him didn't just stab him, Titch." Arthur looked close to tears.

"What else did they do?" My voice was barely a whisper.

My brother put the soup on the carpet and hugged me. I think it was because he couldn't face looking at me.

"They took his eyes, Titch. Whoever killed him gouged out his eyes as well."

3 STARLIGHT

Three days after we had buried Mr. Rochester and I was still reeling. Slurpy didn't seem to care. Her giggling, the moaning, and the creaking of Arthur's brass bed shook every inch of the cottage. Even a pillow over my ears failed to smother the noise. The nasty part of me, the one that we all possess but keep hidden most of the time, wanted to place the pillow over SS's face. That would shut her up.

The idea for her SS nickname came to me one day when I was reading a book about Adolf Hitler and the Nazis. His organisation was called the Schutzsstaffel. That's where the abbreviation SS comes from. History is for people who care enough to remember, or those who simply can't forget. People like me.

So I was trapped in the house. I couldn't run outside because the autumn skies had blackened the day after Mr. Rochester's funeral and the rain started.

The darkness matched my guilt.

Even my mother had shed a couple of tears for Mr. Rochester. Then she got on the phone to my father – who was in Brussels – and her crocodile tears were

23

matched by the gnashing of teeth.

"This place is feral. We cannot live here."

I couldn't hear my father. I didn't want to hear my mother.

"That is not a choice, Luther. I do not want to live in London. You are asking me to choose between terrorists with bombs or terrorists with knives."

Silence, apart from the sound of my mother twisting the cap from a bottle of pills.

"Luther, you need to come home. I cannot deal with this by myself."

More silence, apart from the clinking of a crystal glass as the pills were washed down with something I would bet on my life wasn't water.

"Arthur is fine, of course Arthur is fine. It's Natasha. You know what she's like. She just won't make any effort."

The stairs creaked as I shifted my butt cheeks, but the noise from Arthur's room couldn't have been drowned out by anything quieter than a jump jet. I couldn't believe that after everything that had happened, my mother was still pissed about a stupid school dance. I really needed to go into the kitchen to get my homework, but I couldn't face my mother, and so I had no choice but to wait until she had finished speaking to my father.

Eventually she went to lie down in her bedroom. She said she had a migraine. Clearly the slurps from Arthur and SS didn't bother her. It was three o'clock in the afternoon. A Sunday. The 20th September and a new school week was approaching. As if to prove the point, a large pile of English homework was on the kitchen table, mocking me.

But I couldn't drag my eyes away from the back garden. The rain lashed against the small leaded windows. Large red leaves streamed down from the trees, like enormous droplets of blood. The wind was frenzied in its assault of the garden, relentlessly whipping branches and stems back and forth, back and forth. It was hypnotic. The teak-stained garden chairs were already lost to the storm. In the distance I saw the spindly legs of one, poking out from under a bush like the Wicked Witch of the East after Dorothy's house has landed on her.

Only the ghosts knew where the other three chairs had landed.

My ears were waiting for the sound of whispers, but above the combined noise of Arthur's bed and the weather outside, they would have been impossible to hear unless they were breathing in my ear.

I knew the ghosts were there though. I could sense them.

Waiting. Biding their time.

My thoughts drifted to Mr. Rochester, and a surge of white hot anger rose from my stomach where it spiked in my mouth. It tasted bitter. He was only a floppy-eared baby. Barely two months in my possession and he was gone, stolen from me in the most brutal of ways. It was murder and someone needed to pay. I shouldn't have run from the voices. I could – I should – have saved him.

"Where are you?" I whispered through gritted teeth. "Where are you, you cowards?"

I looked down. In my right hand was a large kitchen knife. I couldn't remember reaching for it, but my fingers were clasped so tightly around the silver metal handle that the tips of my blunt nails were turning white.

"Titch, what the hell are you doing?" cried a voice behind me.

I pirouetted on the spot. Arthur and Slurpy were standing at the kitchen door, their faces frozen in horror.

Without replying, I slipped the knife back into the large wooden block on the kitchen worktop as my rage dissolved into embarrassment.

My eyes went back to the garden, but I knew my brother and his girlfriend were still behind me because I could hear them breathing: short and shallow. I had frightened them.

You do realise how that looked, said my inner voice, as my stitched head throbbed. *Arthur and Sammy walk in and find you holding a kitchen knife, just a few days after your rabbit has been filleted. Could you appear more psycho?*

"It wasn't me," I said.

"No one said it was," said Arthur, slowly walking up to me, "but you gave us a scare there, Titch. Some people shouldn't hold sharp objects, and you are one of them."

I looked at him with as much disgust as I could gather, but I'm not a very good actress. I probably looked constipated.

"Shock, horror, Natasha is in the kitchen with a knife in her hand. Call the police, the Foreign Office, the FBI, call our bloody mother, because clearly the world is about to implode."

"Don't get snarkey with me. I am better at it than you, little sister."

"You don't need to remind me, big brother. I've been told for seventeen years that you are better than me at everything."

We stood there on the cold limestone tiles, eyeballing each other. Then the corners of Arthur's lips – which were miraculously still in place despite Slurpy's best efforts to remove them – started to twitch.

I thumped him. Hard.

"Don't laugh at me, Arthur."

"I'm not laughing *at* you, Titch," he replied. "It's just when you are angry, that big vein on your forehead starts to vibrate. It looks funny, that's all."

I moved my hand up to my forehead and rubbed at it. Arthur was right. It felt like I had a long strand of cooked spaghetti above my left eyebrow.

"I'm stressed out."

"Do your homework then," replied Arthur sarcastically, walking over to the fridge. He grabbed two cans of soda from the top shelf and threw one to Slurpy. He didn't bother passing one to me.

"There's no point. I'm not going into school tomorrow."

"Why?"

"Because I can't concentrate on anything. I may as well go mad here at home where people can't see me."

"Titch…"

"Arthur, can you drive me home now?" interrupted Slurpy, with a nasal whine.

"Just a second, Sammy," replied Arthur, finally passing me a soda can. I opened it and sprayed frothy coke all over my newly washed, white skinny jeans. "Look, Titch, leave the homework for a couple of hours, and come for a drive with us. The fresh air might help clear that banged-up head of yours. Plus I could do with the company on the way back. If the car breaks down, you can get out and push."

My brother: the chivalrous knight, but I didn't have the energy to argue anymore. I nodded pathetically and reached for my short leather jacket, hanging on a hook by the back door. My eyes wandered to the back garden again, just in time to see the fallen trellis fly through the air.

And then I saw him.

My stomach fell into my shoes and then bounced up into my mouth. I was going to hurl or scream.

I decided to run.

Within seconds I was drenched, as I threw back the

door bolt and launched myself into the rain and tornado-like wind.

"What is she doing?" screamed Slurpy.

"Titch, get back in here now," yelled Arthur.

Too late. I was already halfway down the gravel path before the wind carried the sound of their voices to me. Slipping and sliding across the long grass, I ran, squelching into the dark mud. It rose up and over my bright red sneakers. I could feel the oozing, cold sludge seeping into my socks.

Then I saw him again, and a dose of warm happiness repelled, albeit briefly, the cold and wet conditions that were threatening to drown me. It was him, definitely him. There was the same honey and white colouring; the same floppy ears that almost reached the ground.

Two hands grabbed my shoulders and pulled me back sharply.

"I swear to something, Titch, you are seriously starting to scare me," yelled Arthur. He was soaked to the skin already; his blue jeans were several shades darker because of the rain, and his white v-neck t-shirt had become transparent. He could barely see through his wet fringe, which was lying flat against his forehead.

"It's Mr. Rochester," I cried. "We've got to catch him before he runs away again."

"What are you talking about? Mr. Rochester is dead, Titch," yelled Arthur.

He turned to his girlfriend, who was standing under the arched frame of the back door. She looked as if she had been force-fed beetles. I wriggled free from Arthur's grasp and continued running after my baby rabbit, which had disappeared from view again.

"Help me, Sammy," cried Arthur.

Stumbling in the wet, grappling like really bad wrestlers, we reached the chicken coop. I was momentarily stunned by the sight of bloody straw which was soaking into the mud.

Slurpy had now joined Arthur. Her long dark hair was hanging in sodden thick tendrils around her face and shoulders. She snatched at my arm and sank her long purple nails into my skin.

"Stop behaving like a little spoilt bitch," spat Slurpy, "and get the hell…"

Her jaw suddenly dropped. She let go of my arm and swayed like she was about to faint. All of the colour – which admittedly wasn't much to begin with – had drained from her face. In the blink of an eye, Slurpy turned the shade of curdled milk.

"The rabbit," she whispered. "I don't believe it."

Both Arthur and I turned to the spot that had mesmerised Slurpy, and sure enough, sitting quite still on all four paws, was Mr. Rochester.

But it wasn't the same baby rabbit that I had lovingly cuddled and kissed before running away that day.

A golden cage surrounded Mr. Rochester, like a protective bubble. The rain bounced off it like dazzling miniature fireworks.

And if that wasn't enough to stun the three of us into silence, where two big black eyes had once been, were two dazzling silver orbs.

Starlight.

"What the…" swore Arthur, wiping his long blonde fringe out of his eyes. My own long blonde hair, which was several shades darker than my brother's, was stuck to my cheeks and eyelashes. Half of it was in my mouth; I gagged.

"That isn't possible," screeched Slurpy, stating the obvious. "What was in that drink? Have we been drugged?"

She started to back away, and I was sorely tempted to join her. My fluffy baby looked ethereal.

But Arthur was transfixed. The starlight from Mr.

Rochester's eyes had infected his own.

"Come here, little guy," cooed Arthur, slowly walking towards Mr. Rochester. His body lowered to the ground with each careful step. "Come on, we won't hurt you."

With a twitch of his nose, Mr. Rochester disappeared under a holly bush. Arthur tore off after him in pursuit. I screamed at Arthur to stop, or at least slow down for me, but he vaulted over a long-slatted gate, and ran into the wood behind our house.

By the time I had levered myself up and over the same gate, Arthur was gone.

Slurpy and I searched in the torrential rain for hours, screaming Arthur's name until we were hoarse. By the time the alarm was raised back at *Avalon Cottage*, darkness had fallen.

The authorities used spotlights from helicopters and trained sniffer dogs to search the woods, but at midnight the search for Arthur was called off. The chief police officer spoke to my mother in a thick Welsh accent and told her that the search would resume again at first light.

She was beyond reason by this point, and her wailing tore at my insides, dredging up memories that should never have been woken. I desperately wanted to put my arms around her, to feel her heart beating against my face as she allowed herself to love me.

But my mother was out of practice. She was still mourning.

Slurpy and I stood in Arthur's bedroom and looked out through the grimy window into the darkness. An eerie stillness had fallen over the world outside. The leaded panes of glass were still covered in crystal raindrops, and for the mere want of something to do, I let my fingers chase each one as they streamed down towards the windowsill.

Slurpy and I had told the investigating team what we knew: that Arthur had run off into the woods after a rabbit.

We certainly didn't mention the strange cage of light, or the starlight eyes. Nobody would have believed us.

We didn't really believe it ourselves.

After an eternity of silence, Slurpy eventually spoke. Her high-pitched voice was unusually low.

"He told me about the voices you heard."

I nodded, unable to speak as tears filled my eyes. I bit down on my bottom lip.

"Were you telling the truth?"

I nodded again.

"Was it true about the people with swords?"

I nodded again.

"I would have called you a liar or a nutcase if I hadn't seen that rabbit."

"Don't worry about it, most people think I'm a liar and a nutcase," I whispered.

"Arthur doesn't."

The longest conversation we had ever shared was over. While we detested the presence of the other, we now had a common goal.

Find Arthur.

Slurpy's parents arrived to pick her up not long after. Words of comfort spoken to my mother were lost to the breeze that constantly swept through our house as doors were opened and shut again. Total strangers tramped through our house as if it were their own.

My mother slept in Arthur's bedroom, but only after a local doctor had tranquilised her. I didn't sleep at all. I just listened to the voices whispering through the trees.

"He is here. He is here."

4 FOLLOW THE RABBIT

The inhabitants of nowhere were true to their word.

As the morning sun stretched over the horizon, the police cars trundled up the gravel drive, and the search for Arthur resumed.

Word had been spread from one house to another about the missing eighteen-year-old boy, and the strangers who had trampled through our house the night before were joined by more. Many, many more. By seven o'clock, over one hundred people had joined the search. Armed with sticks, plastic boots and waxed jackets, the brigade of locals set off in groups of ten, marching along the stone lanes like green knights.

"They'll find him," said Mrs. Pratchett repeatedly, as she took command of our kitchen.

I couldn't eat or drink anything. Neither could my mother who had to be sedated once more. My father was due to arrive later in the morning, and already more senior police officers had turned up for the Foreign Office de-briefing.

"A terrorist kidnapping is not being ruled in or out at this stage," said a tall thin officer with crooked yellow teeth to no one in particular.

They really didn't have a clue what had been awoken underneath them after all this time, I thought.

My intention had been to slip away unnoticed and go in search of Arthur myself, but that was proving difficult. First, the tall thin officer with crooked yellow teeth had told a junior constable to shadow my every move. I ended up locking myself in the bathroom just to get away from her. Then Mrs. Pratchett and the post mistress of the village, Mrs. Lancelyn-Green, took it upon themselves to force feed me like a turkey at Christmas. They wanted to make sure I didn't have another fainting spell *in my delicate state*.

My opportunity to run came from the most unexpected source. Slurpy and her younger brother arrived with their parents, not long after the second search party had been debriefed and sent out into the woods. Her brother, who saw the whole thing as a great excuse to skive off school, sat at the kitchen table and wolfed down slice after slice of cold toast, before burping the alphabet backwards.

Slurpy's parents were slightly more helpful, and while her father took command of the third search party, Mrs. Slurpy went to keep an eye on my mother.

Slurpy motioned to me to follow her the second our police shadow went to the bathroom. We slipped into the garden and walked down to the empty chicken coop. The first thing I noticed was that the bloody straw had been removed. Yellow police tape was wound around the chicken coop and several trees.

"So what's the plan?" whispered Slurpy, once we were sure no one was within earshot.

We were dressed very similar: skinny black jeans, black t-shirts and unbuttoned red and black plaid shirts. The only difference in our appearance was that my sweatshirt was tied around my waist, while Slurpy had hers draped over her shoulders. She also had a purple backpack.

"We need to find that tomb again," I replied. "The one I fell down last week."

"And what do we do then?"

I shrugged. "I don't know. I'm making this up as I go along. All I know is that we can't tell the police about Mr. Rochester, the ancient soldiers with swords, or the voices, because they'll immediately think we are crazy or on drugs. Then it will look as if we had something do to with Arthur going missing, and that policewoman hasn't let me out of her sight since she got here."

"Then we have to leave now," said Slurpy, glancing around the man-sized holly bush we were hiding behind, "before they realise you are missing. Do you know the way back to this hole?"

I shook my head. Slurpy rolled her eyes.

"It's not my fault," I hissed under my breath. "I was just running through the woods after mum started having a go at me about the school dance. I wasn't paying attention to where I was going, and I certainly didn't expect to fall into a grave."

Slurpy made a *humph* sound in the back of her throat. I wanted to slap her on the back to dislodge it.

Slap her hard.

"Well, at least I'm organised," she said sarcastically, grabbing hold of my shirt and pulling me along to the long-slatted gate that Arthur was last seen vaulting over. She patted her backpack. "I've got food, drink, my mobile, cigarettes, gum, and a torch."

Now it was my turn to roll my eyes. What the hell were we going to need cigarettes for? We could hardly kill them with cancer.

"I think it's that way," I said, pointing east away from *Avalon Cottage*. As we followed a well worn path, I allowed myself one last look behind. There was a figure at my bedroom window; I could see the glint of something silver, like jewellery, but the leaded glass was too dark to determine who it was.

It never occurred to me that it was someone who didn't belong here.

We met the first search party within twenty minutes. They were hacking at the undergrowth with large knobbly sticks. Several nodded at the sight of us. My only thought was that if Arthur was lying underneath the brambles and dead logs, then he would probably end up with a fractured skull if they continued to smack away like that.

I didn't say anything to stop them though. I knew Arthur wasn't going to be found there.

Hours passed. The further we went into the wood, the denser the trees became as the ground became more difficult to navigate. Twice Slurpy went head over arse as she tripped over hidden tree roots, but at least I didn't laugh the second time it happened.

Eventually we came to a small clearing. The green grass was long and fine, and scores of thick toadstools and wild mushrooms carpeted the ground like miniature stepping stones.

"I think we should stop for something to eat," suggested Slurpy, lighting up a cigarette.

"I think we are hopelessly lost," I replied, snatching the unlit cigarette from her lips.

"What did you do that for?"

"You can't smoke in an uncleared wood. It's a fire hazard."

"Fire hazard? Are you kidding me? There was enough rain dumped on this place yesterday to dampen hell. This is Wales, not the Australian Outback."

"You're not smoking around me," I replied angrily. "It's a disgusting habit, and Arthur hates it. He says it's like kissing an ashtray."

"Doesn't stop him though," sneered Slurpy.

That was enough for me. I didn't know what had possessed me to think that the two of us could actually work together to find Arthur. If I had to go into the hole alone, I would. Give me a tomb of rotting warrior zombies over another minute in the company of Slurpy Sammy.

Without another word, I stormed off - or at least attempted to.

I had gone four strides when I saw him. Just like the day before, Mr. Rochester had suddenly appeared like a magician's rabbit out of a hat. He was nibbling at a ring of velvety-looking toadstools. The effect of his twinkling eyes had not been lessened by daylight, and I felt myself drawn towards him. Hypnotised.

"Can you see him too?" whispered Slurpy, drawing level with me. Her voice had taken on a strange deep accent, and her eyes looked glassy, almost white.

"Do you think we should follow him?"

But Slurpy was already treading a path towards the rabbit. Teasing us, Mr. Rochester bounded away. Then he stopped, deliberately looked back at us, and then jumped away again. His gold and white fur appeared impervious to the black wet sludge on the forest floor.

He was playing a game.

This is stupid. You need to go back to the cottage.

I ignored my inner voice, choosing instead to shadow Slurpy's footsteps.

Forget stupid then, you stubborn idiot. This is downright dangerous.

"Will you shut up," I snapped, smacking my forehead with the palm of my hand.

"I didn't say anything," said Slurpy.

"I wasn't talking to you."

"More voices?" asked Slurpy sarcastically.

"Yeah, mine if you must know."

"You really are weird, Natasha."

"Just shut up."

"Voices not playing nicely?"

"Actually I *was* talking to you this time."

Our bickering had led us away from the clearing and into the densest part of the wood so far. Twisted tree trunks encased in thick flaking bark, rose out of the ground. The rain and wind of yesterday had felled several branches, and we had to clamber over them as we followed my baby rabbit. The smell of damp dirt and wet foliage filled my nostrils, but there was also an unpleasant dirty smell, like recently laid fertilizer.

"Can you remember this place?" called Slurpy.

"No," I replied panting. "I'm sure the trees weren't this close together."

The lack of air in the wood was suffocating, but there was an unnatural stillness too. No wind, no birds, no rustling in the carpet of dying leaves that had been shed in the storm. And then I remembered.

"Wait a moment," I called, as Mr. Rochester disappeared behind a tree. Slurpy stopped.

"What...is...it?" she asked breathlessly.

"Can you hear that?"

"I can't hear anything above your breathing," replied Slurpy, who was now making the same noise as a steam engine.

"Exactly," I replied, taking two steps forward. The sound of snapping twigs magnified.

"It's *too* quiet," said Slurpy slowly.

I could feel a chill in the air that hadn't been there before, like the blast you receive when you open the freezer to get an ice-cream. The hairs on my arms were rigid; I could sense the stubble on my recently shaved legs as well. It felt prickly against my jeans.

"I think we're close," I whispered. "I had this feeling after I escaped from the grave."

"Arthur," yelled Slurpy, in her screeching Welsh

accent that was like nails down a blackboard. "Arthur, can you hear me, babe?"

I was expecting an echo, but the sound of Slurpy's voice dropped like a stone weight.

"Arthur," I screamed, "Arthur, its Titch. I'm here with SS. Yell if you can hear me."

Slurpy yanked my arm around so hard my body had no alternative but to follow. She stared at me with her mouth open, and her tired, bloodshot eyes wide.

"What did you just call me?"

"Nothing," I mumbled.

"SS," screeched Slurpy. "Were you calling me a Nazi?"

The Schutzsstaffel may have been the inspiration, but I was certain that she didn't want to know that the full nickname was *Slurpy Sammy* either.

"It's just a joke," I mumbled again, as my cheeks flamed. Despite my occasional snarkey attitude, I really hated confrontations.

"You're on your own, freak," spat Slurpy, and she let go of my arm, but only after her nails had left their mark. She turned on her heels and marched away. Feeling ashamed, I didn't have the heart to laugh when she tripped and disappeared from view with a muffled scream.

Then it registered: Slurpy had disappeared.

Completely.

"Natasha…Natasha…" screamed Slurpy. Her voice was suppressed, like someone had placed a pillow over some speakers.

I reached the hole, and on my hands and knees, peered down. Slurpy was lying sprawled on her back. I knew she was conscious because she was making an awful lot of noise.

"Hang on, I'm coming down," I called.

"Don't come down," screamed Slurpy, "I want to come out."

But it was too late. I grabbed two thick roots and lowered myself into the hole. Slurpy was still sprawled on her back.

No difference there then.

A quick scan of the tomb was enough to confirm it was the same one I had fallen into six days earlier.

With one exception: it was completely deserted.

The blind warrior and his sleeping friends were gone, and by the deep tracks in the earth, it was clear something, or someone, had unwillingly gone the same way as them.

I looked up and saw two twinkling stars peering down at me. Then, with a goodbye twitch, Mr. Rochester was gone, having led us like the White Rabbit into the hole.

I never saw my baby rabbit again.

5 THE LADY AND THE BELL

An unfamiliar sense of bravery had me in its grip. In the past week, I had come face to face with ancient zombies with swords, whispering ghosts and a baby rabbit that had come back from the dead. Nothing could faze me now.

As Slurpy scrambled around in the dirt, I grabbed her backpack and unzipped it. I wanted the torch, which I eventually found under several silver boxes of cigarettes, and enough Jaffa Cakes to turn a person into an orange Oompa Loompa.

A weak white beam illuminated the tomb as I flicked it on.

"What are you doing?" gasped Slurpy, who was now standing, albeit bent double, trying to catch her breath.

"We have to follow the tracks," I replied, scanning the tomb with the beam.

"I'm not following any tracks. We need to get out and find help."

"Then go," I said quietly. "I won't stop you."

"I can't leave you now, and you know it. Arthur would never forgive me if you got lost, which knowing your track record, would totally happen."

"Then shut the hell up and come with me," I replied, "but I am going to find my brother, whether you follow me or not."

I meant it. I really didn't care what Slurpy did, but I intended to follow those tracks in the dirt. Slowly, I started to walk to the back of the tomb, passing scores of empty stone plinths.

There really had been an entire army of warriors, just waiting to feast on my tender – slightly spotty – flesh.

A noise from behind was enough to tell me that Slurpy was shadowing my footsteps. The smell of cigarette smoke started to fill the air which had been surprisingly clean and clear, despite the fact we were underground.

"Do you have to smoke?"

"It calms my nerves."

I decided to let Slurpy kill herself. At least that way I could eat all of the Jaffa Cakes and drink all of the Red Bull without feeling too guilty.

The further we walked, the narrower the tomb became, so much so that after a while it had morphed into a tunnel. The bravery that I had embraced so wholeheartedly deserted me, as the dirty terracotta walls closed in around us. It was claustrophobic, dark and scary. My imagination started to fill with thoughts of the roof collapsing in on us, burying us alive under a mountain of heavy earth.

Every so often one of us would squeal as something fine brushed against our skin. Spiders I could cope with, but I was starting to pray under my breath that bats never entered the equation. I don't like things that flap. It was why I didn't complain when my mother got rid of the chickens.

The tunnel eventually came out into a circular

opening. It was still earth-made, but the soil was a lot darker, like it was wet or stained with something that I hoped wasn't blood. It wasn't wide, about six metres at most, and it was completely empty, apart from a thick wooden beam that arched across the roof of the earth cave. Hanging from that was a pulley, which in turn was attached to a bell.

At first glance it looked like an ordinary church bell: cup shaped with a thick rim. Inside was a long metal clapper, hung like an engorged uvula. Whether it was made of copper, brass or silver was impossible to say, as the metal surface was badly tarnished with a grey-green coating. It looked hundreds of years old, and unused for all of them.

"Can you read what it says?" I asked Slurpy, who was examining the thick rim closely. There were letters and symbols stencilled into the metal, but it was too hard to decipher.

A musical voice in the dark made us both scream and fall back against the earth wall. I dropped the torch in my panic.

"Sleepers of the cave awaken, for glory has come to the Kingdom of Logres once more."

I had bitten through my tongue in fright; I could taste the metallic saltiness of blood. Slurpy was crouching beside me, shaking with fear, as the strange female voice swept through the circular cave, like a gust of warm wind.

Someone, or something, had finally had the decency to scare the absolute crap out of me.

"Do not be afraid for now," said the voice, "for I know of your quest."

The white beam of the dropped torch was fixed on a thick tree root that had grown out through the earth wall. I threw myself forward, grabbed the only source of light we had, and then lurched back towards Slurpy, landing on her in the process. She quickly secured her arms around my waist - not for comfort, but because she clearly intended to use me as a human shield.

I scanned every inch of that circular cave with the torch, but could see nothing. A chuckle echoed back in the dark, and a cold sweat broke out on my forehead, as a dizzying wave of sickness swept over me.

"It's a ghost," whispered Slurpy, digging her nails into my stomach. "We're going to die."

"I am not a ghost," said the voice, "although it is true that my spirit has been waiting a long time for his glorious return."

A fuzzy ball of pale blue light started to rapidly expand in front of us. It grew taller and taller, stretching like elastic, as the form of a woman appeared. Slurpy was swearing rapidly under her breath; I had stopped breathing.

Then the torch failed.

An eerie blue sheen now bathed the entire cave. Slurpy and I were trapped in the shadow cast by the bell. The earth started to vibrate, and powder dry pockets of brown earth fell from the roof, sprinkling us with layers of dirt.

"We should never have come down here," cried Slurpy, dry sobbing. "This is all your fault, Natasha."

The woman raised her arms and held her palms flat against the circular walls. The earth stopped shaking.

She was dressed in a long, pale blue dress. It looked like silk, but it rippled like water. Around her slim waist was a golden belt, woven and plaited. She had long blonde hair which fell to her waist, but it contained a natural wave which gave it the appearance of air.

"My name is Nimue. Do not be afraid, for now."

Easier said than done, I thought, almost heaving with fear. I had never realised that rigor mortis could actually set into a body while it was still alive.

"You are searching for Arthur," said the apparition. It was a statement, not a question.

I couldn't take my eyes off of her. She was achingly beautiful. Even in the blue haze, her skin reflected with a warm buttermilk colouring. I felt the rigidity starting to slowly leave my limbs.

"Do you know where my brother is?" I asked bravely.

"He has been taken," said the lady, Nimue.

"We knew that already," I replied without thinking. I gave myself an internal brain slap.

Do not provoke her. Not unless you want to be turned into a slug.

But to my surprise, the lady laughed. It was musical, like wind chimes.

"Your spirit amuses me, Natasha," said Nimue smiling, although her eyes looked like ice.

"She knows your name," squealed Slurpy. "How does she know your name? You never told her your name. We're gonna die. We're gonna die."

"I have been waiting a long time to reclaim what was mine," repeated Nimue, "but the knights have been complacent in their sleep, and now they have been punished. You, Natasha, must ring the bell until it sounds in all four corners of the realm of Logres. The knights must be rallied to your call."

"The who must be what now?" I spluttered, not having understood a single word the beautiful lady had said.

"Ring the bell, Natasha," said Nimue, "and then travel onwards, until you find the knight you met before. Be forewarned though, for he has changed and he may not see either of you for what you are, or what you will become."

As she spoke, I realised the edges of her pale blue gown were becoming blurred. The haze was thickening, like blue fog. The lady was dissolving away.

SEARCHING FOR ARTHUR

"Don't leave now," I cried, jumping to my feet. "The old men I saw before, the ones who were sleeping back there. Did they take Arthur?"

"Find them in their true form," whispered Nimue. "Now ring the bell, Natasha. Ring the bell and awaken all of Logres."

Her wind chime voice faded with one last burst of air that filtered through the earth chamber. The hair on my head fluttered in the breeze, and then fell flat. The bell rocked slightly, but not enough to ring out. The torch illuminated again, and so I picked it up and started to walk towards the rope.

Slurpy cried out.

"Don't touch it. If we ring that bell, a thousand things could happen, and I bet not one of them would be good for me."

"The lady said we had to ring it," I replied.

Slurpy started choking.

"A lady who magically appeared and then disappeared again," she screeched with a voice pitched high enough to shatter glass. "How can you be so calm about all of this? This sort of insanity doesn't happen to normal people. I'M NORMAL," she wailed loudly. "Your brother is normal. It's you…" now her finger was jabbing perilously close to my face, "…it's you. You're the weirdo. You attract weirdness. You live on Planet Freak. You're like a freak beacon, a magnet for freaks."

Even in the pale beam of light, I could see Slurpy had turned the colour of stewed beetroot.

"Have you finished?" I asked calmly, as Slurpy started to breathe again.

"I haven't even started yet, you freakoid from hell," yelled Slurpy.

"In that case, you won't mind if I do this then," and I grabbed the rope and pulled it down hard.

The first chime was dull, muffled. The second was slightly clearer, as flakes of decrepit rust started to peel back its layers. The third was louder still, metal on metal. Four rings, five. As the ancient bell started to toll its message, the floor started to vibrate once more. Six peals, then seven. Suddenly the world was filled with the sound of baritone bell chimes. I had never heard anything like it. So deep, so powerful. A sound to wake the dead.

"What are you doing?" cried Slurpy, grabbing her purple backpack. "Have you completely lost your mind?"

I started to laugh. Crazy, maniacal joy burst from my lungs as the frayed rope slid up through my hands. I caught the end and yanked it down hard again. I felt more alive than I had done in years. I could hear the words of the bell singing its message:

"Sleepers of the cave awaken, for glory has come to the Kingdom of Logres once more."

Huge shards of earth were now splintering from the dirt ceiling, raining down on us as the bell chimed louder and louder.

"Titch, we have to get out of here now," screamed Slurpy. "The roof is going to collapse."

If she had called me anything other than by my nickname, I'm sure I would have remained. In fact I think that was the first time Slurpy had ever used it - normally I was *it, freak* or *her* - but the sound of Arthur's pet name brought me back to my senses with a sudden thud.

Arthur. I needed to find my brother.

The circular bell chamber had another exit, the same size and shape as the tunnel we had entered from. In single file we ran for our lives, as the earth roof collapsed with a roar behind us.

And still the grandfather of bells continued to ring.

We turned another bend and saw daylight. The dirt walls ahead of us were crumbling, as the noise induced quake continued to shake the foundations of the earth.

With our shirts wrapped over our mouths, we threw ourselves into the blue sky. As we rolled down a grassy verge, the tunnel entrance belched out an enormous plume of terracotta dust and dirt, as the way back collapsed.

The earth stopped shaking, and eventually we stopped rolling.

6 FIVE STRANGERS

I opened my eyes and stared into the red sky. Eventually the dust and dirt settled and the blue returned. The sky was cloudless, and the small sun hovered high above.

All of the wind had been knocked out of my lungs, and a painful stabbing gripped my sides. My first thought was that I had broken several ribs in the fall, but as my breathing steadied, the pain dissolved.

I pushed myself up onto my elbows and looked over to Slurpy. Her eyes were closed, and a thin trickle of blood was leaking from her nose. I rolled over and crawled towards her.

"Sammy, wake up."

"It was a bad dream, wasn't it," she groaned. "Please tell me that was all a nightmare."

Well, at least she was alive. I didn't reply, and instead went searching for her backpack. My throat was clogged with dirt that needed dislodging and Slurpy had soda. Not that I needed the sugar rush, I was still shaking with raw shock.

After a few minutes searching, I found the backpack under a blackberry bush. Thick swollen fruit hung from the branches, like miniature bunches of grapes. I popped several into my mouth and squished them against the roof of my mouth with my tongue. The delicious sweetness slowly trickled down my throat. It was time for lunch: ten Jaffa cakes, two cans of Red Bull and about six pounds of wild blackberries.

By the time Slurpy had accepted the fact that this was not a nightmare and had opened her eyes, I was on the verge of puking.

"So what do we do *now*?" asked Slurpy spitefully, wiping the blood away from her face with her sleeve.

I shrugged. "We find Arthur."

"You don't think a better idea would be to try and find our way back to the cottage and the police? My mum and dad are going to go mad when I come home looking like this."

I doubted whether my parents would even notice I was gone, but there was too much sugar rushing around my brain to attempt a conversation with Little Miss Slurpy-Snarkey-Pants. I looked down at my digital watch. It was still blinking, and the date still read September 21. With wobbly legs, I turned my back to Slurpy and attempted to climb back up the green hill we had rolled down.

The grass was lush and long. It was the perfect tool in my attempt to reach the summit. Bent double, I grabbed handful after handful and used it to pull myself skyward. With green streaked hands, I reached the top in no time at all.

The panoramic view over the valley was stunning, just like a picture postcard. Undulating mountain ranges dominated the distance. Each one covered in towering dark pines. Despite the fact that the sun was high in the sky, pockets of thick mist remained at lower ground, most of which were scattered around several small islands situated in a huge blue lake that was a mirror copy of the sky above. Green grass lined the shore, which was also carpeted with rugs of yellow, purple and pink flowers. It reminded me of the patchwork quilt on my bed back at *Avalon Cottage*.

A clean fresh smell like laundry liquid filled the air. The sound of singing birds occasionally broke the silence, but for all intents and purposes, at that moment in time, I was the only person alive in paradise.

And then Slurpy arrived at the summit to remind me I wasn't.

"Where the hell are we?" she asked bluntly.

I continued looking around the unfamiliar landscape. I had lived in the middle of nowhere for less than six months, and so I wasn't concerned that I didn't immediately recognise any landmarks. What did become worrying was the fact that Slurpy didn't know where we were either.

"You must recognise something," I said, after a short argument in which she called me "a freak" at least three times, and I called her "a dense piece of wood" twice.

"I'm telling you I have never seen this place before," snarled Slurpy, her top lip curling like an angry dog. "Those mountains and this valley do not exist near our village."

"We live in Wales," I cried with exasperation, "there's nothing in Wales *but* mountains and valleys."

"Are you calling me a liar?"

"I'm calling you stupid."

That was the prelude to another, slightly longer, argument, in which she called me "a freak" at least twelve times, and I called her "a colossal waste of space with the brain matter of an amoeba" once.

My insult was worth extra points though. It had more syllables.

Slurpy pulled out her mobile phone and held it into the air.

"There's no reception," she muttered under her breath, adding a few swear words in the process.

My eyes were continually being drawn to the enormous lake and the mist-hidden islands which were dotted around its rippling mass. I shuddered, despite the heat. I would not be fooled by the duplicitous calm of the water. I knew better. A voice whispered in my head, but for once, it wasn't mine.

"...travel onwards until you find the knight you met before. Be forewarned though, for he has changed and he may not see either of you for what you are, or what you will become..."

"What did you say?" snapped Slurpy.

"I didn't say anything."

"Yes you did. You were mumbling about the night changing."

My head had started throbbing. I rubbed at my temples as I came down from the sugar rush. I was on the verge of repeating Nimue's words, but the thought of arguing with Slurpy again was exhausting.

Self-preservation and Arthur were all that mattered now.

"I think we should head towards the lake," I said. "If we walk the perimeter, then we may find a track that leads away. It would be better to do that than go through the woods. We'll definitely get lost if we stay in the trees."

Slurpy nodded, although she wasn't happy. Her bottom lip was stuck out, and her shoulders were slumped. It was really hot, far warmer than when we had left *Avalon Cottage*, and so by the time we had trampled back down the hill and made our way to the water, both Slurpy and I had tied our shirts around our waists. As my sweatshirt was already there, the question, "does my bum look big in this?" really didn't need asking. From the back I must have looked like a sumo

51

wrestler with all that padding.

The closer we got to the lake, the colder the air became, despite the best efforts of the sun's rays to cook us alive. The sound of wind chimes floated through the bluebells, which rocked gently from side to side as Slurpy and I trudged through the ankle-length undergrowth. The movement of the flowers was ominous. There wasn't any wind for a start.

After an hour of silent walking, we came to an exposed area of shoreline. The green grass and pockets of flowers fell away to reveal golden, gritty sand and perfectly round, grey pebbles. The water of the lake was utterly still, as if made of glass. Several bare tree stumps stuck out of the ground like thumbs. A small boat was tied to one of the stumps by a short piece of rope. The barge was made of wood with curved edges, although the bow was raised far higher, with one single piece of wood planed to a point.

Be brave, said my inner voice. *Nothing is going to happen if you just walk into the water up to your ankles, which by the way are swelling up like table legs, Little Miss Cankles.*

"Fancy a paddle?" I asked Slurpy. "I could do with soaking my feet, they're killing me."

"You paddle, if you want," she replied. "I'll keep lookout. This place is giving me the creeps."

Slurpy had a strange abstract glaze over her face. Her nose and forehead were wrinkled, like she was thinking - something that clearly took a lot of effort.

"What's the matter?" I asked, not really caring.

"This place," replied Slurpy slowly. "It seems familiar. I think I've been here before, but I can't remember when."

That was a positive sign, I thought, and it was a feeling I had started to have myself, the closer we got to the lake. I *had* been here before, I was certain of it.

I slipped off my sneakers. Off came my sweaty white socks, and then I rolled up the bottom of my black skinny jeans. They were so tight I could barely raise them above my calves. And my inner voice could go to hell because I did not have cankles! I turned around to check on Slurpy, but she was now lost in her own little nicotine-enhanced world. Her idea of keeping lookout went no further than her smokes.

The water of the lake was ice-cold. It was painful at first, and I scrunched up my face as I waded in. I didn't want to go further than a few inches. It wasn't as if I couldn't swim, because I could. My father had forced twice-weekly lessons on Arthur and I for years, and no amount of begging or pleading made him change his mind. Yet the fact I could swim four hundred metres in less than ten minutes did little to remove my absolute belief that even the most inviting stretch of water was dangerous.

My body adapted slowly to the shocking cold temperature of the water. I could feel the sensation of sliding sand beneath my toes. I felt like I was on a tightrope. One more step, I would still be safe taking one more step. I closed my eyes, tilted my head back and inhaled deeply, as I allowed the water to massage my aches away.

But true fear doesn't go away that easily.

Then I heard the whispers. Voices. Male.

My eyes sprang open. I staggered, as the bank of sand gave way beneath my bare feet.

"Sammy," I screamed. "Sammy."

My jeans were soaked to my knees as I splashed clumsily out of the water to my brother's girlfriend.

"It's the voices. They're here."

"I know," whispered Slurpy, trembling. Her cigarette had fallen from her fingertips, and was now lying an inch from my bare right foot.

"You heard them too?"

Slurpy shook her head, and pointed away from the lake towards the wood, where five males were standing staring at us.

"I don't need to hear them. I can see them."

Five sets of mistrusting eyes were fixed upon the two of us. I suddenly felt very vulnerable without shoes on my feet.

All five of the strangers were dressed in tight fitting trousers and smock-like tunics: the kind pregnant women wear. The colours of their clothes were earthy: browns, creams and various shades of green. They all wore dusty, laced leather boots, and two were wearing long cloaks, which were fastened at the neck by silver clasps.

More worrying than their strange outfits was the fact that every single one of them was armed.

Two of the males carried long spears in their right hands. Another two had a sword at their side.

The fifth person, who I assumed was their gang leader, had broken away and was several paces in front of them. A sword was clasped tightly in his left hand, glinting under the sun. Its sharp point was aimed directly at Slurpy and me.

"Who are you?" said the stranger. The first thing I noticed was his accent. My mother and father would have called it *common*; I just thought it was gruff, like his voice box was lined with gravel. The second thought I had was that he possessed the greenest eyes I had ever seen. The kind that are wasted on a boy because they are so pretty.

"My name is Natasha, and this is Slurpy...I mean, this is Samantha," I replied, in a barely audible whisper. The growl that came from SS was louder.

"Caution, Sir Bedivere," called another male. "I do not see fair maidens abroad. They could be witches. Their words laced with evil magic."

"What are you doing near the shores of the lake?" asked the green-eyed stranger. "What is your business here, and whom do you travel with?"

Despite his appearance: long, straggly chestnut hair, and a stubbly beard that made me want to itch, I had the impression the male was younger than he looked. His face was lined and weary, and he was clearly in need of a shower or ten, but those eyes sparkled like fizzing limes.

"We are looking for my brother," I replied slowly, but my carefully considered words were suddenly interrupted by the mouth on long legs standing next to me.

"And we are with at least one hundred armed men," yelled Slurpy, "and they are looking for us now, as well as Arthur, so you had better leave us alone, or the Foreign Office will hang you for treason or something."

"You idiot," I screamed, as the manner of the five strangers went from cautious observing to rapid movement. They span around, and those who had not drawn swords quickly did so. The cold sound of metal swords being drawn from scabbards burrowed deep into my bones. The one called Bedivere rushed forward and grabbed Slurpy around the wrist. She cried out in pain as he twisted her arm.

"What do you know of Arthur?" he cried. "Speak now, witch, before I remove your head."

Arthur had always told me that if someone attacked, the best chance of survival was fighting back, so I jumped onto the stranger's back and secured my arms around his neck. Squeezing tightly, I wrapped my legs around his body and started to scream.

"HELP, HELP US. ANYBODY."

"Hold the dark haired witch, Sir Gareth," choked the male, as he struggled to release me from his throat. "Sir Tristram, help me with this she-devil."

Despite scratching, spitting, kicking and thumping for all we were worth, Slurpy and I were no match for the five strangers. They dragged us to two trees, where we were bound and gagged.

"In all my days as a knight, I have never seen anything like this," gasped the one called Tristram. He was holding a rag to his bloody mouth, and I was still holding several strands of his curly blonde hair in my hand.

"We should kill them, Sir Bedivere," said another gravely. "Evil times have swept these lands. Our quest to find Arthur will be made all the more perilous if we do not deal out swift justice to enemies of Logres."

But both Slurpy and I had started to make frantic gestures at the sound of Arthur's name, and Bedivere appeared to realise this. Despite the dirty cloth that had been forced into my mouth, I started to choke out the name of my brother.

"This she-devil is familiar," said Bedivere to the one called Tristram. "I have seen her before, I am certain of it." He approached me, and pulled the gag from my mouth with a hard tug. "You have one chance to save your lives," he said in a cold, harsh tone. "What do you know of Arthur?"

"He's my brother," I choked. "He's gone missing and we're searching for him. We met a lady called Nimue, and she told me to ring a bell and awaken the sleepers." I looked desperately at Slurpy, trying to remember any detail, however ridiculous, that might save us.

"The Lady of the Lake came to *you*?" snorted Tristram with derision. A little bubble of blood burst at the corner of his mouth.

"Yes," I cried. "We only want to find Arthur. I'm his sister, and this is his girlfriend. We love him and we need him to come home. That's all we want."

I started to sob. Uncontrolled spasms of pain bounced through my chest and into my shoulders. The fear and worry of the past week finally beached itself in my heart. It felt so heavy I couldn't breathe. Arthur was all I had left, and I had failed him completely.

"Release them," ordered Bedivere. "We will take them with us. If they speak the truth, then the others will be rallying."

"And if they lie?" asked Tristram.

Bedivere shrugged, as if it was of little consequence.

"Then we will kill them."

7 DWARF-RIDERS

Our plan to find Arthur was not going to plan.

Slurpy stayed silent as we trudged through the wood, guarded on all sides by four of the strangers. The light started to fail as we walked away from the lake, and the temperature plummeted even further. Our kidnappers allowed us to put our shirts and sweaters back on, but my feet were numb with the cold, and I could see the tips of my fingers were turning a strange shade of violet.

The five strangers rarely spoke to us, although they kept a constant watch on our movements. Slurpy's bag had been taken from her at the shore and its contents confiscated by the blonde one called Tristram. He kept everything as evidence and threw the bag into the water. It had bubbled up like a flotation device and then sunk quickly, as if dragged down by something hidden under the water.

As we walked, I kept my head down, but my ears alert. The five were friends, that much was obvious, and as I listened to their conversations, I started to feel less afraid. They were far too polite for a start, constantly referring to each other as *sir*.

"Sir Gareth," called Bedivere.

"Yes, Sir Bedivere?" replied the one presumably called Gareth. He had a round face, hazel eyes, and was the same height as me.

"Did Sir Percivale's messenger say any more of your brothers?"

"Alas, he did not. I will pray for more news once we reach the castle of Caerleon."

"We *will* find them, Sir Gareth," said another in an Irish accent. "I long to make merry and laugh with Sir Agravaine once more."

"Sir Talan," said the plump one called Gareth to the Irishman. "Sir Agravaine has not yet forgiven you for the riddle you served upon him before the enchanted sleep took hold over Logres. You may ride to meet my brother and yet you may ride to meet your doom."

As the five laughed, Slurpy muttered under her breath, "I'm at a bloody freak convention."

The fifth one was called David. He looked younger than the others, and was several inches shorter. His voice had barely broken, and small tufts of baby soft hair were dotted around his chin.

"Will we make camp tonight or ride on to Caerleon, Sir Bedivere?" asked David.

"We will make camp," replied Bedivere. Then he looked at me; he appeared hesitant, like he wanted to say something.

Talan was singing as we walked. He had a really gorgeous soulful voice, although all of the songs had the same theme: rescuing fair damsels in distress. It was all very strange. By the way his grey eyes kept darting towards Slurpy, it was clear he was hoping she may need his heroic services at some point. Perhaps he doubled as a manicurist? She had chipped a long purple nail in the struggle by the lake and was very upset about it.

The path we were following had reached a crossroads. Tied to several trees were five horses. Both Slurpy and I cooed at the sight of them; they were gorgeous. Three were dapple grey with white bodies that looked like they had been sprinkled with grey ash. The other two were dark chestnut, glossy and warm. All five pawed at the ground and whinnied at the sight of the men.

For the first time, I saw a glimmer of affection on Bedivere's face. It totally transformed him. He smiled, and deep dimples formed on his cheeks. For a yeti he was actually pretty good-looking. He immediately went to one of the chestnuts, pulled something grainy out of a worn leather saddle bag, and nuzzled into the horse as it fed from his hand. The other men did the same, leaving Slurpy and I alone for the first time.

If it entered Slurpy's head to attempt a run for freedom, she didn't show it. Instead she went straight to the smallest dapple grey, pulling at her bonds as she went. Talan pulled out a short knife and released her hands.

The curly-haired blonde called Tristram glared at him, but Talan didn't seem to care.

"If they were witches, we would be under their spell by now," he said in his Irish accent. "They are strange to be sure, but I see no malevolent intent in their eyes."

"Sir Talan is in love," laughed the young one called David, and the others, with the exception of Tristram, laughed along with him. "He is bewitched already."

This led into a song, although David's breaking voice was no competition for Talan's.

I felt a tugging at the ropes tying my hands, and then they were free. A spasm of tension immediately flooded my upper back and shoulders, as the pain in my wrists registered. As I rubbed my fingers over the deep red welts that had appeared on my skin, Bedivere placed his own knife back in its sheath.

"Thank you," I croaked.

Bedivere opened his saddle bag once more and pulled out a triangular leather pouch. He threw it at me. I fumbled with the stopper and sniffed at the liquid inside. It smelt like flowers.

"You should drink," he ordered, although his voice, while still gruff, sounded softer. I could see him out of the corner of my eye; he was watching me, but when I looked back, his green eyes quickly moved away to his horse.

"Thank you," I said quietly, handing him back the water pouch. His fingers touched mine as he took the pouch. He flinched and dropped it.

Excellent. I was capable of repelling other freaks just by my touch.

"Brother knights, we'll need to make camp for the night soon," said Bedivere to the others, quickly side-stepping me. "We'll make for Caerleon at first light."

"And what do we do with the witches?" asked Tristram.

"The dark one can ride with Sir Talan," replied Bedivere. "If she really has bewitched him, then maybe she can cease his singing."

"Not even witchcraft could slay the magic of song," said Talan, as Tristram and David jumped onto their horses like they had springs on their feet. Talan held out his hand to Slurpy, and helped her climb onto the back of a grey.

"And the fair one?" asked Gareth.

"She rides with me."

Bedivere had already mounted his horse. I stroked its long nose as I stumbled forward. Bedivere grabbed my forearm and pulled me up in front of him. His arm then clamped itself in front of my stomach, like one of those padded rests that secures you into your seat on a white-knuckle rollercoaster. His legs were against mine; his whole body pressed up against me. I'd never been this close to a guy before in my life. I didn't know where to put my hands, legs. Should I lean back? Why couldn't I just walk behind them?

"Yonder is the court of Caerleon," said Bedivere into my ear. Just the sensation of his breath down my neck sent spasmic goosebumps down my back. I shifted my weight to the right and leant around to my left. Not to look at Bedivere, but to move away from his mouth, but the second we locked eyes again I had that feeling of familiarity that I had experienced down by the lake. Bedivere's throat bobbed as he swallowed. Why was I looking at his throat? Because I couldn't look into his eyes, that's why. I should look down – NO – don't look down, look up.

Without another word, Bedivere kicked his heels into the ribs of the horse and we galloped away.

I thought I knew discomfort and pain. When I was nine, Arthur accidentally knocked me off a swing. The sun-parched ground was like concrete and the fall had broken my arm. At the age of eleven, I was deliberately targeted by a human elephant wielding a hockey stick on the school playing fields. That resulted in a broken cheekbone. Then just a year ago, my appendix had burst during a rather gruesome family holiday to Disneyland Paris.

Yet nothing could compare to the sheer agony that was riding bareback in a pair of skinny jeans for over three hours. By the time Bedivere had dismounted his horse, my buttocks were threatening to disengage themselves from the rest of my body and run off to a far corner of the wood, where they would no doubt weep at the misfortune of being mine. I had chaffing on my chaffing.

Slurpy had drawn the long straw. Sir Talan was

proving himself quite the knight in shining armour, and had, at some point, placed his cloak under her butt cheeks which had absorbed the shock.

"The cloth you wear is strange," said Bedivere gruffly, as I fell onto my back and attempted to remove my jeans from my arse. "They are not suitable for a quest."

"You don't say," I snapped back.

Bedivere snorted, but it was more from amusement than annoyance. The cracked edges of his thin mouth started to rise. It would have been optimistic to call it a smile, but it was an attempt.

And then I knew. We both knew: the cave; the blind ancient warrior; me, falling into the grave.

"Are you Arthur?"

But the voice this time was mine.

Bedivere's eyes sparkled, no longer the light sucking black voids of before.

"It wasn't a dream, was it?" he said, his voice low, wary.

I stood staring at Bedivere, catching flies with my open mouth. It was six days since I had fallen through the hole in the forest ground. Six days since the blind ancient warrior had asked me, "Are you Arthur?" In six days my world had turned upside down and inside out, and one half of my brain was now trying to tell the other half that this Bedivere was the same person.

And he knew it as well.

"How is this happening?" I asked. "I don't understand any of this."

"Your name, it is Lady Natasha?"

I nodded. Hey, if they could be sirs, then why couldn't I be a lady? Bedivere pulled out a woollen blanket from beneath a strap on the back of his horse, and placed it around my shoulders. His movements were clumsy and self-conscious. Was I really that repulsive?

"I knew I had seen you before, but I was certain it was in a dream. The longest dream of all," he said, staring into the ground. "I do not have words of comfort for you, Lady Natasha, for I am ashamed that I do not understand all of it myself. Long have we borne our penance for the damage inflicted to Arthur and the court of Camelot. We must earn absolution, and yet rumours of dark magic and a Saxon invasion have persisted in the short time that has elapsed since we were allowed to awaken from our sleep."

Nope. I still didn't understand any of this. But at least I had gone from being a witch to being a lady. My mother would be so proud.

Bedivere turned to the others. "We'll make camp here. Sir Gareth, the first watch is yours."

Tristram was walking back to the group; his arms filled with sticks of various lengths. He threw them onto the ground by Gareth's feet, but claimed the longest stick for himself. With a violent stab, he plunged it into the earth and then unclasped his cloak, which he draped over the stick to make a small tent. David had been charged with settling the horses, but once that was done, he followed and within minutes, he was snoring softly.

"Sir Talan, sleep will forsake me whilst you continue to sing," called Tristram. "Have pity, sir."

Talan grinned at me, and the tension in my shoulders lifted even more. They may have had swords and spears, but they weren't going to hurt me, not now.

I had been totally thrown by the realisation that Bedivere, this bedraggled stranger with the chestnut hair and penetrating green eyes, was the same person I had met on that fateful day when I fell through the earth.

It just wasn't possible.

But then ghostly baby rabbits with starlight eyes aren't possible either are they, and yet there it was, guiding you to this strange land. Time to suck it up and start believing.

Bedivere was lying down on his back, and from the flickering amber light of the fire I could see his eyes were closed. I knew he wasn't asleep though. His body was too rigid; his breathing too controlled. He was faking, and he wasn't very good at it.

"I know you aren't asleep," I whispered, crawling over to him like a caterpillar with his cloak wrapped around my body. "Tell me about Arthur. What do you know about my brother? Do you know where he is?"

Bedivere opened one eye, then the other. Close up they were even more beautiful, framed by long black lashes that most girls would kill for. I noticed he also had another dimple, set deep into his square chin. I shuffled back; I had gotten too close for comfort.

"Arthur is the only one who can unite the kingdom of Logres once more," said Bedivere quietly. "Without him, there is only darkness."

"But my brother is eighteen. He can be brilliant, but you've taken the wrong Arthur. He isn't a king – he's a math student."

"We did not take Arthur," replied Bedivere.

"Then who has him, Bedivere?"

A chilling howl echoed through the air. It was followed by high-pitched cackling, and the swift, shallow sound of something airborne flying through the sky towards our camp.

"Dwarf-riders," yelled Bedivere. "Arm yourselves, knights of Logres, and protect the maidens."

In one fluid movement, Tristram, Gareth and Talan rose and drew their swords. The sleepy David was a little slower.

"For Logres," they cried, as four monstrous black wolves leapt out of the wood and hurtled towards us.

The shadows cast by the amber firelight made the monsters appear the size of elephants. The drooling beasts were on the five knights in three bounds, and if their sharp blood stained teeth were not frightening enough, sitting on their backs, holding onto scraggy tufts of oily black fur, were four hideous little creatures. They were naked, apart from filthy loincloths which barely covered their skin. Even in the firelight, the green pus-filled boils that covered their hairy bodies were too easy to see – and smell.

The dwarves – who possessed wide, bright yellow eyes that glowed like headlamps – were armed with small bows. Their thick stubby fingers were amazingly dextrous, as arrow after arrow was slotted and fired, before being immediately refilled from a fringed quiver that was strapped to their humped, hairy backs.

Bedivere beheaded the first wolf and sent its rider the same way before it had time to strike. David was not so fortunate. An arrow pierced his sword arm and another quickly followed into his thigh. With a blood-curdling howl, a wolf lunged for him and pinned the knight to the ground. Sparks from our camp fire exploded as the wolf ran straight through the flames. The beast was about to bite a chunk out of David's throat, when Tristram and Talan combined to gut and slice the wolf until its guts fell sizzling and smoking onto the ground, like a mass of roasted grey snakes. The dwarf-rider lost both his arms before Gareth leapt forward to slit his throat. Even in the darkness, I could see the spilled blood was dirty green in colour. The ground beneath the blood appeared to sink down, like water draining from a bath.

"The sword," I yelled at Slurpy, who was standing like a stone statue in a frozen silent scream. "Use David's sword."

She picked it up, and howling like a banshee, started twirling it around her head like a mace. It was bizarre.

The firelight seemed to frame her in a blue haze. Slurpy didn't look real. I frantically searched for something sharp in the darkness, and noticed one of the spears lying on the ground by Bedivere's cloak. I picked it up and charged. My brain and body filled with thoughts of Arthur and a primal instinct to survive.

Bedivere and I combined to bring down another dwarf that had shot several arrows at Talan, while Gareth and Slurpy joined forces to slice the head off another wolf. Slurpy's high-pitched screeching accompanied every hack she made at the oily fur neck of the wolf. She continued to scream and stab long after the beast had stopped shuddering on the ground.

The wolf that had lost its rider, and the lone surviving dwarf, ran back into the wood with Talan and Tristram in pursuit. Only the wolf made it.

Slurpy and I slumped to the ground. It was only when I registered the snot running down into my mouth that I realised I was sobbing. Slurpy bypassed the tears and started heaving up the contents of her stomach. Bedivere had no time for hysteria. He pulled us up onto our feet.

"We cannot tarry," he said seriously. "The arrows of the dwarf-riders are riddled with poison. We must ride now to Caerleon, or it will be too late to save Sir David."

The embers of the hastily-doused fire were still flickering as we rode away into the darkness. I kept my ears primed for the howl of wolves, but only the heavy hooves of our horses, the groans of a dying knight, and the shallow breathing of Bedivere accompanied us.

8 CAERLEON

Exhaustion totally owned me. The rocking motion of the horse, the physical exercise of the strange day, and the fear in my system combined to send me to sleep, secured firmly by Bedivere's arm.

It was still dark when we arrived at Caerleon castle, but the hasty opening of the iron portcullis, and the teeth-grinding crunch of rusty metal were enough to wake me. The five horses were led through a narrow stone passageway and into a large rectangular courtyard. Blazing torch brackets lined the cobbled walls, and the smell of horse manure burned the inside of my nostrils.

"My lord Bedivere," cried a barefoot man in rags. "Sir Percivale and Sir Ronan have been awaiting your arrival; they are in the Great Hall. I will call for the men to take you there immediately."

Bedivere jumped down from his horse and opened his arms to help me. The ragged man gasped as he saw my shadow in the light of his own torch, which was spitting sparks at his filthy feet. I looked around for Slurpy, wanting an ally for my strangeness, but several horses were blocking my view of her.

"Advise Sir Percivale that I will come soon," replied Bedivere, "but first you must send for the new court physician. Sir David has been wounded – mortally I fear – by the arrows of a dwarf-rider. We were ambushed as we made camp."

"And the witches, sire?"

"They are not witches; they are kin to Arthur. Take them to the ladies quarters, and ensure they are attended to as befits a lady of the court."

The ragged man bowed deeply, but as he rose, Bedivere grabbed his wrist.

"Ensure she is not harmed. I will personally remove your head if a single hair on hers is damaged."

"Yes, sire," whimpered the man, and his bare feet scuttled away into a dark tunnel.

I was confused why Bedivere was now acting as protector, when several hours earlier he had held me captive. He threw the reins of his horse into the outstretched fingers of a tiny stable boy, who couldn't have been older than six.

"Is it safe for us here?" I asked.

"You are safer here than out there." Bedivere jerked his head towards the castle walls. He stared at me. I felt very self-conscious, but not in a bad way. Bedivere's face wasn't hard and angry, it was softening. It made my chest tighten.

"I want to stay with David...and you," I stammered, thinking safety in numbers.

Bedivere shook his head. Beads of sweat scattered in all directions, like a dog drying itself after a bath.

"The physician's quarters are no place for a maiden," answered Bedivere brusquely, "even one as able as you."

David was pulled from Tristram's horse and gently laid onto a frayed woollen blanket. Even in the eerie firelight, I could see he had gone a strange yellowish-green colour. The veins on his face were swollen, filled with the same pus that had marked the deformed bodies of the dwarves. His eyes were shut, and his throat was making rapid gasping noises. The poison was suffocating him.

Bedivere, Tristram, Gareth and Talan formed a guard of honour around the blanket, and then each picked up a corner and gently raised it. I was sure I saw tears in Tristram's eyes. They were helped by several more servants, who had scurried out of the dark corners of the courtyard like mice. David was carried away into a tunnel, and Slurpy and I were left alone.

"Should we run for it?" whispered Slurpy. Her words echoed back at us.

"And go where?" I replied, without sarcasm for once. "Now we know what's out there, do you honestly think we would last the rest of the night?"

"We should never have come here."

"I think it's too late for that."

"Will that boy live, do you reckon?"

I shook my head, unable to speak. David could not have been more than fifteen years old: two years younger than me, and three years younger than Arthur.

But the same age my other brother, Patrick, would have been now - if he had lived.

The men had gone, but a group of scared-looking women had replaced them. They approached us cautiously, and then flinched back as I sniffed loudly and wiped my nose on the sleeve of my sweatshirt. All of them were dressed in horrible A-line dresses that skimmed their ankles and appeared to add at least twenty pounds to their weight.

They still looked malnourished.

"Please, come with us," squeaked one woman. "We are ordered to take you to the ladies chamber."

"I hope there is hot water," sighed Slurpy, "because right now I would kill for a bath."

I couldn't help but snort as two of the women appeared to sway with fright. I leant over to Slurpy and whispered in her ear.

"As they think we are witches, we should probably leave talk of death and killing for another time."

Slurpy threw her hands out in frustration and slapped them down on her hips. She was still swearing and cursing the land of bizarre a full five minutes later.

We were led in the opposite direction to the one the knights had taken the injured David. Across the courtyard and into a circular tower. Up and round we climbed on narrow, slippery stone steps that were already starting to wear down with use. The now familiar sight and smell of burning torch brackets lit the way. We were shown along several long stone corridors, most of which were lined with long velvet standards that were covered in silvery cobwebs. Various mythical beasts had been sewn across them: dragons, unicorns, and even a one-eyed giant.

A quick glance at Slurpy was enough to tell me that she had that wrinkled quizzical look about her again.

"Is this familiar as well?"

She nodded. "Perhaps it was a school trip," she mumbled.

"That's what I thought."

"You recognise it?"

"Perhaps I've seen it in a book."

"Well, I don't read books."

A heavy oak door groaned as it was opened, and we were led through it. A large four-poster bed, covered in white linen sheets and heavy satin fabrics, dominated the room. A roaring fireplace, set deep into the stone wall, blazed directly opposite us. In front of that, two steaming tin baths were waiting.

Two young women approached us. They were dressed in pale pastel coloured dresses which fell to the floor, and they wore ballet type slippers on their feet.

Their long red hair was left loose where it fell in waves around their shoulders. They were very pretty.

The girls – who I thought were probably sisters – curtsied, and the shoeless servants pattered away to the other side of the heavy door without another word.

"Your bath awaits, m'lady," announced one of the girls. Then she stepped forward and immediately started to pull at my clothes.

"It's okay, I can do it," I mumbled, although I had to ask for help in removing my skinny jeans, which had glued themselves to my sweaty, swollen legs.

I asked the girls to turn around for the final part of undressing. I never showed my body off to anyone, and this reminded me too much of the torture that was the school changing rooms. Naked, I slipped into the bath water and submerged myself up to my neck. It was oily and smelt of lavender. The water was warm, but the roaring heat from the fire made it feel much hotter. Once my maid had stopped playing with the hook and eye fastening of my bra - which she found fascinating - she skipped over and started washing my hair, gently massaging a musky ointment deep into the roots before gently lathering and rinsing. It was peaceful and calm, with the silence only broken by the snapping of logs on the fire, and a strange wheezy rattling that seemed to come from the maid's chest. She was tender though, and I was particularly grateful that she paid attention to my stitches, carefully rubbing around the wound on my head that had been slowly healing for a week.

It seemed a lifetime ago now.

"Spa treatment – medieval style," I said to Slurpy.

I don't think she heard me. Her maid was not as gentle as mine and had ducked Slurpy under the water. Perhaps she was checking to see if Slurpy would sink or swim - wasn't that what they did to witches centuries ago?

Long, white linen nightgowns were then slipped over our heads and our long hair dried, combed and then wrapped up in segments and tied with suede ribbon.

"You look ridiculous," said Slurpy, as she flung herself onto the end of the four-poster bed.

"You should just be thankful Arthur isn't here to see how stupid you look," I replied.

And then we both fell silent. We had forgotten the reason we were there.

Arthur.

"May I ask a question, m'lady?" said the girl who had been helping me. Her arms were filled with my filthy clothes.

"Of course," I replied, "and please, call me Natasha, or Titch. Everyone else does." Well, those that don't call me *freak*, but then I wasn't going to tell her that.

The two sisters swapped looks. Then, urged on by the other, my maid spoke again.

"Is it true what the men of the castle are saying, m'lady? About Arthur?"

"Why, what are they saying?" I sat upright, desperate for news of my brother.

The girl had swallowed her top lip.

"The men are saying the bell has tolled once more. They are saying that Arthur has come again, and the great and brave have finally awoken. That the Knights of the Round Table shall meet the barbarian Saxon kings, and that the battles to come shall be the greatest ever seen in the kingdom of Logres."

She may as well have spoken to me in Mandarin for all the sense it made. How on earth could I answer that? I looked to Slurpy for help, but her mouth had dropped into a perfect circle, and her eyes were so wide the whites had swallowed her irises.

It was time for diplomatic relations again.

"My brother is the bravest, smartest boy I know.

Arthur has stood by me, and believed in me when no one else would. If he can help, in any way, I believe he will."

My statement - taken straight from my father's book on Foreign Affairs speak - seemed to please the two girls. A small hand bell was rung, and a fat woman, as wide as she was tall, then waddled into the room and placed a wooden flat tray on a table. It was filled with roast chicken, bread and fruit. Two golden goblets with dark red wine were also put down.

The maids curtsied, and Slurpy and I were left alone once more.

"I suppose now wouldn't be a good time to go and ask that Tristram dude for my cigarettes," said Slurpy, grabbing a chicken leg.

I was so hungry that, for a moment, my brain was willing to fool my conscience that I was a vegetarian. The smell from the roast chicken just oozed into the room. I had been a vegetarian for a year, and if I was honest, I desperately missed bacon and chicken nuggets. This delicious feast wasn't helping.

"I hope the court physician has helped David," I said, grabbing several tomatoes and tearing off a chunk of bread. My conscience would win the battle with my stomach this night.

"Who do you think lives here?" asked Slurpy. "I didn't think people, other than the Queen, lived in castles anymore."

"One of the servants mentioned the names Percivale and Ronan to Bedivere," I replied, reaching for the wine. "My guess is one of them is in charge here."

Slurpy started snorting into her wine. Some of it dribbled out of her nose. I laughed as she choked.

"This is mental," she gasped. "I still think we're tripping out on something. Does your mother grow funny mushrooms in your garden?"

"My mother wouldn't know a mushroom if it grew

on her face," I replied. "She's literally starved herself since Patrick…"

I trailed off. The heat from the fire, the aroma of the oils, and the very strong alcohol content of the castle-brewed wine had caught me off guard and dulled my sense of self-preservation. Patrick was a banned subject.

"Arthur told me about Patrick," said Slurpy, and there was something sly in her voice that immediately raised my defences.

"Good for him," I replied bluntly, slamming the goblet down. Thick red liquid slopped over the sides, trailing down the rim like blood.

I walked over to a bronze basin and poured cold water from a jug into its hollow. My hair was already tied up, and so I didn't need to worry about holding it back, as I threw my head forward and submerged my face in the freezing shallows. The giddiness quickly left me.

With my appetite gone, I climbed in between the sheets and closed my eyes. Slurpy followed, after blowing out the candles. The fire burnt down to cinders, and I eventually fell asleep.

I was back in *Avalon Cottage*, watching my two brothers play in the garden from an upstairs window. The room wasn't mine; it was Arthur's bedroom. I had space to breathe. There was a river running through the garden, fast-flowing and black as coal. It disappeared from view at the same spot where the chicken coop and Mr. Rochester had lived. Arthur was calling to me to watch Patrick, just for a minute. Then Arthur turned into a honey white rabbit and disappeared into the long grass. Patrick was laughing with his infectious giggle. Then he started running after Arthur. I wanted to call out to him, but I couldn't speak. My fingers grasped inside my mouth and found nothing but space. My throat was screaming at Patrick to stop, to stay away from the water, but no noise came out. I turned from the window to run downstairs, but my mother was blocking the door. In one hand she held a silver knife; in the other she held a purple slab of meat. It was my tongue.

"This is what we do to liars," she snarled, and then her scaly nostrils started to smoke as white flame shot from her mouth.

"Natasha, Natasha," screamed a voice in the dark. "Titch, wake up, wake up."

My eyes sprang open. I was back in the hospital bed. I could feel Arthur holding my pinkie finger, and hear the bleeping of the hospital machines.

My eyes focused, and Slurpy came into view. Another vision in white. I looked for Arthur, but instead saw the grim faces of Tristram and Talan standing beside the bed. Their swords were raised over my digital watch which was beeping away.

Sweat was pouring down my face and neck. Every muscle I possessed ached.

"You were screaming, but I couldn't wake you," sniffed Slurpy, "even when I slapped you around the face, and then *they* rushed in with their swords and I thought I was going to die." She looked whiter than the nightdress she was wearing.

"How is Patrick?" I gasped. "I mean David."

"Alive," was the reply. I wasn't sure whether it came from Tristram or Talan.

"Why are you here?" I said to the men, pulling the sheets up around my neck. "Isn't it against some knight's code to enter a girl's bedroom without an invitation or something?"

To my surprise, both looked embarrassed.

"We heard screaming," mumbled Talan, glancing at Slurpy. "Sir Bedivere had placed us outside the door to guard you both. We feared you to be in danger."

"From my watch?" I silenced it with two pushes of the same button.

The knights looked confused and slightly fearful.

"Tell Bedivere that we are perfectly well," I said, "and you can both get lost."

Tristram and Talan couldn't get out of the bedroom quick enough. The door slammed with a solid thump as the temperature finally registered on my skin. I looked down at my arms, which bore more than a passing resemblance to a plucked turkey, as the skin pimpled with the cold.

"Bad dream?" asked Slurpy, lying back down beside me.

"Yes."

"Well, I hope the nightmares stay inside your head, freak girl."

I didn't reply. It would seem like tempting fate. The terrors of my sleep were bad enough. I didn't need them invading the waking moments too.

9 BEDIVERE REVEALED

Roosters. Hundreds of them. Rising in one symphony of tuneless screeching. It reminded me of Arthur's dreadful singing in the shower, and my heart ached for what I had lost: past and present.

The two maids - who both looked far too happy for such an obscene hour - skipped into the bedroom. Slurpy had dived under the bed covers in an attempt to block out the noise from outside the castle walls. I had resorted to jamming two feather pillows against my ears.

"It is time for the women of the court to waken, m'lady," said my maid, as she started stoking the fire with a long blackened stick. It sparked to life like a cracker, and then simmered down as more logs were placed into the centre of the grate. I noticed the strange wheeze in my maid's chest again. She rattled with phlegm.

I wasn't exactly dragged out of bed, but it was close. With my eyes still glued shut with sleepy dust and that corner gunk you get whether you wear mascara or not, I was led, cold feet on even colder tiles, to a long wooden bench. My maid started tugging the ribbon out of my hair. Each portion cascaded down like a dirty blonde waterfall until my entire head was covered in a wave.

My maid beamed as I touched my hair with my fingertips. My reflection was shown back to me from a large polished plate.

"I love it." And I really did.

"You are very beautiful, m'lady," said my maid. "We just had to clean you up, that was all."

Slurpy's long dark hair looked even more stunning as it cascaded over her shoulders. It had a midnight blue sheen to it. She looked calculating, scary. Definitely witch-like. She even cackled as she gazed at her reflection. I felt jealous just watching her. I was pretty in a typical blonde hair, blue eyes kind of way, but Slurpy looked utterly gorgeous at times. I was mesmerised by her eyebrows. They were thick and arched low above her chocolate brown eyes. Keira Knightley eyebrows.

Hair combed. Teeth brushed with hot water and my finger. Face washed and eye gunk removed. It was time to get dressed, but my clothes from yesterday were gone.

The maid – who, after much prompting, had revealed that her name was Eve – had placed a sapphire blue dress on the bed. To my horror, I realised I was about to become a medieval Barbie doll. The satin was stitched so tightly that it made me gasp, as it was yanked and pulled down over my chest and hips, and then tightened like a corset. It was full length to my ankles and had long flared sleeves. Bands of silver embroidery were sewn into the hems and neckline. Upon closer inspection, they looked like linked hearts.

It was hideous.

I turned to Slurpy, who was wearing a magenta coloured dress with black and white fur edging.

"Arthur would love this," she sighed, flaunting her hourglass figure one way and then the other in the copper plate mirror.

I thought that my brother would probably love the plunging neckline, but I wasn't so sure he would be too keen on the dead badger that was hanging from the cuffs.

"I'm going to see Bedivere as soon as we're finished here," I said, as Eve tied a silver chain belt around my waist. "I want to know where Arthur is, or at least who they think took him."

"Oh, that would be the heathen king, m'lady," said Eve interrupting. Her little hands immediately flew up to her mouth, and she choked with an involuntary reflex as her chest gave way.

"Heathen king!" cried Slurpy. "What on earth are you talking about?"

"It's okay, Eve," I said softly. "If you know something, anything, about Arthur, you must tell me. My brother has been missing for two days now. I *have* to find him."

Eve's eyes were bulging in their sockets; her freckled face was on fire. She shook her head.

"It's just gossip in the kitchens, m'lady," she said weakly, although she wouldn't meet my eyes. I knew when a person was lying, especially when they weren't very good at it.

"Eve, where is my brother?"

"Tell the lady," prompted Slurpy's maid, nudging Eve in the back. "Tell them what we heard."

"You won't get into trouble, Eve. I promise you."

"King Balvidore has him, m'lady," whispered Eve. "At least that's what Sir Percivale told your Sir Bedivere last night, m'lady."

"Tell me everything you know about this Balvidore man," I replied. "Quickly, before we have to leave."

"Well, he isn't a king for a start," interrupted Slurpy's maid. "He just calls himself that. If you can't pay the taxes he sets, then he takes one of your family to work it off. Dirty old man, he likes the girls, 'specially the young 'uns," she added, narrowing her eyes. "Right nasty he is – pure evil, like the devil himself. Instead of the joust, he'll watch people burn at the stake for his jolly."

"But why has he got my brother?"

"Because Arthur is the only one who can stop him," replied the other maid, incredulously. "At least that is what folk here are saying. Now that the enchanted sleep has been lifted, all the court can talk about is the bell ringing once more. Balvidore has set up a rival court in Camelot, but the table and the sword won't accept him and his men, you see. It won't reveal their names. He can't be the true king without the table. They say it's cursed."

Slurpy was pinching the slim bridge of her nose between two fingertips. At first I thought she might have a nose bleed, but then her patience finally snapped.

"THIS IS MENTAL," she screamed.

"There's no need to get angry at them," I yelled. "If Arthur has been taken, then we need to know by who and why."

"But not one single word any of you says makes any sense," cried Slurpy, backing away as she jabbed her finger at each of us. "You're all insane, and I'm getting out of this asylum before every one of you infects me with your madness."

I made to follow her, but Eve grabbed my arm and pulled me back.

"You must watch yourself, m'lady," she whispered. "Watch yourself with that one."

"Sammy's just highly strung, that's all," I replied, but Eve gritted her teeth and vigorously shook her head, as the door slammed and a high-pitched scream of anger echoed through the castle corridors.

"When she realises the power she has, no one will be able to stop her. Mark my words, m'lady's companion has been touched by the dark arts."

While I was more than happy to refer to my brother's girlfriend as a witch, even I thought the girls were taking their suspicions to the extreme, and neither maid made any effort to stop me as I walked away. The satin ballet flats I wore on my feet made no sound on the stone floor, which was uneven and jagged. After stubbing my toes three times before I had even reached the door, I made a mental note to find my real clothes at the earliest opportunity. Dress up time was definitely over.

I made my way along several stone corridors, all of which were identical, down to the tapestries that hung from wrought iron hooks. Slurpy was nowhere to be seen, and I soon became hopelessly lost. Eventually I found a staircase that descended. Following its winding track, I waddled like a duck in a dress that was too long and far too tight. Along another, paler stone, corridor that was lined with shelves of leather bound books and dusty scrolls. It was deserted within the castle walls. I checked my watch, safely hidden under the flared satin sleeve of my dress. The date displayed was now the 22 September, but I had given up trying to guess the year.

And still I had the strangest feeling that I had been here before.

I came to a large set of oak doors. A dented shield, painted with a red dragon, was hanging above the arched frame. By now I was convinced the seams of my dress were starting to unravel with the strain of trying to contain me. Skinny jeans were positively loose when compared to the outfit of torture that Eve had forced me into.

The castle was silent. I pushed one of the large doors, which creaked like my grandmother's joints in the morning, and went through into a large hall. Several stone pillars were spaced evenly apart along its full length. At the far end were hung three banners, all portraying the same red dragon that had been painted onto the shield above the door. Below the banners was a raised dais made of pale shiny stone, like yellow marble. As the morning sun reflected through the slit windows, it bathed the dais with golden rays. Three high-backed seats were positioned below the banners. They were the kind of seats you find in churches. One sermon and you leave with haemorrhoids.

"Have you eaten, m'lady?" said a deep gruff voice behind me.

I squeaked as my feet lifted from the floor.

"My apologies, Lady Natasha. I didn't mean to scare you," said a tall male from the shadows. His voice and accent were familiar. Was he one of the men we had passed last night on the way to our room?

"I'm looking for a knight called Bedivere," I called, looking around for something that could be used as a weapon – just in case. "I arrived here last night with him and several others. One was injured. A boy called David."

"Sir David is being tended to by the new physician of Caerleon," replied the man from the shadows. "They say the physician is highly skilled and Sir David will quickly recover under his care."

"Well, that's good then," I said, spying a heavy-looking silver candlestick that had been left on a long table.

"You have nothing to fear, Lady Natasha," said the male, and he stepped out of the shadows. He was tall, very good-looking, clean shaven with a square dimpled jaw and pale pink lips. For every stride he took towards me, I took three stumbling steps back. His legs were longer though, and within seconds he was only a couple of metres away.

His thick hair was shoulder length and chestnut coloured. He wore dark, slim fitting trousers which were half covered by a pair of long, cracked leather boots. A sleeved tunic covered his body. It was olive green with a vertical slit at the chest, which revealed a small smattering of hair.

He smiled at me. His teeth didn't dazzle like Arthur's, but then no one had teeth that white. My braces had only just been removed and so my teeth hadn't been whitened yet. For some reason, the thought of teeth made me slide my tongue over my own. Then I started to nervously wind my wavy hair around my fingers. And what were my hips doing? They were swaying. Stay still. Oh help.

The young guard smiled again. His huge green eyes caught the sun streaming into the hall and I gasped.

It was Bedivere.

Without that matted hairy carpet covering his face, he looked so much younger than before. He still had a few lines, mainly creased into his forehead, but then I had a friend – no, it was just someone I knew – at a school in Amsterdam who had worry lines when she was seven.

How was this possible? The first time I met Bedivere, he must have been a thousand years old. Crumbling and blind. Then, down by the lake for our second meeting, he had been given life, a purpose – and eyes. Those gorgeous fizzy green eyes. Now he appeared even younger, only a year older than Arthur at the most. At this rate he would be running around the castle screaming for an ice-cream by supper time.

"How do you do that?" I asked.

"Do what, m'lady?"

"Manage to look younger every time I see you."

Bedivere shrugged. Without his beard, his mannerisms seemed younger as well. The hair was his own personal shield.

"These are strange and dark times," said Bedivere, stepping closer. "Nothing is how it appears, and I too look for answers. Now Lady Natasha, perchance you would care to tell me how *you* came to be here? Everything about you differs from the maidens of Logres, and it intrigues me. I accept you are no witch, but you are a rare breed for sure. So help me now. The knights and I are needed for the fight that is coming against an enemy we know. If more strangers arrive from your land with malevolent intent, then we may lose the battle before the first blade is drawn."

"I don't think you need to worry about more coming from our land," I replied. "The tunnel that brought us here collapsed. Our way back is blocked."

"I see." Bedivere smiled to himself. "I must counsel that Sir Percivale has ordered that you and your companion remain here at Caerleon while we go in search of Arthur."

"Percivale can go stuff himself. I'm leaving to find Arthur. Today in fact, once I've found my clothes."

Bedivere laughed and I immediately wanted to hear it again.

"I told Sir Percivale and Sir Ronan that you could not be contained."

"Then you know me pretty well already," I replied, feeling unnerved as a strange sensation started to tingle inside my body. "Well, it was nice speaking to you again, Bedivere, and I am very glad that David is getting better, but I need to go."

The slice of metal against metal then echoed through the cavernous hall; Bedivere had drawn his sword from a steel scabbard. From hilt to tip, it was longer than my arm. My mind raced back to our first meeting inside the tomb. Oh no – now he had his strength back he really was going to skewer me like a kebab.

"I am a Knight of the Round Table," cried Bedivere, "and by my honour and life, I swear an oath this day to protect you, Lady Natasha. You will ride with us, and we will reunite you with Arthur. For glory *will* come to

Logres once more, and my heart tells me that you have a part to play for the good of us all."

Bedivere went down onto a bended knee, kissed my hand, stood and saluted me with a curt bow and then strode from the court.

I staggered back onto the dais and collapsed into the centre chair. A blue satin seam across my stomach exploded. It was the most uncomfortable seat I had ever sat in, yet I stayed there for several minutes until my heart had stopped banging against my ribcage, oxygen had returned to my lungs, and my stomach realised gravity still existed. My skin tingled at the spot where Bedivere had kissed it.

Well, this is starting to get complicated, isn't it?

10 DECISION TIME

Several things in my life were absolutely guaranteed: I would get at least three Facebook friend requests a week from people who had barely said five words to me; it would rain at least three hundred days of the year in Britain, and all of them would be when I was outside without a jacket; my zits could get so big they could be seen from the International Space Station; and a television show would become uncool, just as I was getting into it and had bought the t-shirt.

Now added to that list – and highlighted for good measure – was another one: I would start thinking the most inappropriate things about the most inappropriate boys at the most inappropriate moments.

I spent the rest of the morning with three aims, the most important of which was to find my real clothes. The second, and it caused physical pain to say this, was to find my brother's ridiculous girlfriend. The third, and it caused physical pain to say this as well, was to stay out of the way of Bedivere and his band of merry men.

When my inner voice noted that was the legend of Robin Hood and not this one, I told it to "sod off." I had enough distractions as it was, without my schizophrenic counterpart voicing its opinion whenever it wanted.

Task number one was ticked off after breakfast. I found Eve sweeping a set of stairs, and she took me down to the kitchens, where my washed clothes were hanging in front of the most enormous fireplace I had ever seen. Getting out of the dress and into my skinny jeans took physics to a whole new level. A crowbar wasn't called for, but it was close. In the end I had to lie flat on my back before I could pull my jeans up over my knees. The warm breakfast that followed was very welcome. It looked like the bread and butter pudding my grandmother used to make, and it was just as delicious. In between spoonfuls, Eve told me that the men didn't take food in the morning.

"It is reserved for the women and children alone. Gluttony is a sin and the breaking of the fast is not undertaken by the men of the court until late morning," she explained.

"More for me then," I said, before burping.

Task number two was next, as Eve and I searched everywhere for Slurpy.

"She's pretty and quite tall," I explained for the millionth time to yet another guard; this particular one had caught us looking in the armoury. "She has long black hair." The guard looked confused, so I cupped my hands and put them in front of my chest. "She has big...you know..."

A smile. Yes, he knew who I was talking about. Then he shrugged.

"I saw the lady from a land afar just as the sun came over the battlements," he said. "She looked most displeased, and so I did not follow her."

"Which direction did she go in?"

"Yonder way," he replied, pointing.

I looked at Eve. "What is yonder way when it's at home?"

"He points to the stables, m'lady."

"Then we'll try there."

But Slurpy wasn't there either.

So with task one dealt with, and task two proving difficult, all that was left was task three.

Steering clear of Bedivere was easy. He had gone riding with Gareth, Talan, Percivale and Ronan and would not be back until sunset, according to a stable boy. So Eve and I went back to the kitchens to help with the cooking.

My thoughts drifted back to school. Would this strange new place be filed under history, literature, drama, or that miscellaneous folder that covers the things you don't know where to place: like what shoes are cool; how much make-up can you get away with before you get detention; and how saying nothing at all can still get you cold-shouldered?

And where would I file it in *my* history? I had never met any of these people before in my life, and yet I knew where things were stored in the kitchens. I instinctively knew what people were called before they were introduced to me.

It was all so weird, and yet all so familiar.

The fat cook, who had appeared the previous evening in my room with a tray of food, proved to be an awesome hostess. I liked her immediately. She kneaded bread with one hand, while hacking chunks of carrots with the other, all the while booming out details of castle life in a deep voice that seriously had me doubting whether she was actually female.

"Our Lord Percivale of Wales is the lord and master of Caerleon," explained cook. "He was married to a

young fair maiden called Lady Matilda, but she was
bewitched by an evil knight called Tarquin the Green.
Lady Matilda now sleeps all day, and only rises when the
full moon is high in the sky."

I thought she just sounded like most of my English
class at school, but I kept quiet.

The cook continued on. "Sir Ronan is a former lord
of Caerleon, and he reappeared just days before your
coming, not long after the enchantment of Logres was
finally lifted. Oh, we slept for such a long time, didn't
we, Eve. Sir Ronan was searching for your Sir
Bedivere."

My heart skipped as I heard Bedivere's name. *Your
Sir Bedivere*, the cook had said.

It was taken as given by those at Caerleon that
Arthur had come once more. The quest now was to find
him. I was happy at the enthusiasm, bordering
adoration, that the kitchen staff showed my brother, but
my inner voice was, as ever, ready and waiting to bring
me back to the land of reality.

They have the wrong Arthur.

I knew that of course, but with so many now willing
to assist, I knew that I stood a greater chance of getting
him back with the help of others than I did on my own.

I had lost one brother – I would not lose another.

A soldier came down to the kitchen. He slapped
cook on her backside and she whacked him back with
her palm. He then buried his face in her neck. I groaned
and diverted my eyes. They were even grosser than
Slurpy trying to eat Arthur flavoured ice-cream.

The soldier eventually pulled his red sweaty face
away from cook's cleavage and looked at me. My first
instinct was to grab a sharp knife. He was going to lose
body parts if he tried that with me. I didn't need to
worry, I was simply being summoned to the Great Hall.
Lord Percivale had returned earlier than expected and

was now requesting an audience.

That meant Bedivere, my new protector, was back as well. I gave Eve a resigned shrug with the promise I would be back. She winked at me and I poked my tongue out at her.

I finally had a friend, and while I was buzzing inside at this thought, it also laid bare the pathetic tragedy of my life to date.

The sex-starved soldier marched ahead of me with a vertical spear in his right hand. Until my adventures down a dark hole, I had been studying Greek mythology and the works of Euripides at school. It was another memory of a legend that seemed to link rather tenuously to this one. It was all very phallic. I just think boys want to have something in their hands. We were joined by several more soldiers on the short journey to the hall, and so by the time I was shown in and my attendance announced, I was flanked by a pentagon of armed men.

The day before I would have found this scary, but now I just found it rather ridiculous. What was far more frightening was the knowledge that with every step, I was getting closer to the gorgeous Bedivere.

"Don't blush, don't blush," I muttered to myself through gritted teeth.

A man, who I presumed was Percivale, was sitting in the centre chair on the raised dais. He looked much older than Bedivere, Tristram, and the other knights. His brown hair was flecked with long wiry streaks of grey, as was his beard, which was groomed into a short point on his long chin. There was a weariness about him, despite the fact his back was upright against the back of the hard wooden seat. His faced was heavily lined, and a long scar marked an ugly purple fissure down his cheek.

The chair to his left was empty, while the chair to his

right was taken by a short man with a shock of red hair. I knew he was small because his boots didn't reach the floor. I took a guess that this was the man they called Sir Ronan. His short body didn't appear to be too fat, but he had a large round face with bulbous cheeks that shone. He grinned broadly at me as I walked in. I smiled back, all the while thinking I was about to be interrogated by an over-ripened tomato.

Percivale and Ronan were the only people on the dais, but loads of others were standing in the hall, lining the walls. All noise had stopped the second I walked into the room. My eyes caught Tristram and Talan and, to my surprise, David who was with them. He was leaning back against a pillar with his eyes closed. A blotchy green rash covered his neck and face, and two thick bulges under his clothes indicated the outline of bandages.

The sight of David made me quietly seethe. The poor boy had been at death's door just hours ago. Why on earth had he been dragged to this farce? Someone should have been spooning him vegetable soup from the comfort of a warm bed.

Abruptly I stopped walking, taking all five guards by surprise. The one behind me actually walked into my back, which caused some suppressed laughter to echo around the stone walls. I scowled at the guard with my contemptible face, and then turned back to the dais and crossed my arms, hoping beyond hope that I hadn't appeared too constipated in front of Bedivere. I wanted to be cool, and calm, and pretty, and smart.

"So this is Lady Natasha," said Percivale slowly, looking at me as if I were a horse to be bought at auction.

"Natasha Amelia Roth, to be exact," I replied.

"Sir Bedivere claims you skewered a dwarf-rider," said Percivale. "Is this true?"

Just the sound of his name turned the tap on under

my arms. Cool, calm, pretty and smart was in danger of becoming sweaty, flustered, blotchy and stupid.

"I helped, I guess," I mumbled.

"And Sir Tristram has finally admitted that it was you that provided him with that fine plump lip."

More laughter around the court as Tristram scowled. His split lip seemed to magnify in size as I remembered the scuffle the day before at the side of the mysterious lake. I couldn't resist smirking back, encouraged by laughter that wasn't aimed at me for once.

"Maidens of Caerleon do not behave in such a way," said Percivale gravely, and immediately a hush descended. It suddenly occurred to me that while Bedivere was convinced I was not a witch, the same may not be said for the rest of the men bearing arms.

"I am not a maiden of Caerleon," I replied, hoping I sounded braver than I actually felt. "I come from a different place, a different land. My only reason for being here is to find my brother, Arthur."

Unintelligible, whispered mutters swept the hall.

"Where is your lady companion?"

"I don't know," I replied truthfully.

Percivale quickly rose from his chair, as if challenged.

"One of our horses is missing from the stables. A fine red mare that belongs to Lady Matilda. She will be sorely aggrieved to discover its loss."

I was sorely tempted to ask *how*, bearing in mind the Lady Matilda did nothing but sleep.

"Your companion, the dark maiden called Lady Samantha, is believed to have stolen the horse," continued Percivale. "It will be grievous indeed if this has come to pass."

"I don't know where Slurpy...I mean Sammy is," I replied anxiously, "but I do know she loves my brother, and if she did take the horse – NOT that I'm saying she did – but if she *borrowed* the horse, then she would only have done it to go in search of Arthur." I looked around the maze of men and finally caught Bedivere's eyes. It was impossible not to.

"Isn't that what you all want?" I cried, blushing furiously. "To find Arthur? He's been in trouble for days, and yet you're all still standing here? It seems to me that Sammy is the only one who actually had the guts to do something about it."

Things were desperate. I was defending Slurpy for a start.

Outside a cloud passed in front of the sun, and the light around the dais darkened. En masse, every pair of superstitious eyes in the Great Hall turned to the blocked window like it was a sign. Percivale held out his hands, and with his long fingers twitching, beckoned people forward. For a terrifying moment, I wasn't sure whether he was calling me, or motioning to his guards to relieve me of my head.

Several men, including Bedivere, Tristram, Gareth, Talan, and a wobbly-looking David, approached the dais. I quickly counted at least twenty five heads now surrounding Percivale and Ronan. A discussion was taking place. It reminded me of the ghostly whispers that had surrounded *Avalon Cottage* and the wooded area behind the house. I couldn't hear what the men were saying, but I knew I was being mentioned because faces would suddenly jerk towards me. Gareth and Talan looked impassive, almost bored; Tristram pouted; little Sir Ronan was licking his lips, and David was clearly about to throw up or die where he stood. Only Bedivere and, to my surprise, Percivale, appeared to display any obvious friendliness towards me.

The men dispersed back into the crowd and Ronan climbed back into his seat like a child, knees first. It was difficult to not giggle. Percivale motioned to a guard, and a silver sword, studded with red jewels, was brought forward. Percivale clutched the sword to his chest, and I was instantly reminded of Bedivere's oath.

Something was about to happen. The tension in the room was palpable.

"Noble knights of Caerleon," announced Percivale loudly, and the weariness I had detected in him earlier just melted away. "The decision has been made. Ready the horses and prepare to ride. For tomorrow, we leave for battle. Tomorrow, we leave for Camelot –," he looked straight at me, "– and Arthur."

"For Arthur," cried the men as one, and every hair I possessed stood to attention. Legends would say someone was walking over my grave. With my sense of direction and luck, it was probably me.

A crescendo of male voices, clanking silver, and the rush of feet on tiles then broke like a wave as the men jostled through the hall. I feared being crushed, but a strong arm appeared from nowhere and pushed me towards the dais and Percivale.

"My instincts tell me that you should remain here at Caerleon, Lady Natasha," said Percivale solemnly, as I approached.

"Your instincts can tell you whatever," I replied, "but I'm going to find Arthur, even if it means stealing a horse and following Slu…Sammy."

"What if we were to lock you in the tallest tower?" squeaked Ronan in a high-pitched voice.

"Then I'll tie my clothes together and make a rope."

Ronan gave a squeak and exclaimed, "I like this maiden, she has spirit."

Percivale stroked his beard with his fingers, thinking.

"Sir Bedivere," he called. "Do you still intend to protect the lady?"

"I have sworn an oath," replied a deep gruff voice behind me, and I realised it was Bedivere's strong hands that had guided me through the crowd. Blood rushed to my head, and other parts that I hadn't realised contained arteries.

"Look," I cried. "If you have me with you, then you stand a better chance of finding Arthur, don't you? He'll immediately recognise me, and my voice. He'll trust me above anyone."

"I marvel at your bravery, Lady Natasha," said Percivale. "You must come from a great and noble house."

I shrugged. "My house is called *Avalon Cottage* if you must know."

"The secret land of Avalon," squeaked Ronan again. "Then Arthur has truly returned after all this time."

Percivale nodded once to Bedivere. Sir Ronan climbed down from his wooden throne, and he and Percivale swept from the hall without another word. Confused, I turned to Bedivere. We were now the only two left in the room.

"Does this mean I'm coming with you?" I asked.

Bedivere smiled, and my stomach was immediately infested with butterflies. He was at least six inches taller than me and so he had to look down. It made his face appear softer. I wanted to touch his lips, play with his hair, flick his earlobes…

What the hell was wrong with me?

"I think we need to get you more suitably attired for the journey," he said. "It is a dangerous road to Camelot."

Arthur. I was finally getting closer to finding my brother. I *whooped* with delight and threw my arms around Bedivere's neck. Before I realised what I was doing, my mouth had clamped down hard on his.

11 LADY SLURPY-TITCH

My parents, Arthur and I had lived in New York before the transfer to nowhere. One evening, my parents went out to an official reception at the French embassy. Arthur and I were left home alone, and so he decided to have a party.

I didn't need to find pretend friends to invite because Arthur always had more than enough to go around. He could make friends with a statue. The texts and invites went viral, and within an hour, all of these rich kids turned up with more alcohol and pills than a Hollywood actress. The Government-loaned apartment was trashed, as was everyone inside it.

I sucked three bottles of vodka and cranberry juice through a straw and developed a cold sweat. I was in my bedroom, watching the ceiling spin from my bed, when one of Arthur's friends walked in.

I can't remember his name, but in light of what happened next, I'm pretty sure he has never asked me to be his friend on Facebook.

I can remember that he was smoking something sickly-sweet smelling because it clashed horribly with the aftershave he had showered in. It didn't help my churning stomach. After talking to me about his car and horse power – none of which I understood or cared about in the slightest – he tried to kiss me with a tongue that was as long as a giraffe's.

I vomited on him. I may have actually been sick in his mouth.

Even moving to the other side of the world did not remove the shame I felt at being the instigator of something so horrible.

So why did I remember this now?

Because I needed some kind of measure on my gross-o-meter when I realised I was doing an impression of Slurpy Sammy all over Bedivere.

At least Bedivere didn't vomit.

At first he froze. Then he parted his own mouth a little before he froze again. It was like kissing a robot that was running out of batteries. Bedivere didn't appear to know what to do.

So he grabbed hold of my arms rather roughly and pushed me away. Then he bowed, and with a face drained of colour, he ran away.

He ran away!

My knees buckled as my brain caught up with my hormones. My inner voice abandoned me like Bedivere, only to be replaced by the voice of a screaming banshee.

WHAT THE HELL DID YOU JUST DO?

In a shamed daze, I staggered back down to the kitchens, where I found Eve; she was slicing bruised apples. I collapsed onto a wooden bench beside her and placed my head in my hands.

"Kill me now, Eve," I whispered. "Just kill me now."

"What has happened?" cried the cook, waddling towards me. "Did that filthy scullion Branor attempt to have his wicked way with ye'?"

Bile was rising in my throat. I wanted the earth to open up and swallow me whole.

"She's been kissed," crowed a voice. I looked up, and saw a toothless woman sitting on a three-legged stool next to the fire. She looked at least one hundred years old, with black shining eyes and crinkled, parchment thin skin, that reminded me of those treasure maps you make at school: a white piece of paper stained brown by tea leaves and then burnt at the edges.

A violent thump made me jump as the table shuddered. Cook had slammed a large rectangular blade into the wood.

"When I get my hands on that Branor," she boomed, "my knife will go hunting for his manhood."

Words bubbled in my mouth; I think I actually drooled a little. I shook my head and my empty brain rattled. I didn't know who Branor was, but I thought I should do my best to stop his impending castration.

"It was me. I kissed Bedivere."

My head collapsed back into my arms as laughter rang through the kitchen.

"Lady Natasha," said Eve, in awe.

"I knew it, I knew it," crowed the old woman, clapping her clawed hands as she rocked to and fro.

Cook simply slid a large piece of pie towards me.

"Eat up, child," she ordered, as a gleam spread across her podgy face. "Sir Bedivere is a fine knight, but you'll need some more meat on your bones if you're to win his heart."

"I don't want to win his heart. I want mine cut out before it does something else really stupid."

Soulful singing interrupted my cries, as a voice from above started to descend the stone steps to the kitchen. Moments later, Talan appeared. Everyone, with the exception of the old woman and me, jumped to their feet and either bowed or curtsied. Clicking arthritic joints echoed around the dimly lit room.

"Lady Natasha," said Talan, grinning. "I've been sent to accompany you to the stables. We are to find a worthy mare for you and your maid for the journey to Camelot."

He started singing again. I distinctly heard him mention kissing, fair maidens, and wondrous lands abroad.

"I don't need a horse. I'll walk – by myself."

My statement was met with another verse from Talan. This time Bedivere and my own name were mentioned, although Talan was cut short mid-sentence because he clearly couldn't think of a word that rhymed with *Natasha*.

Cook and the old woman were roaring with laughter. Even Eve was giggling, although she had the decency to muffle her sniggers with her fist. Then she broke into a coughing fit, and that was enough to distract cook from her amusement.

I wasn't the only one worried about Eve's health.

"M'lady," said Talan smiling, "I am certainly more akin to assisting damsels in distress than carrying them, but you would be foolish to entertain the notion that I am beyond sweeping you over my shoulder and into the courtyard. Before the age of Logres' enchanted sleep, I slayed evil knights, dragons and pestilent dwarves. My duty today is to prepare you for the quest, and I will fulfil that deed. Now do you yield, or do I carry?"

I yielded. I had been embarrassed enough for one lifetime.

Talan led me and Eve out into the courtyard and towards the stables. Percivale had ordered that Eve was to come with me on the journey to find Arthur, and as Slurpy had still not been found, I was very thankful for the company. As a replacement, Eve was way better than the original.

Bedivere's horse was gone, which of course gave Talan the perfect excuse for another song. It was quite amazing how many words Talan could arrange to rhyme with *Bedivere*. When that became boring, I taught him the words to "Hey Jude", which he picked up with ease. It sounded gorgeous in his Irish voice.

Eve was terrified of the horses and she refused to go anywhere near them. While I was certainly no equestrian, I had been riding since the age of seven. After trying out several, we eventually agreed that a dappled mare with white socks was the best choice. Talan had a little stable boy take it away to be made ready for departure.

As the morning went on, Talan hung out with us and explained more about the castle of Caerleon.

"For sure, Lady Matilda is trapped in a dreamless state. Sir Percivale is weary with worry. And did you know that Sir Ronan is her brother? Their father was Lord of Caerleon before Sir Percivale, and he pressed for the marriage to ensure the castle stayed in the family. Sir Ronan may not have the look of wildness, but he had disappeared long before Arthur was lost to Avalon, and the enchantment over Logres was born. Sir Ronan turning up was quite the shock, for he had been long presumed dead."

What a charming father, I thought to myself. Pimping out his daughter. No wonder she still slept all the time.

"So how old are you, Talan?"

"I have seen twenty winters, Lady Natasha. I have no kin left now, and I crossed the sea from my beloved Ireland to join the court of Camelot as soon as I was old enough to ride a horse and stay on it."

"Twenty winters? So you're twenty years old. What a cute way of saying it. Well, I have seen seventeen winters."

"Seventeen? And you are not yet married to a noble knight of your land? Your father should not tarry any longer."

"Seventeen isn't old," I spluttered, "and my father doesn't get a say, thank you very much."

"Why, seventeen is ancient," replied the knight.

Spinster. Witch. Lady Slurpy-Titch. Just how many insults would come my way in this place?

Don't forget freak?

"How old are you, Eve?" I asked. She was sitting on the courtyard steps, quietly sewing away as her chest rattled. I was starting to wonder whether she was asthmatic.

"I am not sure, m'lady. I believe I have seen fifteen winters, but I'm not well versed with numbers."

"Sir Bedivere has counted off nineteen winters, Lady Natasha," said Talan with a sly grin, "and eight of those as a knight."

Which means Bedivere is far too old for me, I immediately thought, as well as being too tall, too green-eyed, and too hairy.

You're convincing no one you know. Slurp, slurp.

After lunch, Eve and I went back to the room that I had slept in. She continued to alter clothes, and I spent an hour picking dirt out of my fingernails. Then I squeezed a couple of new spots. The whereabouts of Arthur - and to my chagrin, Slurpy - played heavily on my mind. I missed Arthur's drawling accent and his smirk-like smile. I replayed memories in my head like a projector, trying to keep his image with me as a prop. He had only been missing for two days according to my watch, but time and events in this fantastical land were eating up the space in my head. Thankfully, Eve was more than happy to hear stories from our childhood, especially Arthur's great deeds, which usually involved scaling walls, running away from police, or kissing girls.

And my brother had kissed a lot of girls.

Tristram and Talan came to visit during the afternoon, and the items from Slurpy's rucksack were handed back to me: the Jaffa cakes, the cans of Red Bull, her mobile telephone, cigarettes and the torch. The gum had gone.

"These are strange objects to be sure, Lady Natasha," said Talan.

"What is their use?" asked Tristram, scowling slightly.

"It isn't witchcraft, if that's what you're thinking," I replied. "Look."

I picked up the can of drink and snapped open the ring pull. The sudden release of gas made Talan, Tristram and Eve jump back. They only inched forward once they saw me drinking from it.

I shuddered. It tasted vile because it was so warm. I held it out to them.

"It should be cold, but you can see for yourself that it isn't poisonous."

To my surprise it was Eve who ventured forward. She took a sip, then a gulp. She convulsed as bubbles got stuck in her nose. I couldn't help laughing. She looked like a baby who had been fed lemons for the first time.

"This is food where I come from," I said, opening the box of Jaffa Cakes. I bit into one of the circular soft biscuits. They were looking a little squashed and crumbly, but still tasted delicious.

Talan tried one of those. Then he sang about it.

I looked at Tristram, who was staring at me with suspicious eyes. His arms were folded in front of his chest in a defensive pose.

"And those?" he said, with a nod towards the cigarettes.

"Damn you, Slurpy," I muttered. The lighter was

tucked inside the packet. I took one of the thin white sticks out and stuck it between my lips.

"Suck and blow," was all I managed to splutter before I started choking.

Tristram was far more interested in the lighter, which he snatched from my hand.

"Fire at her fingertips," he muttered.

"This is grievous indeed," replied Talan thickly; he had stuffed three biscuits into his mouth at once.

"Here we go again," I muttered, rolling my eyes. I looked over to Eve who was twitching. I grabbed the drink and realised it was nearly empty. My new friend was overdosing on caffeine, and showing the wonders of butane gas to two armed knights hadn't been the greatest idea I had ever had. The day was going from bad to worse.

"We have had word from an outpost that your companion has been sighted," said Tristram.

"You've found Sammy?"

"She was long gone by the time Sir Bedivere arrived," said Talan, and his handsome face suddenly darkened.

"What's wrong?"

Tristram & Talan exchanged looks; they appeared fearful.

"She is with Sir Mordred," they replied together.

Outside the castle walls, a bell started tolling.

12 A FLASH OF WHITE

I paid attention in history and English class, and so I knew the myths, the legends.

I was also hopeful that this strange land where time had gone mental, was working to different rules now. They had the wrong Arthur, I was sure of it, so perhaps the knights' worries about Mordred and Slurpy were off the mark as well.

Yet my second night within the castle walls of Caerleon did not produce the dreamless sleep I craved. Tossing and turning, too hot one minute, freezing cold the next. I heard whispers when my eyes were shut, and I saw shadows moving in the room when they were open. For the first time I wondered whether Arthur was frightened too, and the thought made me cry.

Eve knew I was upset when she crept into the bedroom. I guess the dying firelight was enough to see in if you were accustomed to it. She hugged me. No fuss, no drama. Just two skinny arms wrapped around my body.

My tears became painful sobs. I wanted this to end. I wanted my brother back.

I washed my blotchy face and allowed Eve to brush my hair. Then I dressed in the clothes she had been altering for me: dark tan coloured trousers that were made of stretched suede, and a dark purple tunic. They were soft to the touch and very comfortable. Perfect for riding *sans* buttock chaffing.

The cobbled courtyard of Caerleon was heaving with men, horses, and wooden carts that were filled to breaking point with supplies. I quickly found Gareth, Talan and David, who were grouped together at the back of the small army. Gareth welcomed me with a friendly smile, and I noticed he had chipped a tooth since I last saw him.

I couldn't help myself from searching the bobbing heads for Bedivere, but he was nowhere to be seen. I hoped he wasn't saying a passionate farewell to some girl - the thought of which sent spasms of jealousy through my stomach.

Women and barefoot children lined the stone walls and threw flowers, as we clip-clopped our way out of the safety of the castle and into the wild. Thin tube trumpets were blown and lifeless banners rose, as the travelling court of Caerleon left for Camelot. We were on our own, with no protection other than sharp slivers of metal.

I hoped swords would be enough.

I couldn't see Eve either. She had hitched a ride on one of the carts from the kitchen. There were hundreds of them also travelling to Camelot.

Camelot. Even saying the word in my head made me feel dizzy. The worst thing was there was no one, other than Arthur, that I would ever be able to share this with - at least not once we were back in the middle of nowhere. The entire world, or at least the people in it who knew me, believed I was a liar.

It wasn't your fault.

Who was I kidding? I hadn't told the truth when it

mattered.

As we slowly made our way along a dusty, pale orange track, I struck up a three-way conversation with Gareth and David. The young knight still looked dreadfully ill. His skin had a dark yellow tinge to it, like jaundice. The whites of his eyes had the same sickly shadow as well.

"Are you sure you are well enough for this journey?" I asked, trotting beside him. "You look awful."

David looked annoyed to be asked.

"Soon I will be a true knight of Camelot," he wheezed. "This is my duty."

"Your duty is to die on us?"

Laughter from behind indicated that Gareth and Talan had overheard.

"Sir David has yet to fully prove himself, Lady Natasha," called out Gareth, who now spoke with a lisp, courtesy of the chipped tooth. "At the joust, he has no equal, yet he cannot fully declare himself a knight of Arthur until he has smote a rival in battle."

"And I take it all of you have *smote rivals*?" I asked.

"Many, Lady Natasha," boasted Gareth. "My brothers and I are renowned for our skills with the blade and spear."

"Have you heard anything about your brothers, Gareth?"

"My younger brothers, Gawain and Gaheris, went straight to Camelot when word of Arthur's capture reached us. Alas, they have not been sighted since. My other brother, Agravaine, was captured by Balvidore's ruffians, and is being held captive east from here."

"So what will Percivale do? Will we try and rescue Agravaine before Arthur?"

"The lord of Caerleon will have his own way, and I will have mine," replied Gareth cryptically, but I noticed he swapped looks with Talan.

"Don't you dare leave me," I said quickly. "You're the only knights I know here."

"Nor leave me," groaned David.

"Your path is with Sir Percivale and the travelling court of Caerleon," replied Gareth softly. "He can protect you better than we can."

"I don't believe that for a second. I'm telling now, if you leave us, Gareth, then we'll follow you, won't we, David?"

The knight gurgled his agreement.

"Why do you care so, Lady Natasha?" asked Gareth. "Your safety is assured with so many around you. Any road we lead you down will be perilous, and certainly no place for a maiden."

"I care because the only person here who really understands me is you," I replied quietly. "Take away the magic and the monsters and the barbarian kings, and at the end of the day we are just two people who are looking for brothers. I feel safe with all of you."

"You are a strange and yet intriguing maiden," said Gareth, massaging his neck.

"Tell me something new."

My sarcasm was lost. Talan merely took it as a request for a song.

After several hours of riding, the travelling court of Caerleon stopped and rations were passed around: bread, water and thin strips of something that looked like beef, but smelt like pickled onions.

Eve caught up with me and spent the first ten minutes fussing, fetching and carrying for the boys, until I told Gareth, Talan and David that they could bloody well get their own food and water. I made Eve sit down with me. She looked pale and worn out, but as soon as my back was turned, she ran off to the court physician to get medicine for David, which he gulped down in one go, smiling shyly at Eve once he had finished.

I looked at Talan, who was also watching the scene with a smile.

"Don't you dare start singing."

"Perhaps, Lady Natasha, you would like to teach me another sonnet?" he asked. "The songs from your land are most interesting."

I grinned. "Where I come from, there is a princess called Lady Gaga. I'll teach you one of her songs. She's very popular."

"I would be honoured," replied Talan, before his eyes switched from me to something over my left shoulder. "Sir Bedivere, Sir Tristram, what is the news from yonder way?"

My stomach shrivelled up and died. I hadn't seen Bedivere since the snog-that-wasn't in the hall. I knew my face had turned a strong shade of puce because I could feel the fire around my eyebrows. I looked over at Eve, desperate for a distraction, but she was busy mopping David's brow.

"Sir Percivale intends to make camp tonight at the border," said a deep gruff voice, which I immediately recognised as Bedivere's.

"Do we break from the travelling court then, or continue further?" asked Talan. He silenced a groan from Tristram by adding, "Lady Natasha has already guessed our noble intentions."

"I would have expected nothing less," replied Bedivere, and even with my back to him, I could tell there was humour in his voice.

Well, now I was really confused. Chivalrous one minute, allergic to me the next, and now he was being playful. I couldn't help thinking that if Bedivere got going, he would be a really good kisser.

Will you stop it. What is wrong with your hormones, girl?

We set off again. Bedivere and Tristram rode side by side, while I rode behind them with Gareth, Talan and

David. I liked it this way. I could check out Bedivere on the pretence of following the crowd.

The further we went, the denser the trees became, until eventually, we were riding single file through a large pine-filled forest. The sky had darkened to a violent purple. The first crack of thunder came as we started a downhill canter.

I had just finished teaching Talan the words to "Bad Romance" when my eyes were dragged to a glint of white, deep in the heart of the forest. It was a long streak, like brilliant white gloss painted onto a thick windowsill.

With barely a rustle, Bedivere jumped down from his chestnut horse, and handed the reins to Tristram.

"Lady Natasha," whispered Bedivere. "Give your steed to Sir Talan and come with me."

I did exactly as he asked, but my dismount was not so elegant. My feet slid into the stones, which sent a crunching noise out into the forest. The white streak moved like a fork of lightning, and disappeared.

Bedivere held his arm out. At first I was unsure how he wanted me to react. Should I hold his hand? Place my arm through the nook of his elbow? Wrestle him to the ground? In the end I followed the example of the women at the court of Caerleon, and placed my left hand on top of Bedivere's right. My grip was left intentionally loose.

"What was it?" I whispered, but Bedivere didn't answer. He placed a long finger to his lips and indicated to me to be quiet, as we wound our way through the trees and across the fern-filled ground. Heat blazed through my skin at the touch of Bedivere. My palm was getting sweatier by the second. Was this normal? I was melting.

I looked back over my right shoulder. Everything and everyone had disappeared from sight.

Bedivere was hunched over, but his movements

through the overgrown forest floor were quick. He placed a hand on the crusty trunk of a tree, and I noticed his hands were scarred with purple welts. He hadn't shaved since our first day at Caerleon, and stubble was starting to sprout over his chin. I removed my hand from his.

Bedivere is not ice-cream. Do not start slurping him.

We came to several fallen trees that had collapsed on top of one another like dominoes. Bedivere crouched down and beckoned me to follow him. He was using a dead tree trunk as a shield.

Look, he mouthed, pointing to a group of enormous, perfectly spherical boulders, that glistened like black marbles.

I heard it before I saw it. A deep snort followed by a sonorous neigh that magnified around the perimeter of the dense stones. I immediately felt the power of something older, wiser. Heavy pressure pushed against my eyeballs and in my eardrums, just like the feeling you get when a plane comes in to land.

Between a gap in the boulders the brilliant white streak appeared again. It was moving slowly, deliberately. As it filled out, the vision showed itself to be a white horse: a stallion.

It was huge. I would have been able to stand under its belly without bending, and I was nearly five feet eight inches in my socks. The stallion's white mane and tail glistened with silver glitter, and above that majestic long nose were two of the bluest eyes I had ever seen, settled deep into a head that was topped with a long pointed horn.

My hands went to my mouth as I failed to smother an excited scream. The creature stopped dead in its tracks. Not a single muscle rippled through its body, although the thin smooth tusk quivered like an antenna.

And then it was gone. The stallion moved so quickly

I couldn't tell which direction it had run. The heavy pressure in the air lifted, and all that was left was an ache in my head.

"They are rare creatures indeed," sighed Bedivere; his delicious eyes still glued to the space left by the unicorn. "It is said they will bring good luck to a quest if witnessed by a virgin."

Is that why Bedivere had wanted me to see it? At least he thought I was a virgin. If Slurpy had seen the unicorn, the world would have imploded into a vortex of doom. I fell back against the tree trunk that had been shielding us. My legs were shaking. I wouldn't have been able to run after the unicorn if I wanted to. This was all becoming too much to handle.

"I cannot believe I have just seen that," I gulped. "I've read about them in books, but they're supposed to be just myths, legends."

"Any legend will have its foundations in a truth," said Bedivere knowingly, taking a seat on the green mossy ground beside me.

Bedivere was staring at me; I could see him through the corner of my eye. A lump, the size and shape of a banana, lodged in my throat. I couldn't breathe. Scarred fingertips reached for my chin and slowly turned my head to the right.

"My behaviour in the hall was shameful," he said quietly.

I shook my head, not trusting myself to open my mouth and not dribble.

"I have sworn to faithfully protect you, Lady Natasha."

Something unintelligible came out of my mouth as my chest roared.

"I will prove myself worthy, to you and to Arthur."

Shut up and kiss me, you bloody fool.

Oy, hands off. He's mine, I thought.

We're the same person, you idiot.

Bedivere continued to stare at me; his eyes were fixed so intently on mine I knew he could read my mind. I felt exposed, as once again, Bedivere made me feel totally aware of myself. My head tilted to one side; Bedivere's slanted in the opposite direction. My fingers reached for his face and stroked his lips. His tanned skin was warm. I locked my arms around his neck and pulled him down onto the forest floor. Bedivere rolled onto his back and pressed me to his chest. His hands were in my hair then spread around my neck, gently teasing the skin that was burning. I couldn't breathe, and I didn't care. We were in each other's mouths and still I needed to get closer.

Magic was real and present and at my fingertips at last.

13 THE PHYSICIAN

The five knights and I caught up with the rest of the travelling court just as the rain started to fall. I couldn't have guessed how many miles from Caerleon castle we were now, and I had even less of an idea how close to Camelot we were. To me, this really was the middle of nowhere.

Riding one-handed, I continually combed my hair with my fingers, removing twigs and moss which had collected in there after my kissing session with Bedivere. I gave up when I found a tiny bottle green caterpillar attached to my scalp. I would have to ask Eve to de-lice me like a monkey when I next saw her. I couldn't wait to gossip. I had never had a friend I could do that with before. Most of the time, I was the subject of it.

Bedivere barely spoke to me for the rest of the afternoon, but he continually turned on his horse to smile in my direction. My stomach flipped and flopped every time I caught his eye. Every part of me tickled. At times it was difficult not to laugh out loud. Nine days before, Bedivere had been an ancient soul connected to my world through magic: an enchanted sleep they called

114

it. Now I was part of his world, his time.

I thought back to that day I fell into the grave. The knights had been sleeping and ageing in the dirt and dust for a thousand years. I looked down at my hands, which were filthy, grazed and blistered. Old hands. What was my fate now? Even if Arthur, Slurpy and I were reunited, how could we return with the way back closed to us under a million tonnes of dirt? Were we destined to grow old here? Would an enchantment revert me back to my old self if we ever found a way back? Would I forget?

One problem at a time. I was becoming an expert at categorising my thoughts. Find Arthur – kiss Bedivere a bit more – find Slurpy…I suppose – kiss Bedivere even more to compensate – find a way back – leave Bedivere.

No.

One problem at a time.

The leaves on the trees were like enormous golden nuggets. Autumn is beautiful in Britain, and at least the seasons in Logres and *Avalon Cottage* were in synch. As the rain stopped teasing us and became heavier, I knew we could only have another hour of daylight at most, and a sneaky glance at my watch confirmed it. Cloaks were pulled from travelling packs; Bedivere helped me with mine. It was made of thick wool, and coloured like red wine. A silver clasp, roughly minted into the shape of a unicorn, held it secure. We both smiled at the connection. Bedivere stayed silent, but his calloused fingers lingered along my jaw line. My bones momentarily forgot they were supposed to keep me upright.

I spent the next hour dreaming of ways to get Bedivere alone under his cloak. It was a good job my horse was concentrating because I didn't have a clue where I was going. No wonder half of my English class was failing. I had a new grudging understanding of the airheads who thought Jane Austen was a clothes store. This love business was very distracting.

Talan was the knight who filled me in about Balvidore: self-proclaimed king of Logres, and leader of the Saxon warlords who had now invaded. Talan claimed that Balvidore ate roasted babies for the break of the fast, and then bathed in the blood of virgins. What I took far more seriously were the rumoured sightings of a bloodied and beaten Arthur being held captive in the dungeons of Camelot.

"I still don't understand how my brother was taken, or by who?"

"Magic - dark and light - graces these lands, Lady Natasha," replied Gareth. "It was foretold that Arthur would return after the battle of Camlann. The fellowship of Camelot was scattered, wounded and lost. Arthur was mortally felled and taken to the land of Avalon to be healed. Sir Bedivere was the knight who placed him in the boat. We were to wait for Arthur's return, and wait we did. An enchantment, a dreamless, ageing sleep was laid over these lands. Now Arthur has returned, and we have awoken to our former selves. Our quest is perilous, but simple: find Arthur, and restore him as the rightful king of Logres."

The rain was pounding against my face. It was brittle, like ice. It felt like hundreds of needles were prickling my skin.

"But what if Arthur doesn't want to be king?" I said, spitting into the rain. "What if he wants to go back to *Avalon Cottage* with me?"

Gareth looked at me like I had asked the most ridiculous question in the world.

"Arthur is the king of Logres," he replied simply. "It is his destiny. There is no other way."

And another problem was just added to the list.

As dusk fell we reached a stone building. From the

outside it looked like an abandoned church. The centre of the structure was long and rectangular, with two tall square towers at either end. Percivale sent some of his guards up, four to each tower. Glass windows sparkled like rubies as fires were lit inside for the knights. The rest of the travelling court of Caerleon was setting up camp for the night outside. I found a drenched Eve, shivering violently by one of the carts. She was trying to lift a heavy black cauldron by herself. I took off my cloak and wrapped it around her.

"Go inside," I said. "I'll do this."

"No, m'lady," replied Eve, coughing. She took the cloak off and wrapped it back around me. "This is servant work."

"I'm hardly a lady, Eve, and I thought we agreed you were going to call me Titch or Natasha from now on."

Refusing to listen to the other, both Eve and I worked together and carried the supplies from her cart into the abandoned church, including – to my horror – several cages of hyperactive chickens.

"Why are we unpacking everything if we're only staying one night?" I asked.

Eve sneezed and coughed. "Balvidore's ruffians have been sighted not four leagues from here, m'lady. Anything left outside could be stolen or burnt during the night."

"What about the horses?" I asked, not wishing to sound stupid by asking exactly how long a league was. It could have been forty metres or forty miles for all I knew.

"Horses are the responsibility of the grooms," explained Eve.

By grooms she meant little boys, no older than ten years, who were expected to handle and comfort terrified animals three times their height and twenty times their weight.

Cracks of lightning speared the sky; Eve whimpered.

I put my arm around her freezing bony shoulders and dragged her inside. I found Gareth, Talan and David huddled around a fire, so I pushed them aside and tried to warm up Eve. Privacy was non-existent, but I desperately needed to get Eve out of her wet clothes and into dry ones.

I put my hand to her forehead. It was clammy, but I didn't know whether that was because she was wet from the storm. Her long red hair had congealed into thick lumps, like tomato-covered spaghetti.

"Talan, could you please ask the court physician to come here," I asked. "David should take more medicine, and I want something for Eve immediately."

"Your bidding is my command, Lady Natasha," replied the knight, and he jumped to his feet and strode off, still clutching a tankard of frothy ale that looked like shaving foam.

"Could you help me arrange these cloaks into a shelter," I said to Gareth. "Eve needs to change out of these wet clothes."

"You first, m'lady," wheezed Eve. She was shivering so violently it was a wonder she hadn't toppled into the fire.

"I would like to assist if I may," offered David, and together, he and Gareth quickly constructed a screen with cloaks and spears.

I found some dry clothes for Eve inside a large wooden chest. There were several women making the journey to Camelot with the travelling court, and while the white cotton tunic was frayed and grubby, it was dry. That was all I needed.

When I returned to our little corner, I saw that Talan had returned with the physician. I had been expecting a much older man, but Percivale's doctor was younger than my father. He was tall and broad, with the muscular body of someone who played a lot of sport. His light brown hair was cropped short, and his large nose was crooked. It looked like it had been broken several times. He stared at me for several seconds, looking at me like a person gazes at a portrait. Then he nodded to himself and went back to mixing a potion for David. My first impression was not good. He could have at least smiled, or introduced himself.

A wooden box, the size of a small suitcase, was by his feet. It was already open, and so I peered inside. It was filled with jars, and strange metal implements that looked rusty and unhygienic and just as likely to kill as cure. One half of the chest was filled with roots and berries and lumps of black rock that looked like coal. Several pieces of fur were jammed into the corners, and a handwritten journal was lying open, its pages torn and stained. Several of the jars contained what appeared to be skin and bone, floating around in a cloudy substance the colour of pee.

Were you expecting a range of paracetamol and flu remedies?

"And now to see to the servant," said the physician, rising from attending to David.

I had gasped at his accent. It was unmistakable. A thick Scouse accent from the city of Liverpool.

Now I knew my geography of the British Isles, and certainly it was plausible that a physician from the north-west would settle in north Wales and the court of Caerleon, but what was beyond the realms of possibility was that an accent so modern was already here.

"Robert of Dawes," he said, finally introducing himself. "I've heard a lot about you, Lady Natasha."

"Nice to meet you," I mumbled. "Eve is just over here."

I led the physician around the screen of cloaks to where Eve lay shivering and white.

"Oh, Eve," I cried, dragging her upright with a struggle. "Let me change her into something dry first," I appealed to the physician, "but please don't leave."

"I will stay unless summoned by Lord Percivale,"

replied Robert of Dawes. "There is much I wish to discuss with you, Lady Natasha, if you will permit my company."

I nodded as the physician disappeared behind the other side of the makeshift screen. The men's voices became louder as more beer was drunk, but my only concern was getting Eve into a state of consciousness. It shocked me how quickly she had deteriorated in such a short period. I should never have left her alone on the cart in the rain.

I pulled and tore at her wet clothes, rubbing her goose-pimpled flesh as I went. I then pulled the borrowed dress over her bony little frame. It was like dressing a rag doll that had lost its stuffing.

"Eve, please wake up," I begged, slapping her face.

She moaned quietly, and her eyelids flickered.

"I'm sorry to be a bother, m'lady," she whispered.

"No bother at all," I replied, "now just stay awake a little longer. The court physician is here. He can help you."

Robert peered around the edge of a cloak.

"May I see her now?" he asked in that thick accent. I nodded, but kept Eve in my arms. She may have seen fifteen winters, but she had the weight of someone who hadn't been fed for most of them.

I watched intently as Robert of Dawes listened to Eve's chest with his ear against her ribcage. Then he checked her limp wrist for a pulse. He called for more light, and it was David who appeared holding a flaming torch. Robert checked her pupils, and then felt under her armpits.

Something wasn't right. Or rather, it was all *too* right. The new court physician was methodical in the way he treated Eve. Even with his medieval tools, he checked measurements and moved his hands across her body in the impersonal manner of a modern doctor.

David was told he could go and we returned to the

shadows. A thick brown sludgy potion was poured down Eve's throat, which made her gag. I wiped her mouth and rocked her to sleep in my arms like a baby. It took just seconds.

"Will she be okay?" I asked.

"She has been ill for some time, I suggest," replied Robert, pausing to check her pulse again. "The infection in her chest is quite advanced."

Now I was certain something was wrong. Robert used the same phrases as a medic from my time.

He leant in towards me. I was already lodged into the corner and his presence so close to my face felt intimidating. I could smell fatty meat on his breath. He quickly turned his head around to check no one was there, before placing a foul-smelling finger to my lips.

"I need to talk to you alone, Natasha, but now is not the time or the place," he hurriedly whispered. "For now, answer me this one question: would you be able to find the tunnel again if we went back to the lake?"

My mouth opened and closed like a fish. He was confirming my suspicions as if they were the most natural thing in the world.

"I...I..."

"I know what you are and where you are from," whispered Robert, with even more urgency in his voice. "Now tell me, could you find the tunnel again?"

I nodded. "I think so, but..."

Robert interrupted me, placed his hands on my ears and kissed the crown of my head.

"Bless you, girl. Tomorrow, I'll find you and we'll speak some more."

He rose to his feet, grabbed his medicine box and swept from my sight.

So Arthur, Slurpy and I were not the first. Just how many more were here from my time? More importantly, how could I break it to Robert that far from giving him

121

faith, I had inadvertently caused his world to collapse?

14 DDRAIG

The strange mixture Robert of Dawes had created for Eve worked like magic. Her fever broke during the night, and by morning she could sit up and drink hot water laced with nettle leaves. It smelt vile, but my new friend drank every drop without a murmur.

I decided that Eve needed to be my priority, and so I tied my horse to a cart, and let it trot alongside us as I sat watching over her. As much as I wanted to be close to Bedivere, I would not become one of those girls who gave up on their friends for the sake of a boy – however hot and kissable.

The storm had moved on, and a warm autumn sun hovered low in the sky. Eve slept most of the morning, and so I made myself sick by gorging on pale green apples that were in another open sack at the rear of the cart. Every so often I would take Eve's pulse. It was a foolish gesture. I had no idea what was quick and what was slow. It just made me feel as if I was doing something useful.

I needed Eve to know I cared.

At some point during the day the travelling court crossed the border from Wales to England. I had spoken to Bedivere, and he had said the road to Camelot would take a couple of days to track, if there were no problems along the way. I made him promise that he and the others would not desert me. He agreed, reluctantly. I waited for him to kiss me, but he didn't. Perhaps he hadn't wanted to make a show in front of the men, or ruin my reputation in some way?

Or perhaps he simply hadn't wanted to, and it was that thought that played on my mind as I continued to eat apple after apple. I seemed to repel boys in the same way Arthur attracted girls. I was the anti-Roth.

We had been bumping along a dusty, pot-holed track for hours when a call went out from the front. It rippled back along the men on horses until it reached us.

Smoke had been spotted in the distance. I gently pushed Eve to one side, and strained my back and neck in an attempt to see past the giant Shire horse that was pulling our cart. Sure enough, two giant plumes of thick black smoke were billowing into the sky. Two small green hills obscured what was on fire, but I assumed it was a building and not a forest, as the smoke was ballooning upwards instead of spreading out.

The men around us reacted quickly. Carts and support wagons were stopped and pulled over into the berry-covered hedgerows. The horses that belonged to knights and armed guards were spurred to the front of the procession; dust and grit flew into the air and settled painfully into the corners of my eyes.

Eve was confused by the sudden increase in noise and whimpered in fright. I attempted to settle her as two horses galloped past me, but I became distracted by the faces of the knights. It was Bedivere and Gareth. I had had no idea they had been right behind me all this time.

Fear gripped many of the servants, who ran around with no purpose other than to make the person nearest to them even more frightened. This was old-age terrorism. Some servants were cowering behind thorny bushes; others were making for a dense copse of trees in the distance.

"Eve, stay where you are until we know what's going on," I shouted. My feet had taken over control of my body and were running in the direction of Bedivere and Gareth. I could see that mass of chestnut hair in the distance, but he was getting further and further away from me.

"No, Natasha," cried a thick Liverpool accent, and I suddenly found myself rugby-tackled by the court physician, Robert of Dawes.

"I have to get to Bedivere," I cried, struggling to remove myself from the two thick arms that held fast around my apple-swollen stomach.

"He won't thank you for it," replied Robert, picking me up with ease. "Trust me, Bedivere will think better of you for keeping order back here. I haven't been here long, but I've already learnt you don't get in the way of a knight and danger."

He placed me back on the ground and started barking instructions. His voice boomed out in all directions, as he ordered supplies to be tipped out and carts and wagons to be overturned.

Robert was making a fortress.

To protect us from what, though? Most of the knights had already galloped away into the distance, towards a third eruption of smoke.

Suddenly, the sky above us was thick with a quick moving mass, which flapped and screeched as one enormous black cloud.

I was terrified of birds, petrified of anything that flapped in such an excited, out of control fashion. I threw myself to the ground and covered my head with my hands. The blackbirds were only a few feet above our heads, and had swarmed out of a wooded area to my right.

"Arm yourselves," cried Robert, and the servants and guards who were left with the supplies quickly grabbed bows and arrows from an upturned armoured wagon. Two women dropped to their knees, and clasped their hands together in prayer.

"How are you at archery, Natasha?" asked Robert.

"Have the birds gone?"

"Something far worse than birds is out there," said Robert, as an unnatural hush descended on those of us left by the side of the track.

A tree to my left burst into flames. A crimson fireball rose into the sky, as a stomach-vibrating roar knocked everyone to the ground with a sonic boom. The praying women started shrieking their devotion to their God.

"Wait," screamed Robert. "Wait until it shows colours."

"What the hell was that?" I screamed back.

"A Ddraig," cried Robert. "Everyone, keep your eyes alert and pray for red."

He grabbed hold of me and pulled me to his side.

"Stay with me, but if you see white then run as fast as you can."

"A white what?"

"You'll know when you see it," replied Robert, his eyes darting in all directions, "although you may not believe it…"

The physician was interrupted by another ear-splitting roar that flattened person, horse and tree alike. An oak tree, at least thirty metres tall, disintegrated into flame and cinder.

"It's an ambush," gagged Robert, as he coughed up a mouthful of smoke. "The evil bastard lured the knights away and left us sitting here like ducks."

I had no idea what was going on, but only one thing was now on my mind: Eve. I had to get back to my friend.

Toxic black smoke was eating at my eyeballs, causing them to stream with tears. An acrid stench had filled my nostrils and was burning the back of my throat.

Eve. Where was Eve?

I couldn't see anything, but I could hear the choking screams of people around me. I strained my ears, listening amongst the cries for one from Liverpool, but if Robert was still yelling, I couldn't hear him.

Then there was a swooping sound, like a huge vibrating heartbeat, and the vague shapes of people stumbling around began to materialise. A piercing scream split the air and was just as quickly silenced. It wasn't a cry of panic. It was pain. People didn't scream that high if they were frightened. A splash of liquid hit my face, splattering against my skin. It felt warm, and thick. I don't know why, it was instinctive, but I touched the fluid with my fingers and then placed it to my lips. I vomited up undigested apples as I realised what had drenched me.

The toxic black cloud that smothered us was clearing. It was a pale grey now, but I still couldn't see into the distance where Bedivere and the other knights had charged. I couldn't see further than the length of a netball court. My eyes were pulled to a young girl with long dirty-blonde hair. She couldn't have been more than eleven years old. She was screaming for her mother; tears were streaming down her pale face. An enormous barrel-shaped man knocked her to the ground in his haste to escape. She sprawled into the dirt. The man did not look back.

I left her as well. Eve. I had to get to Eve.

Blind in the cloud, with my blood-splattered hands groping in the smoke, I made my way to where I thought I had left the cart and Eve. Or what was now left of it. It had been tipped over and dragged along the dirt on its side. One large wheel was lodged upright in a soot-covered bush; the other wheel was in pieces. My horse and the Shire had panicked and pulled themselves free, wrenching and splintering the wood into matchsticks.

Eve was gone.

I started yelling her name. Another pain-ridden scream shot through the air. The cry was so high, I couldn't tell whether it was male or female. I wouldn't allow myself to think of that little girl. She would be safe. *Her* mother would have come for her.

Whatever had trapped us had everyone running around like ants in a rainstorm. We knew we had to get away, but we didn't know where. We couldn't see, we couldn't breathe.

"EVE!" I screamed again. "EVE!"

A huge Shire horse galloped past me; the feathering around its long lean legs made it look like it was wearing four fluffy white boots. It was dragging a man along the ground. His fat ankles had become caught up in the leather straps that were fixed to the horse's back. The man was clawing at the long pockets of grass that lined the hedgerows, trying desperately to hold onto something. Horse and man disappeared into the smoke.

The back of my throat was dissolving. Huge chunks of skin were shredding into my gullet. I bent over and puked again, just as a large object appeared in the sky and swooped over my head.

The force pushed me into the hard ground. I heard a bone-splintering crack. Agonising pain fired like a furnace through my face. I put my hands up to smother the flames, but there was nothing there except warm wet blood. Excruciating spasms juddered down my jaw and spine.

The sky and horizon were almost clear of smoke now. Whatever was flying at us had dissolved the haze it had caused. In the distance, through my tear-filled eyes, I could make out the mass of charging horses galloping towards us. The glint of raised swords and spears reflecting like mirrors in the sunlight. Help was returning.

"EVE!" I cried, as tears of pain and terror streamed down my bloodied face.

"M'lady."

The voice was faint, but I knew it was hers. I stood up and made my eyes search the scene of carnage for her image. Eve was running across a field from the small copse of trees, which were, miraculously, still unscathed. She was running straight towards me through ankle-length grass. Bright yellow buttercups danced around her feet. She was safe.

But Eve wasn't looking at me. Her head was tilted back; her wide eyes fixed on the sky.

More screams, and then the crushed remains of a food cart exploded beside me, sending pulped potatoes and beets flying through the air. The shockwave lifted me off my feet, and threw me several metres into a blackened hollow. The earth was hot and crumbly, like ground coffee beans.

I lunged at the edge of the hollow and pulled myself out. The first face I noticed was Robert's. He saw me and cried out, flapping his arms. I couldn't hear his words, though, because the world had fallen silent. There was no sound, except a painful ringing vibration which rattled my skull.

Then there was Eve; a fierce determination spread across her pale freckled face. Her long red hair flew behind her as she ran towards me, her arms pounding like pistons. In the deathly silence, I watched my friend, ready to hug her tightly, but she collided with me with such force I was thrown back into the blackened hollow.

It came from the sky. A mass of sinewy white scales. An army of one designed to kill.

Two huge, purple clawed feet, with talons like

daggers, struck at Eve. She must have screamed because I saw the blood spurt out of her neck and stomach, but I couldn't hear her. I couldn't hear myself. Yet I knew I was screeching because the force of my voice was bleeding into my mouth.

I lunged at the dragon's claws, but with another sonic beat, the white beast flapped its enormous sail-like wings and took off into the sky. Fragile Eve, lifeless beneath its hideous frame. Limp and broken.

I watched the terrorist of the sky fly away from the total devastation it had reaped, and the world fell into darkness.

15 A WARRIOR IS BORN

Voices. Hundreds of them. Rising in one symphony of tuneless screeching. Yet there was no memory of Arthur resurrected amidst the pain. Not this time.

I felt hands pulling at me, dragging me. Too many directions. Ripping me apart.

There wasn't a part of me that wasn't covered in blood, but I didn't know which red streaks belonged to me. My body was a metro map of pain and suffering. Outlines of bodies ripped and torn like paper.

We are nothing.

We are irrelevant.

The hope that I had maintained for days of finding Arthur was gone. Snuffed out with Eve's death. I would never see him again, and we would both die in this timeless land.

What were the last words I said to my brother? I couldn't remember. Were they words of anger? Words of sarcasm? They wouldn't have been words of love, I knew that for sure. I loved Arthur with all my heart, but I had never told him. We were too close to *not* fight. With us it was sarcasm and angst. We didn't *exchange* words. Not ones that mattered.

Why had Eve done that? Stupid, stupid girl. Why didn't she listen to me and stay near the cart?

Because the horses bolted.

Then why hadn't she stayed in the trees? She was safe there. The stupid fool.

She was trying to save you.

"SHUT UP, SHUT UP, SHUT UP."

"Natasha is in shock," said a voice. It was that thick Scouse accent again.

"LEAVE ME ALONE."

Hands were pulling me. Strong hands, calloused hands. Wet and cold hands. My own balled into tight fists and I started fighting back, but it was too little, too late.

Voices. Hundreds of them. Issuing orders, drawing together groups, searching for loved ones. My loved ones were gone. I had no reason to speak.

I just wanted to scream.

It started in my stomach, and like a tsunami, it drew back and then unleashed hell from my voice box. I doubled over and fell forward, as gravity owned my grief. I screamed and clawed at the dirt.

Two arms swooped under my body. They held me tightly.

"I should never have left her," said a gruff voice.

"It was an ambush. When you are dealing with the devil itself, you need to think like evil."

"Will she recover?"

"Get away from this place. It has been poisoned by the Ddraig's breath. The former physician of Caerleon wrote about it in quite some detail, and gruesome reading it makes too. Advise Sir Percivale to regroup the knights at least five leagues away. More will be lost before night, but we can contain it if we act quickly."

"I should never have left her."

"You are a knight. You had no choice."

My eyes were closed again. I saw nothing but

blackness and flashing streaks of strange white light. I knew the voices belonged to Bedivere and Robert of Dawes, but I didn't want to see them. I couldn't face seeing what was beyond them.

I always thought ghost stories were worse than the reality of death, but that was psychology crap. Fed to me by the child shrink I saw after Patrick died. The thought of my little brother haunting me had caused me to regress. I was eight years old and living in a world of nightmares. I wet the bed. Cried until my eyes were red raw. Cut my bed sheets with scissors. Did anything I could in an attempt to stop bedtime and the inevitability of darkness that comes with it.

Death was acceptable because it was part of life, explained the shrink. I was afraid of the unknown, which was why I was terrified of the ghosts.

But nothing in this world was worse than death. I should have realised that nine years ago when my six-year-old brother drowned. My parents knew it. My mother had spent every moment since that day grieving for what had gone, instead of loving what she had left. Arthur knew it too, even though he was only a year older than me when *it* happened. He had tried to protect me by backing up my lies, but he had realised, even then, there was nothing more horrific than how it all ends.

And it was so easy to die.

We are nothing.

We are irrelevant.

And there are always more fools to replace us.

I felt Bedivere's cold mouth against mine. His fingers scrunched tightly into my hair. It wasn't passion; he was trying to revive me.

"Sir Bedivere," called a voice, but he dismissed it with a bark-like command.

"Come back to me," he whispered. "Come back to

me."

"Give her this," said the voice belonging to the physician.

I felt a hand leave my back, and then a rough rim of metal pressed against my lips. The battle I was waging against my eyes started to weaken.

"She's rousing," cried Bedivere.

"Come on, Natasha," encouraged Robert, "that's a girl, open your eyes."

I allowed Bedivere to pour the liquid down my throat. Menthol vapours washed over me. It reminded me of the cream my grandmother rubbed onto my chest when I was sick. It was a memory of a place that should have been called home, but never was.

My eyes opened further. A smoky haze existed around everything that was solid. The sky had turned a pale diluted yellow.

"Can you ride?" asked Bedivere.

I nodded weakly.

"My horse will carry her," said Bedivere, rising to his feet with my whole body still in his arms. "Tell Sir Gareth and Sir Tristram I am taking Natasha to the monastery of Solsbury Hill. They will follow."

"But Bedivere…"

"Do not argue with me, just do it."

"Lord Percivale will be very unhappy if some of his knights leave the travelling court now," protested Robert.

I felt the anger ripple through Bedivere's body.

"I am not one of Lord Percivale's knights, and his travelling court is not my concern. My allegiance is to Arthur and him alone."

"Then leave Natasha with me. I have the means to protect her. She should not be riding in her weakened state."

While they continued to argue, my mind slipped back to Eve. Desperate Eve. Foolish Eve. Weakened

Eve.

The bravest person I had ever met.

"Put me down."

"I am not weary. I can bear your burden."

"Put me down."

"You are in no condition…"

"PUT ME THE HELL DOWN BEFORE I KILL SOMEONE."

My feet were gently lowered to the ground as anger surged through me. My hands, bloodied and filthy, grabbed the hilt of Bedivere's sword and pulled it from its scabbard.

"Get the others," I shouted. "Gareth, Talan, David, and even Tristram if you must, but you are going to show me how to use one of these. You are going to train me how to fight, how to kill."

Bedivere took a step towards me, but I raised the sword with both hands and held the point to his neck.

"You swore an oath to protect me," I cried, shaking violently with the weight of the blade. "So do it. You will not leave me defenceless again. I will not lie on the ground like a coward while those around me die – not ever again. Do you understand me, Bedivere?"

He pushed the gleaming blade from his neck. A small droplet of blood started to swell on his skin. I had cut him. Gently prising my fingers, one at a time, away from the leather grip, Bedivere took back his sword.

"I will never leave you again," he said quietly.

"Swear you will train me to fight."

"If that is what you desire."

"It isn't desire, Bedivere, it is worse than that. If I don't learn how to protect myself in this land with your rules and your monsters, then I will die, and my brother will die as well. I can't let that happen, not again."

"Natasha…" started Robert of Dawes, but I had neither the time nor the interest in hearing what he had to say. With my palm open, I slapped him as hard as I could.

"And you're even worse," I cried, balling my fist, ready to hit him even harder. "You're like me, but you knew what was coming at us, and you chose not to tell me. You let me stumble around like an idiot. If I had known, I could have saved her. I would have saved her."

"You could not have saved the maid, Natasha," replied Robert, his eyes blazing with the reflection of the fire that was still burning all around us. "That beast had you in its sight and was coming right at you. If the girl had not reacted when she did, then we would be mourning your loss, not hers."

"We will honour the girl," said Bedivere.

"HER NAME WAS EVE," I screamed. "How can you honour her when you don't even know her name?"

Three more knights on horses pulled up alongside us: Tristram, Gareth and Talan. Their faces were sweaty and pink. Talan had an oozing raw burn seared across his cheekbone.

"Sir David has gone after the white beast, Sir Bedivere," cried Tristram. "He believes the girl may still be saved."

"You have to stop him," exclaimed Robert vehemently. "We all saw the girl – Eve – we saw her die before our eyes. The Ddraig pierced one of her arteries. She is gone."

"Bring him back, Sir Gareth," said Bedivere quietly. "Sir David's health is still waning and he will not have gone far. Sir Tristram, you must ride with him, the boy will listen to you."

Both knights nodded, and spurred their horses with their heels. The ground thundered as they galloped away across an open ploughed field. Robert turned to Bedivere.

"What are your intentions, Sir Bedivere?"

"My intentions are not your concern, Robert of

Dawes," replied Bedivere, and his arm wrapped around my waist. "Now go attend to the lord of Caerleon and his travelling court. If what you say is true and this land has been poisoned, your counsel will be required elsewhere."

"I will not leave Natasha," argued Robert, glancing at me. I knew what he was thinking behind those narrowed eyes. It wasn't my safety or health he cared about. It was my memory and passage through a tunnel that would lead us all back to civilisation.

"My brother is being held captive at Camelot," I said to Robert. "That's where you'll find me."

"We are making to leave now?" asked Talan.

Bedivere nodded. "We leave for Solsbury Hill. If our timing is true, we will reunite with the travelling court of Caerleon at Camelot. For now, Sir Talan, Natasha requires her steed and weapons."

The singing knight, now so unnaturally quiet and pensive, pulled at the reins of his own horse and trotted away towards the armoury. All around us, people were crying, screaming and yelling. They wouldn't notice a few more departures from hell.

"Promise me, Natasha, that you will find me," begged Robert, taking my hand.

Bedivere tightened his grip around my waist. It suddenly occurred to me that he saw Robert of Dawes as a rival. It was ludicrous, but no more so than the truth.

"Find me at Camelot," I replied dully.

It was as near to a promise as I could get without lying. Robert kissed my bloodied hand, bowed to Bedivere and turned away. He disappeared into the crowd, and I didn't search for him once he was gone.

"Don't hold back on me," I said, twisting my body into Bedivere's.

"I loved Arthur as a brother," whispered Bedivere, wiping blood from my mouth with his fingers. "He is a brother to me once more, and I will defend you both to the end."

He bent his head down and kissed me again.

A new warrior had been born, and she was coming to unleash hell on those who had turned her world upside down.

16 GORE

Bedivere, Talan and I left the travelling court of Caerleon to deal with the aftermath of the Ddraig's attack. We now had our own journey to make. There were no road signs to Solsbury Hill, no obvious landmarks to follow other than the sun and the landscape of mountains, and yet Bedivere and Talan were totally confident that Gareth, Tristram and David would find us.

As we rode further away from the devastation unleashed by the Ddraig, I felt the poisonous cloud I had been covered in, start to lift. We stopped to allow the horses to drink from a fast-flowing river. Bedivere and Talan stripped off and washed themselves in the cold crystal shallows. I desperately wanted to get the stains of death off my skin, but the water took me back to another memory of death I had tried so hard to repress. I started shaking. All I could see was the colour blue. Bedivere and Talan had to combine to hold me upright as I scooped water over my skin.

Death may have been removed from my body, but it was now tattooed inside my head. I thought back to the little girl who had been screaming for her mother. Had she found her? Was she even alive? My own mother swam into a pain-filled haze before my eyes. Slurpy and I had set out from *Avalon Cottage* just three days earlier. Arthur had been gone a day longer. Was my mother screaming for me? Had she even noticed I was gone?

Who was really doing the running here?

I was now armed. Talan had given me a silver sword and a dagger with a curved blade. The smaller weapon was already attached to my waist by a leather scabbard. The sword was wrapped in a dark red cloth and tied to my saddlebag. Bedivere had promised he would show me the basics of sword movement, and as we dried off, he took me through the steps of grip and stance. Talan was left to clean the horses of the Ddraig's toxic residue. Their chestnut and dapple grey hides had already started to bubble up with yellow weeping sores, and huge pink blisters were forming around their gums. Their pain was very upsetting to watch, but the horses trusted Talan; their long noses nuzzled him constantly for reassurance as he washed them down.

Tristram, Gareth and David rejoined us not long after. The men hailed each other as knights, but I was now all too aware of their young age, especially David, who looked like a child playing with older brothers.

At least in my time I was allowed to be a teenager. We wanted to grow up. Here, people had no choice.

"Lady Natasha," called a voice. To my surprise, it was Tristram.

"Sorry," I mumbled. "I was miles away."

"We thought you would wish to know that your lady companion has been sighted," he said.

My heart surged – they had found Eve. Then it plummeted again as I realised they were talking about Slurpy. From the dark furrowed looks on the five knights' brows, it was also clear she was still with the one they called Mordred.

"Is she safe?" My question was for Arthur's sake, not mine.

"She and Sir Mordred are also tracking the road to Camelot," replied Gareth. "They have been joined by others."

"An army?" asked Bedivere.

"Of sorts," replied Tristram.

"Sir Mordred is now leading the druids of Gore," said Gareth.

"It was to be expected," sighed Bedivere.

"Who, or what, are the druids of Gore?" I asked.

"The druids of Gore have long dealt in the dark arts of this land," replied Bedivere. "There are many like them, using sorcery and witchcraft for their own purposes, but they have other weapons too."

"Such as?"

"These are not tales that should be told to a lady," interrupted an ashen-faced David.

"If this Mordred has Arthur's girlfriend, then you had better believe I need to be told," I snapped back.

"Fire at her fingertips," mumbled Tristram, walking away. I wasn't sure whether this was simply another comment about Slurpy, or something new. Tristram did not elaborate, not at first.

"The druids of Gore have the malevolent sight," explained Bedivere, taking my arm. "It is said they have visions of things not yet come to pass. They can forge weaponry and armour that is stronger than anything these lands have seen in war, and their knowledge of medicine and tools is unsurpassed. They are few in number, but they are dangerous."

"I thought druids were peaceful people."

"Most are," said Talan, "but the druids of Gore are a man apart from anything that walks these blessed lands. They are cursed. It is said they can see and travel through time itself."

An unsettled giddy feeling swept over me. Had my

141

brother's girlfriend found more like us, like the new court physician, Robert of Dawes? With our original way back blocked, I couldn't understand why the thought of others here from my time upset me so much. They may know of another route back. Then again, they may be more dangerous. My world was also filled with evil. The news was constantly filled with it.

"You look pale, Natasha," said Bedivere softly. "You should take some food before we set saddle once more."

I shook my head, registering for the first time that Bedivere had stopped calling me *Lady* Natasha.

Stop being so paranoid.

"Tell me more about Mordred and the druids of Gore?"

Gareth looked over his shoulder towards Tristram, who was crouched down at the edge of the river; he was filling his leather-skinned water bottle. His eyes were fixed on the water, but his ears were still listening because he took up the story.

"Sir Mordred was Arthur's greatest foe," said Tristram. "Many of us tried to warn Arthur before the battle of Camlann that Mordred was a traitor to the Round Table, but Arthur, who saw the good in all hearts, would not take heed. Mordred betrayed Arthur, and smote him with the mortal stroke."

"Is Mordred now riding to Camelot to hurt Arthur again?"

"We believe so."

"Then we have to ride on."

"We will reach Camelot and Arthur before Mordred and the druids of Gore," said Bedivere, stroking my hair. "Yet Solsbury Hill must be our next stop, and this is why we have split from the travelling court of Caerleon. We have received news that Sir Gareth's brother, the noble Sir Agravaine, is being cared for there by the Maidens of the White Cloth. We must heed another knight's call, especially when that knight is kin. You of all people will understand that."

Bedivere was looking at me with such a gentle, soft look that I understood completely why the other four followed him. Why knights like Ronan would look for him above all others.

"Wait," interrupted Tristram, just as Talan and David mounted their horses, and I was about to jump up onto mine. "We have not told Lady Natasha about her companion. If we are to go forth with her at our side, then she must hear of the new evil that has arisen."

How could this land get more evil? Someone – and I still didn't know who – had gutted my baby rabbit and stolen its eyes; a band of barbarians had apparently kidnapped my brother; I had been attacked by pus-filled dwarves on wolves; and my friend had been ripped apart by a white dragon in front of my eyes. This world was dripping in evil. Every particle of air was contaminated with it.

Tristram walked towards me. Worry lines were creased into his pale pink skin. How many winters had he seen? I had never bothered to find out. If David had seen fifteen and Bedivere nineteen, then Tristram was almost certainly the same age as me, which would explain why I found him so annoying. I never did like the boys in my school year very much. They were far too stupid and full of themselves.

"Your companion, the one you call Lady Samantha," started Tristram, "has gone through a rebirthing ceremony with Sir Mordred and the druids of Gore."

I knew he meant Slurpy, but I don't think I had ever referred to her as a *lady* before.

"What does that mean, rebirthing?" I replied, imagining it to be some kind of religious event like a baptism, or that service where baby boys have their bits snipped.

"Your companion has embraced the dark arts,"

continued Tristram. "She will have made a vow to use them against the court of Camelot for her own use."

"What!" I exclaimed. "Look, Sammy is an idiot, I'll agree with anyone who thinks that, but you really are giving her way too much credit. The only dark art she knows is how to trick a boy with brains into going out with her."

"Rebirthing is the stripping away of customs and traditions," continued Tristram, but I interrupted him with a raise of my hand.

"Stop, Tristram. Just stop. Look, you have real enemies out there," I said in a mildly irritated voice. "This king Balvidore for one, and even Mordred and his druids perhaps, but you have to trust me when I say Sammy isn't dangerous. She's a fool, and I wish Arthur didn't love her so much, love her at all, especially as he hasn't known her for very long, but you have to stop giving her so much attention. She's a moron, and I can and will handle her."

"It is *you* who does not understand, Lady Natasha," snapped Tristram, his own anger now rising. "I do not care for your language and strange words that fall from your tongue, but Sir Bedivere believes you are true. So listen to *my* words. Your companion, the one you have called Sammy, is no longer travelling by that name. As Arthur has come to the land of Logres once more, so has one of his greatest enemies. Morgana has been reborn, and now she is in the companionship of Mordred and the druids of Gore, our quest to restore Arthur to the throne will be more perilous than ever."

My mind raced through my own private history files. Morgana: the Queen of Gore, according to the legends and myths. An evil sorceress who tried to destroy Arthur.

I looked at Bedivere and the others. This was a joke, right? A snort leapt from my nose, causing a fresh bubble of blood to leak over my top lip. Then I started laughing. My diaphragm ached as my shoulders heaved with ever louder gasps. It had been days since I had laughed, and the muscles in my stomach were too tense to let go properly.

They were not seriously telling me that the ridiculous idiot had decided to call herself Morgana? This was precious. Slurpy had finally realised she wasn't tripping out on magic mushrooms and had come to understand where she was. I was just amazed she knew enough myths of the past to change her name to that of a legendary witch.

In fact Slurpy grew a little in my estimation. She had displayed wit and brains in one go. I often forgot she had a hyphenated surname because I concentrated my nastiness on the two initials of SS: Slurpy Sammy, or to be more exact, Samantha Scholes. Yet there was another surname added in there. Whether the Morgan came from her mother or father, I didn't know. I didn't care.

Samantha Scholes-Morgan. Slurpy Sammy with the hyphenated surname was still one of the un-dead, but now she no longer wanted to share her name with cute rabbits or hamsters. Instead, she was telling this ancient world she was a queen with magical powers.

Morgana. It was like an episode of Countdown. I'll take an A and add it to my name please.

My laughter had offended Tristram. He jumped onto the back of his horse and kicked it so hard it reared. Dust flew into the air as Tristram, Talan and David galloped away.

I was still trying to smother my laughter as Bedivere helped me mount my horse. I didn't expect any of the knights to share or even understand my sense of ridiculousness at the game Sammy - sorry, Morgana - was playing, but they would get it in time.

17 ARTHUR'S LETTER

A night under the stars. If this had been the movies, then this would be the mushy romantic scene. Reality was a little different. The temperature dropped as soon as the sun set, but that didn't put off the bugs and insects that arrived en masse to eat us alive.

And Natasha "Tartare" Roth was the main course.

Tristram and David combined to get a fire going, while Bedivere and Talan provided supper: three rabbits, which were skinned and roasted on sharpened sticks.

Needless to say, my appetite had not returned, and even if it had, thoughts of my own baby rabbit were at the surface. I rolled over and showed my back to the knights as they pulled at the shrivelled grey flesh with their fingers and teeth. Even the moon disapproved. The crescent was high in the black sky, down turned like an unhappy mouth. Twinkling above it were two bright stars. It looked like a face.

The sky was watching us, and it wasn't pleased.

Talan started to sing. The chorus was unmistakable: "Hey Jude". He had remembered. It seemed like a fitting lament to things that are lost.

I took the watch with Gareth while the others slept. Finally a chance to bond over missing brothers, but while Gareth worshipped his, all I could think about was Arthur's faults.

His main lameness was with girls. Arthur was a total sucker for long dark hair and even longer legs. It was how that witch, Slurpy Morgana, had snatched him up within a week of our arrival in the middle of nowhere. Tiny denim shorts that barely covered her arse, and long, midnight black hair.

Why hadn't I just tried to find Arthur on my own? If she now got to him first, then my efforts and sacrifices would mean nothing. I would be the little sister, coming along for the ride with the grown-ups.

I didn't need an inner voice to tell me what I really felt towards Slurpy was just jealousy. I was in danger of losing my brother to a gazelle in hot pants, and it made me seethe at how pathetic some of the opposite sex could be. Bedivere was different, I was sure of it, but then I started to wonder about how many girlfriends he had had before me, and that just made my jealousy worse.

I was in quite a bad mood by the time Gareth started snoring.

Unable to sleep, I also took the next watch, this time with Bedivere. He wrapped his cloak around me, and played with my diamond stud earrings as we huddled and kissed in front of the fire. I swivelled around onto his lap and wrapped my legs around his body. We moulded together perfectly. Bedivere liked stroking my skin, especially on my neck and on the inside of my forearms. He said it was smooth and reminded him of his horse. I decided to take that as a compliment. I got a little annoyed when I realised he was kissing me with his eyes open, but then we were supposed to be keeping watch. My ears were primed for the swish of an arrow or the howl of a wolf, yet nothing more exciting than a weathered-looking fox came towards our camp.

The next morning the six of us galloped onwards to the monastery of Solsbury Hill. Gareth took the lead, excited at the thought of being reunited with his brother, Agravaine.

An enormous stone building, at least four storeys high, eventually loomed up on the horizon. It was set on a hill, surrounded by trees. As we reached the stone steps which led up to the entrance, two women, veiled and dressed in long white gowns, came out to greet us.

I watched the other knights, not wishing to draw attention to myself. Bedivere took the lead once more. He jumped down from his horse and bowed deeply to the two women. I liked it when he took charge. It made me feel important because he was now mine.

"You are most welcome here, Sir Bedivere," said one of the women in a slow voice. "We have been praying for your safe arrival."

Deep male voices were singing beyond the open doorway. I looked towards Talan and smiled at the expression on his face. He would love my time with its constant supply of music. I should have packed my iPod. He would have gone nuts for it.

Because of course everyone packs for a romp through a mythical medieval land, don't they?

Go away, I thought to my inner voice.

Next time you should bring your brother's old DS. You could all play Dragon Quest together.

"Leave me alone," I hissed through gritted teeth. Tristram was the only one who heard me. By the look on his face, I was doing little to remove his opinion that I was a crazy witch.

"Sir Bedivere," cried another voice, quickly dragging me back a thousand years from the 21st Century. A thin man, dressed entirely in black, came running down the steps.

I glanced over to Bedivere, and was shocked by the sudden look of horror that had frozen his face. His mouth was open and the colour had drained from his skin. Even his eyes had muted to the colour of green glass bottles. He didn't look fearless and capable of anything anymore. He looked like he was going to pass out.

The man continued to run towards Bedivere, and my instincts screamed at me to do something, especially as no one else was. I jumped from the horse and pulled out my dagger. Gareth reacted just as quickly, but instead of protecting Bedivere from the man in black, Gareth placed himself between me and the stranger.

"Brother," cried the man, and he threw his arms around a shocked and immobile Bedivere. Slowly, Bedivere's arms raised and he reluctantly returned the hug.

"Sir Archibald," stammered Bedivere, pulling away. "I was not told you would be passing this way. Are you alone?"

Archibald grinned, displaying a set of crooked, grey teeth.

"I am not alone, brother," he replied. "Lady Fleur rests here also."

It was like someone had opened a plug to Bedivere's heart and drained his entire body of blood. My own jealousy, which I had barricaded behind an imaginary door, gatecrashed back through. Who the hell was Lady Fleur, and why had her name had such an effect on Bedivere?

Gareth now had my arm in a vice-like grip. He turned to Archibald as well.

"Sir Archibald, my name is Sir Gareth of Orkney. I am seeking my brother, Sir Agravaine. I was told to look for him amongst the Maidens of the White Cloth."

Archibald did not have time to answer. One of the

veiled women had interrupted the exchange.

"Sir Gareth," she replied, "your brother is indeed being cared for in the monastery, but it is not Sir Agravaine that lies within its walls. It is Sir Gawain."

"Sir Gawain," gasped Tristram, Talan and David at the same time. Gareth's sword fell to the ground with a clatter; I hadn't realised he had drawn it.

"We were told Sir Gawain was held captive by the barbarian, Balvidore," said Bedivere urgently. "A prisoner in the dungeons of Camelot."

"Sir Gawain escaped."

I rushed forward, only to be pulled back like a spring as Gareth's grip remained.

"Is Arthur with him?" I cried. "Did my brother escape with Gawain?"

"Is this fair maiden the Lady Natasha?" asked Archibald. His eyes had narrowed, cutting out all colour with the exception of his inky black pupils.

"It is."

"Miriam, take the lady to the Golden Chamber," ordered Archibald. "I'm sure she requires resting after such an arduous journey."

"But my brother," cried both Gareth and I.

"I will take you to Sir Gawain," said Archibald to Gareth, "but Arthur is not here," he added, looking at me with a strange expression on his sunken features. "To our knowledge, he is still being held prisoner at the whim of the Saxons."

"Then I want to speak to Gawain as well," I demanded, shaking my arm up and down in an attempt to release it from Gareth's grip, but he was like a puppy with a shoe and wouldn't let go.

"You may accompany Sir Gareth - if he permits it," said Archibald eventually.

"I favour her company," replied Gareth, and he smiled at me.

Thank you, I mouthed, and he nodded. I would have

gone with him regardless of the man in black. I was sick of people telling me what I could and couldn't do, and Archibald really needed to know that wearing black merely showed up his dandruff.

"Then Sir Bedivere, if you and your knights would care to join me, I will ensure your every need is attended to," said Archibald, clapping his hands three times. "Miriam, if you could interrupt Lady Fleur from her tapestry, I am certain Sir Bedivere is eager to be reacquainted with his betrothed."

I registered the exchange on Tristram and Talan's faces before I understood the words Archibald had spoken.

"Betrothed?"

"Natasha…"

"Betrothed?"

"This is not how it…"

"BETROTHED?" I screamed. "Are you telling me that you're engaged?"

Not even Gareth could keep me from launching myself at Bedivere, who was taken by surprise as I fell on top of him. My fists pummelled his chest and face as we sprawled into the dirt.

"You disgusting, two-timing piece of crap," I yelled, as Gareth, Talan and David lunged forward and attempted to pull me off their friend. Two had my arms and one went for my legs. Big mistake. I kicked and writhed until my boot connected with something solid. It might have been David's head, or it could have been his ribs. Either way, he collapsed onto the dirt.

"Get off me," I cried, as Archibald, bug-eyed and appalled, looked to Tristram to restore order. Yet while Tristram's lip had recovered, his ego had not. He was not going to be seen going up a mere girl and losing – again.

"Let Natasha go," appealed Bedivere, climbing to his feet and clutching his stubbly jaw.

"I urge caution, Sir Bedivere," said Tristram, "you named Lady Natasha a she-devil yourself when we tarried by the lake. You, one of the greatest knights of Logres, have taught her how to handle a blade. Do you want to be skewered?"

"I wouldn't waste my energy," I screamed, before collecting a globule of spit in my mouth and lobbing it at Bedivere's feet for good measure. "I never want to speak to you again, you revolting worthless slimeball."

It was Gareth who restored order.

"I will keep Lady Natasha with me, Sir Bedivere," he said to his friend. "I am anxious to pay attendance to my brother, and Sir Gawain may have news of Arthur. We will meet later, when m'lady has had an opportunity to become herself once more."

"PIG!"

I turned on my heels and ran up the steps into the monastery, past several white limestone statues of knights bearing swords and round shields. I realised once inside I was going to look pretty stupid if I had run the wrong way, but I was past caring. No one cheated on me and got away with it. Bedivere was going to regret arming me - big time. I would castrate him when I got the chance.

Then I turned a dark corner, slumped to the mosaic-tiled floor, and burst into hot, heart-broken tears.

I'm not stupid. Far from it. But I had truly believed that Bedivere was different from other boys.

I was wrong.

A dry spasm was still ricocheting through my chest as Gareth, a maiden in white, and I climbed a narrow set of stone steps. Gareth had not said a word, but he had a sad expression of understanding on his face. He had found me sobbing into my knees on the cold terracotta tiles. The knight had pulled me to my feet, taken a square piece of transparent material from within his vest, and gently wiped my face. The cartilage in my nose went into spasms of pain, that shot into my jaw and eyeballs like red hot needles.

There really wasn't a part of me that wasn't broken now.

The maiden led us into a circular chamber. It was plainly fitted with a single wooden bed, a bench covered in rags, and a low-lying table. All around the walls were iron brackets containing melted candles. The wax dripped in long stalactites, frozen by daylight. Only one remained lit, flickering feebly in the morning shadow.

"Brother," moaned a male from the bed. He raised his hand weakly at the wrist as Gareth rushed forward, falling to his knees.

"Sir Gawain," cried Gareth softly. "My noble brother."

"Is he badly hurt?" I asked. The maiden who had led us into the chamber was several inches smaller than me, stout like a barrel, and her face was covered in a sheer white veil.

"Sir Gawain will recover in time," she replied, "but the chains of Camelot have left their mark on the skin of his limbs, and we believe he has been poisoned. He is very weak, as he made the journey from Camelot to Solsbury Hill in one ride, and he cannot yet stomach the food of our halls. Sir Gawain needs time and prayer."

He needed some good antibiotics, I thought to myself, looking at the festering red welts on his wrists. Then I had the image of Arthur, chained, beaten and starved, and bile rose in my throat.

No. I would not allow such thoughts. My own brother was healthy, strong, and far more likely to survive this kind of brutality than boys of a medieval age. I needed to stay positive, for my own sanity,

DONNA HOSIE

however difficult that was proving to be.

Gawain was mumbling and flapping his other hand towards the bench. Gareth bent down and allowed his ailing brother to whisper into his ear.

"Lady Natasha," said Gareth, "my brother says he has something for you in his saddle bag. A letter – most urgent."

"I will retrieve it," said the white maiden, and she glided over to the bench like her feet were on rails. I was rather glad she offered. The foul-smelling pile of rags lying on top of the bench were so matted with dirt and dark streaks of blood that I couldn't understand why they hadn't been burnt. They were a health hazard, and probably contaminated with fleas at best, the Ebola virus at worst. My teeth clenched together as I thought about throwing them at Bedivere, but I had to stop thinking about ways to hurt him, because any thought – bad or positively evil – just brought back the tears.

A brown piece of parchment, torn and crumbled, was passed to me. At first I didn't want to touch it, but then I saw my nickname, *Titch*, written on the outside, just above a bloody thumb print.

It was Arthur's scrawl.

I know I cried out; I think I swore. I unfolded the parchment and sank to the floor. My cold hands were trembling so much I could barely read the first sentence.

Titch
I don't have time to explain everything here. Just know that I'm okay.
You know I would never lie to you, so you MUST listen to me now.
Trust Bedivere.
I know this will be hard to understand, but we get each other, you and me. We're a team. Us against the world, and we've seen

154

most of it. TRUST BEDIVERE. OK!

Try not to break any bones on the way to Camelot. I will explain everything when I see you. Bedivere will get you to me. You must trust him.

Arthur

18 A MAZE OF INFORMATION

I read the letter. Nine times. The quickly-scrawled words never changed, but that didn't stop me from willing them to rearrange into something I could understand.

Trust Bedivere.

This was insane. Arthur didn't know Bedivere. He had never met Bedivere. They had been born over a thousand years apart. It was ridiculous. The letter must be a forgery – or worse, one written under torture. There was even a bloody thumb print on it.

Gareth and Gawain had not disturbed me during my efforts to decode the torn piece of parchment, but I was not going to be so polite to them. I rose to my feet and walked over to the bed, brandishing the letter in my right hand, like a lawyer in a courtroom.

"Who made Arthur write this?" I demanded. "Was it Bedivere?"

Gawain made an effort to pull his body upright; Gareth tucked two hands under his brother's hollowed armpits and yanked him skyward. He was so frail. His poisoned, starved skin was puckered and loose like an old man's, yet Gareth had already told me that Gawain was the youngest brother and not yet sixteen.

"The word is from Arthur," said Gawain slowly. "I saw him write it in his own hand, before he entrusted me with its safe keeping and delivery."

I shook my head. "It isn't possible. Arthur has never met Bedivere. He has never known any of you. You've got the wrong person."

Gawain smiled. His gums were white and had withdrawn away from his yellow teeth. They looked twice as long as a normal set of teeth. Dog-like.

"I would know Arthur as I know my own brothers," replied Gawain, as Gareth placed a hand on his shoulder.

I kicked at the foot of the bed in frustration. Gawain was obviously delirious, so I turned my attention to Gareth.

"Arthur couldn't have written this," I said, willing myself not to cry with helplessness, and failing miserably.

"Why?"

"Because my Arthur, my brother, has never been to this place before. He wouldn't admit to knowing Bedivere - or any of you for that matter - if his life depended on it."

"Is Arthur's tongue untruthful?"

"Of course not, and that's my point."

"Then why do you doubt him, Lady Natasha?"

"Because…because…"

Gareth rose from the bed and took the letter from my shaking hand.

"If you believe - truly believe in your heart - that this is a falsehood, that my noble brother is deceitful in his word. If you, Lady Natasha, doubt that Arthur wrote on this parchment, then burn it."

Gareth had called my bluff. He walked towards the burning candle and held a corner of the letter close to the small flame.

"Your want, Lady Natasha?"

Why were they all so desperate to play along with this charade? Was this medieval kingdom so hungry for the return of its king that they would come after the first Arthur that fell their way? Even after a thousand years?

"Why would my brother tell me to trust Bedivere?" I sobbed. "He has another girlfriend. He's engaged to someone else, and you all knew this. I can't trust any of you."

Humiliated, I ran. Down the steps I flew, stumbling and tripping over my own feet. In the distance I noticed a thin shaft of light. I ran towards it, praying that it was a door through which I could escape this hell.

I came out into a blanket of green. Tall hedgerows, at least seven feet high, twisted up into the overcast sky. Perfect square tiles had been cut deep into the thick green grass. Each one was filled with rose bushes.

It was perversely serene. A couple of white butterflies chased each other through a bank of blood red flowers. Butterflies didn't live for very long, and it was almost as if they knew it. Death was looming over them, but they didn't care. They were just having fun.

I wiped my streaming nose on the back of my filthy hand. It left a long disgusting streak on my skin which I knew had been transferred to my face. I was a mess. Inside and out.

A gruff voice spoke through the silence.

"Natasha."

"Piss off," I replied, not daring to take my eyes off the butterflies. I was waiting for them to die. Everything else around here did.

"You will hear what I have to say."

"Like hell I will."

"You are a stubborn wilful maiden." I felt two hands around my waist.

"And you are a cheating, two-timing pig and I wish you were dead," I cried, and I span around and aimed my right knee as high as it would go.

Bedivere gasped, his eyes rolled as he sank to the ground.

"Give my apologies to Lady Fleur, won't you," I hissed. "I would hate to have deprived her of an exciting wedding night."

I turned and ran off into the garden. The hedgerows closed in around me as I turned left, right, left again and onwards. Any direction to avoid my spiteful, broken heart from finding me.

Only when I stopped to catch my breath did I realise, to my horror, that I had run into a maze.

"Oh, bloody perfect."

I tried to pull apart the tightly packed vines that had been deliberately twisted around thin wooden poles. They wouldn't give an inch, but were more than willing to slash retribution on my hands with tiny thorns. I took my frustration out on the world by repeatedly kicking a stump that was poking out of the earth.

"You are lost I gather, Lady Natasha?" asked a voice, and I looked up to see Tristram leaning against a topiary sculpture of a unicorn.

"Fabulous," I muttered to myself. "That's all I need."

"At least I am now convinced you are no witch," he said smirking. "If you were cursed with the dark arts then you would have burnt a hole by which to escape."

"Actually, I would have set the whole place on fire," I replied, rolling my eyes and flicking my fingers in his direction. "Fire at my fingertips, remember."

"It was most unladylike of you to attack Sir Bedivere, Lady Natasha. He is quite hopelessly enamoured with you," said Tristram, walking towards me. "For my part, I think his mind has been slain by madness, but one can never tell what is forged in the souls of even the most brilliant of knights."

"Bedivere is betrothed to Lady Fleur, and the only

person with whom he is enamoured is himself," I replied, placing great emphasis on the name of my rival. It sounded like the noise a person makes when they vomit. In fact, that's what I would call her from now on: Lady Puke.

Tristram laughed.

"It is not a betrothal of love, Lady Natasha. Any fool can see that."

"Then what the hell is it? Not that I care," I lied.

"Lady Fleur and Sir Bedivere were promised to one another as infants in the crib. Their parents believed it to be a worthy match, as long as Sir Bedivere proved himself in manhood to be the knight his father once was. Of course, Sir Bedivere surpassed their expectations."

I wanted to say something witty in response, but my inner voice was enjoying the struggle. I settled for pouting.

"Sir Bedivere is not in love with Lady Fleur," continued Tristram, encouraging me to walk on with a wave of his hand, "but he is of noble breeding. He had no intention of dishonouring her reputation by ending the attachment. That was until he met you."

"What do you mean – until he met me? Are you saying he's going to finish with her?" I mumbled. My nails had found their way into my mouth, and I was busy ripping off my cuticles. My jealous temper was going to be the death of me, and it wasn't even my time of the month.

"I do not know what you mean by finish with her," replied Tristram, taking a left turn, "but until you thwarted his procession, Sir Bedivere had been intending to ask Sir Archibald for release from the bond of their parents."

"Oh."

Idiot.

It was back, and I knew my inner voice was referring

to me and not Tristram. I wanted the ground to open up and swallow me whole. Better still, could someone make me a time machine? I would go back a couple of hours and try yet again to be cool, calm, pretty and smart, instead of angry, violent, snidey and dumb.

"Bedivere should have told me that he was engaged," I said righteously.

"I have no doubt that he is cursing his folly now."

"And even if he does get released, or whatever you said, it doesn't make it okay that he didn't tell me. He shouldn't keep secrets from me, especially ones like that."

"Indeed."

"It wasn't fair, finding out like that. It was completely humiliating."

"You see yourself as his equal?"

Tristram had guided me through the maze. We were now in a new garden that had vines of dusty purple grapes, hung in long rows as far as the eye could see.

"Of course I'm his equal."

"It is strange," said Tristram. "For I do believe that Sir Bedivere also sees you as such, but would you fight the glorious fight if called to, Lady Natasha?"

"For heavens sake, you boys talk of war as if it's something glorious and romantic, but there's nothing wonderful about death."

"You are wrong, Lady Natasha. There is nothing in this land nobler than fighting for what you believe in, fighting for those you love. Why, isn't that exactly what you are prepared to do?"

"That's different," I said, taking a left turn away from the vines, back to the monastery. "Arthur is my brother, and he would do this and more for me. I just didn't think it would take this long to find him."

Tristram snorted. "You are now amongst knights who have been searching and waiting for Arthur for an entire millennia, m'lady. Time is nothing in these lands, not any more."

"Which one do you fear the most, Tristram?" We had arrived back at the tall stone walls of the monastery. "Mordred or Balvidore?"

"I fear nothing and no man," he replied, but I knew he was lying. The knight had taken too long to answer.

"I don't believe you."

Tristram sniffed, took out his knife and wiped it down on the edge of his suede waistcoat. He didn't answer me, choosing instead to gaze at his reflection in the blade.

I took that as my cue to leave him. I needed to find Bedivere. I would apologise to him if he apologised to me first. I also wanted to stalk out the opposition: Lady Puke. Would we be expected to duel for his affection? Mud wrestle? We could run a race. I would totally win that, especially if she was in a dress. Then again, if she was beautiful like Slurpy, I wouldn't stand a chance.

Perhaps I could just hit her over the head with something heavy?

As I pushed open the oak door to the monastery, hinged with creaking, rusty brackets, Tristram answered my question.

"There is only one true danger to a knight of Logres - to any mortal man - Lady Natasha," he called, "and today you have proven it."

"And what's that?"

"The subtle craft of a maiden. One who ensnares the heart and renders a man as helpless as a baby. Love is a powerful ally, but it is also the most dangerous foe there is."

19 THE ARMY OF BLUE FLAME

I tried to follow the direction of the male voices at first, but everything was distorted back inside the walls of the colossal monastery, and I soon became lost once more. The deep tenor of the singers vibrated along the brickwork. Musical vines that were trapped in the stones. At every turn I could hear their chants, but I couldn't find them. They were invisible. Ghosts.

I wanted to find Talan. I knew Gareth wouldn't have left his brother's bedside, and David would probably be sleeping. Where there was singing, Talan wouldn't be far behind. If I had the friendly Irishman on my side, then finding and apologising to Bedivere might be easier. As it was, Bedivere was probably having his balls removed from his throat.

I wasn't alone during my search for Talan - far from it. The Maidens of the White Cloth glided along the halls like spectres. Their white woollen slippers made no sound on the tiled floors, and several times I jumped out of my skin as I turned a corner and ran straight into them. They seemed to breed like bacteria. They all walked in the same way: shoulders thrust back and hands pushed together in prayer; their long white fingertips just grazing the edge of their veils.

You are in a monastery, what did you expect them to do? Stagger along in high heels and daisy dukes?

They all had another thing in common as well: not one of them would speak to me. I was nothing to them. I asked for help, begged and yelled, and yet they seemed to walk through me like I wasn't there.

With my temper and frustration rising, I eventually found a familiar face. It was David. He had removed his cloak and waistcoat and was sitting on a long wooden bench beneath a window. His whole body was hunched forward.

David heard me clumping towards him like a rhino because his head rose. When he saw me he jumped up and bowed.

"Lady Natasha," he cried. "How is Sir Gawain? I am eager for news, but everyone seems to have forsaken me."

"He looks pretty crap," I replied bluntly, "but you looked far worse after the attack by the dwarf-riders. I have no doubt that Gawain will feel obliged to get back on a horse within the hour."

"And word from Arthur?"

"There was a letter."

David's face lit up with a beaming smile and my heart suddenly ached. The sensation was so quick, so out of the blue, that I felt the overwhelming urge to throw my arms around David, to squeeze and mould him into the shape of someone new.

"Lady Natasha, are you unwell? Should I get a physician?"

I shook my head. Spots of perspiration had gathered on my top lip. I wiped them away with the back of my hand.

"You just reminded me of a person I knew, many years ago."

"Sir Patrick, perchance?"

"What do you know of Patrick?" I gasped.

"Sir Bedivere asked us if we knew of a noble knight called Sir Patrick. He said you spoke of him when you slept."

I thought I was silent in my nightmares. My fire-breathing mother had sliced my tongue out. Obviously this wasn't the case.

"Patrick is my brother," I replied quietly.

"Arthur has more kin? Why, this is glorious news."

I went to open my mouth to correct David, but my tongue really was gone. Why couldn't I pretend, just for a little while?

Because that would be a lie, said a muffled voice inside my head. It was fighting a war with my heart. My tongue returned.

"Our brother's dead," I whispered. "He drowned when he was little."

"Drowned?"

"Water, a river."

David clenched his fist, brought his knuckles to his mouth and kissed them. He was muttering under his breath, a prayer of sorts, but I didn't care. I had listened to enough words for Patrick. Eulogies at the funeral; inscriptions on a white angel tombstone; the screams of my mother; the accusations; my own lies...

David and I spent the rest of the afternoon keeping one another company.

We played checkers, and I kicked his ass.

We played chess, and I kicked his ass in that.

We played cards, and I let him win a hand.

And then I kicked his ass.

Knights – 1. My self-esteem – 3.

We talked about Arthur – who was now everyone's obsession – and David's dead family. His mother, brother and three sisters had all been killed during an outbreak of the plague, many years before the battle that had broken the fellowship of the Round Table.

"I pledged myself to Arthur and the court of Camelot as a boy of ten winters, and I have risen through the ranks to be unrivalled in the sport of jousting," he said proudly. "I am still an apprentice to Tristram, but the knights regard me as their equal. Sirs Bedivere, Tristram, Gareth and Talan are my family now."

"Tell me more about the enchanted sleep, David. Were you all really in that grave for a thousand years?"

"I remember little of the battle of Camlann, but I recall the aftermath as if it were yesterday. A vision came to us, a lady who rippled with the water of the lake," said David, a faraway look in his eyes. "She spoke to Sir Bedivere, and told him that we must wait for Arthur to return. Then glory would follow, and the hand of evil would be smote down and left in ash and shadow. The kingdom was to sleep whilst we waited. We aged – a punishment for allowing the mortal stroke to fall. It is strange to sense the body weakening whilst the mind remains strong, but we were not afraid because we knew we were not dying. Not like that, not without honour. Nimue would appear in our enchanted dreams to tell us that there could be no penitence without suffering, and that the day of Arthur's return was close, and we would soon be returned to our former glory."

"That seems rather cruel," I replied. "Why would Nimue make you age while you waited? I bet she didn't get any older." I stopped talking and quickly checked up and down the corridor for a blue haze. Nimue didn't strike me as the kind of woman who would take kindly to being called cruel.

"To be honest," I continued, "Nimue scared the life out of me when I first met her, but sometimes I wish she would come back and just tell me what I'm supposed to do here. I'm just stumbling around, making a fool of myself, and people are dying because of me."

"She was indeed a treasure to behold," sighed David sadly.

"Nimue is very beautiful."

"Not the lady Nimue, your lady companion. The one who perished in the claws of the white Ddraig."

"You mean Eve?"

"She was the loveliest maiden I had ever set eyes upon."

"I knew so little about her. I know so little about everyone here."

"Including Sir Bedivere?" asked David wisely.

"Bedivere most of all," I replied, shooing away a mouse with my boot. "I know nothing about him, except that he's *betrothed* to Lady Puke." I stabbed my heels into the floor with anger and frustration.

David's face and neck were now bathed in a blotchy pink blush. He wouldn't meet my eye.

"What is it?" I asked. "There's something else you're not telling me."

"There is to be a tournament in their honour," said David reluctantly. "Sir Archibald has declared it. He wants to see Sir Bedivere and Lady Fleur wed before we depart Solsbury Hill for Camelot."

An icy hand had plunged into my chest and was slowly squeezing the last drop of life I had left in me. I was only being my normal sarcastic self when I screamed at Bedivere about depriving Lady Fleur of her wedding night. Had he known? Did he now believe that I knew and that I didn't care? This wasn't happening. I'm not that kind of girl. I don't shove my tongue down the throat of every boy I meet. I'm not Slurpy. Bedivere was different, special. He was *my* special. I had never felt like this about anyone – ever. The feelings I had for Bedivere were in my blood, in my breath. They were now part of me.

"When are they getting married?"

David shook his head and flapped his hands.

"I know not, m'lady," he replied. "I am merely repeating what Sir Talan has been told. He was asked by Sir Archibald to prepare a sonnet of confirmation. I had the measure that Sir Talan was not happy about the idea, because of your place now in Sir Bedivere's heart."

I grabbed hold of David's shirt and pulled him up to my height. It was a good job he was still too young to have chest hair, because I would have scalped him in the process.

"You have to help me, David," I begged. "Swear an oath that you'll help me. Swear it now."

David meant to go down on one knee, but I yanked him up again. This time I definitely took a layer of skin from his chest as he winced in pain.

"Forget the knee, and I don't need you to kiss my hand, or say Hail Mary, turn around three times or do any of those knightly things, just say you'll help me find Bedivere."

"It is getting late, Lady Natasha," said David, squirming under my grip. I realised to my horror that I probably had his nipples twisted in the fabric of his shirt. I let go quickly and he gasped with relief.

"Are you saying they may have already married?" My voice box felt like a python was squeezing the life out of it.

"No, no," stammered David, taking two steps back in case I grabbed him once more, "but you will be expected to retire to your chambers, now that the sun has set."

"Retire to my chamber? Do you want a slap around the head? You sound like my brother."

"Then you would do well to heed to your brother's judgment," said David, rather pompously. "Arthur's word is law and must be obeyed."

"And pigs will fly," I snapped back. "Now are you

going to prove yourself a knight and help me find Bedivere, or will your honour fail me."

I could totally get used to having knights at my beck and call. David's nostrils flared with indignation. He puffed out his chest, and was on the verge of declaring himself my undying slave when a deep boom shook the solid stone walls.

David's hands instinctively went to draw his sword, but he had taken it off and he was now unarmed. He span around, lost and confused, as another deeper explosion was unleashed. Pale dust from the ceiling rained down on the two of us.

"David, what is that?" I cried, as the first screams started to echo through the walls of the Solsbury Hill monastery.

"It is the sound of evil," yelled David, grabbing my hand. "You need to reach safety, Lady Natasha, and I must retrieve my sword."

My first thought was that Solsbury Hill was under attack from another Ddraig, but as David and I ran past a shattered window, I saw a tall, wide panel of blue light outside.

"David, wait," I said, suddenly stopping. Cautiously, we crunched over the broken fragments of thin glass and peered outside.

There was an immense wall of flame, similar to the Nimue-made haze that had appeared in the tunnel. Except this was bigger, much bigger. The swirling, powder blue vortex was at least thirty feet in length. It had a strange three-dimensional appearance as traces of white smoke churned inside the flickering mass. The tips of the flames darkened the higher they went, so they blended into the starless sky. And then there was the smell. It was sickly-sweet, like toffee.

"Have you ever seen anything like that before, David?" I asked the knight. Both of us were trembling, not through fear, but because a bitter wind was now howling through the lower level of the monastery.

"Never in all my days have I seen such a sight," replied David. "Come, we must not tarry, Lady Natasha. I must arm myself."

"Wait," I cried again. I had seen black shadows moving in the flame. "Something else is out there. In the blue fire."

"My sword, Lady Natasha," begged David. "I implore you."

Without warning, a swirling ball of flame erupted from the bank of blue in the garden. David and I dived for cover as it sped like a cannonball directly at us. As it connected with the stonework, a mass of electrical currents swarmed out across the walls.

"What is this devilry?" yelled David.

The wall disintegrated, choking us in a plume of white dust and crumbled stone. A cry went out.

"The walls of the monastery have been breached."

Whatever was attacking the building was not friendly. Coughing, both David and I climbed to our feet and ran for the nearest set of stairs.

We were only five steps up when we were met by four visions in white. Their conical headdresses were slightly askew, indicating they had also been flattened by the blast of blue flame. Miraculously, their faces remained veiled.

"Sir David," said one of the women, and I recognised the voice as that of Miriam who had greeted us upon our arrival earlier that day. "We are gathering in the chapel. Prayer will be our salvation."

"Take Lady Natasha," commanded David. "I must arm myself, and go out in battle with the other knights and smote down this evil."

But I pushed my way through the barricade of white and continued up the stairs, ignoring David's cries and the screams of the terrified women, as another blast rocked the monastery. I had already made my decision.

If Gareth was as decent as I believed him to be, then he would not leave his brother. Whether they stayed in the chamber or attempted to leave, Gareth would need an extra pair of hands. I would make myself useful for once. I certainly wouldn't cower, or look to a higher being for guidance, not this time.

As I reached the next level, which was lined with a long stone balcony, a wrought iron chandelier, filled with tens of candles, came crashing down. I jumped over the twisted wreckage, but slipped on a rolling candlestick. My left shoulder bore the brunt of my weight as I crashed into the limestone base of a statue. Dazed, and in pain, I looked up into the face of an angel staring down at me. Powder blue smoke was twisting around the wings, making them look like they had been draped in chiffon.

"Natasha."

The gruff voice had cried out from below. I peered through a gap in the stone columns of the balustrade, and saw Bedivere and Tristram, struggling through a swarm of terrified people. Both were armed with swords.

"Stay where you are, Natasha," shouted Bedivere frantically. "I am coming."

Another ball of blue flame pierced the outer wall and shot through into the corridor below. It came through with such ease, the stone walls may as well have been made of paper mache. Bedivere, Tristram and twenty more were swallowed by falling masonry. Thoughts of a September morning in New York flooded into my head. My family and I had been there when the towers fell. I hadn't really understood the panic and worry back then; I was too little. Now I did. Fear for your own safety starts to play second to the panic you feel for those you love.

I screamed Bedivere's name, but plumes of choking dust were already rising swiftly in a mushroom cloud.

Everything below was obscured. More women in white came running towards me; they were quickly followed by men in long brown robes which looked like potato sacks. All of the men were bald, but their hands glistened like gold.

They were saving the treasures of the monastery.

I screamed for Bedivere again, but the attack on the building was now so ferocious that I knew he wouldn't be able to hear me. Blue sparks spat at the walls, setting fire to the fringed tapestries that lined every window. Blue and amber flame combined to create an enormous brown monster that was intent on devouring everything in its path. The sickly smell of toffee stuck everywhere.

Yet again I could hear cries of "mother, mother." This time though it was something more Godly: a mother called Mary.

But I wasn't waiting to find out if she had any intention of helping.

Black smoke was starting to fill the corridors. With the sleeve of my tunic covering my mouth, I crawled along the stone floor until I reached a turn where the air was clearer. I got to my feet and ran, choking and screaming for Gareth and Gawain.

A black mass surged towards me. It was moving so quickly, at first, I thought it was a gigantic lizard slithering along the narrow corridor.

"Get the girl."

The voice was cold and oily. It oozed out of the black-hooded shapes. I screamed. Someone at the front of the surging crowd held out his hands, which were tanned from the sun. He had long pointed nails that were painted black. A fizzing ball of light formed in his palms. I had never witnessed anything like it, but I instinctively knew it was going to be used as a weapon. I turned direction, and then dodged to my left and then to my right. The flame shot past my earlobe. From the burning smell, I knew it had come close enough to singe my hair.

I ran back towards the stairs, but the way was now blocked by a wall that had collapsed. I heard my name again, and almost cried with relief as I realised that Bedivere was still alive. I reached the balcony and threw my upper body over the edge, screaming his name.

Bedivere had moved further away from the carnage below, and was looking for another way to climb to the next level. He turned around and looked straight at me.

"My love," he cried.

Another blast of blue flame shot through the wall. This one was thinner, like a laser beam. Bedivere fell to his knees, and with his body stretched backwards, slid underneath it with his sword clenched tightly in his left hand. A wooden cross on the wall exploded into lethal splinters. One, shaped like a pointed dagger, pierced a veiled maiden in the face. She collapsed to the ground, jerking and screaming, as the gauzy material that fell from her headpiece quickly soaked with blood.

A cold hand then pressed down hard over my mouth as a fist connected with my stomach. I choked as the wind left me. I saw the look of horror on Bedivere's face and knew he wouldn't be able to reach me. I had to defend myself. My right arm was free, and so I pulled the small curved dagger from the sheath that was attached to my side. My attacker was not expecting the blade that was plunged into his right thigh. A pain shot through my forearm and shoulder; it was harder than it looked, stabbing through skin, muscle and tendon.

My attacker cried out and dropped me, but someone else was there to willingly take his place. Another black-robed figure stepped forward and punched me in the face. That was quickly followed by two more blows to my stomach.

I fell to my knees and stayed conscious enough to register the hood that was placed over my head. I kicked out in the darkness, and then felt the weight of something hard and solid against the back of my neck.

Starlight and Bedivere's face invaded my thoughts. Then nothing.

20 M AND M

The first sense to come back to me was smell. Onions. Rotting food. I gagged.

Then I registered the scratchy material that was smothering my face.

I couldn't breathe, panic gripped me.

I was lying on my side with my hands tied behind my back. Painful stabbing sensations were shooting through my arm and shoulder. How long had I been lying in this position? It could have been hours, judging by the loss of circulation in the left side of my body.

I tried to twist my face and head, but the sack simply tightened across my neck. I screamed out.

Then I heard giggling. High-pitched, definitely female.

I fell silent, although inside my head I was screaming every swear word I knew, and I knew plenty – in several languages. I hated that laugh. I had heard it enough times back at *Avalon Cottage*.

"I'll let you go if you promise not to try anything stupid," said the Welsh voice of Slurpy.

"When my brother finds out what you've done to me…"

"I didn't do anything," said Slurpy, "but I'm sure Arthur will be fascinated to hear about your little adventure with knives. Stabbing someone, *tsk tsk*. Now that's serious, even more awful than killing your baby rabbit, you murdering little freak."

I had never hated anyone so much in my entire life, and that was saying something.

The hood was pulled off my head, and I coughed up the lungful of fibres that I had inhaled.

We were in a large tepee that had been made out of scaly red leather. In the centre was a small fire of blue flame, miniature versions of the ones that had exploded around the Solsbury Hill monastery. Now that disgusting piece of cloth had been removed from my nostrils, I could smell sweet toffee once more. The unnatural flames were warm, and I started to feel light-headed again, with a sensation that I knew had nothing to do with the fact I had been knocked out. It was hallucinogenic. It reminded me of the boy with the giraffe tongue.

"You look hideous," said Slurpy. She was sitting crossed-legged near the flapping entrance to the tent. Her eyes flickered between me and her nails. There were strange henna tattoos on her hands.

"I didn't have time to tart myself up like you."

"I wouldn't speak to me like that if you know what's good for you." Slurpy's top lip curled.

"What are you going to do, bitch me to death?"

Slurpy rose to her full height and arched her neck back. She was dressed in skin-tight black leggings, with a black fitted tunic over the top. The front was laced, but left a gap of pale white flesh for its entire length. It was on back to front, and deliberately so. Slurpy wasn't wearing underwear. Dark blue jewels, set in thick gold, were draped around her neck. I would never admit it, but she looked quite stunning - in a medieval, high-class hooker kind of way.

Then she started to mutter in a deep voice that sounded alien, not even male. The tendons in her throat stood to attention. Now it was my turn to giggle. Slurpy had finally gone insane. It was either that, or she was stoned.

Then her head snapped forward and I screamed. Slurpy's eyes had gone completely white. She clapped her hands together. A tiny ball of blue flame zapped away from the fire in the centre of the tepee, and hovered above her interlocked fingers.

And she had the nerve to call me a freak.

I started to panic. My arms and legs were still tied, and I was in so much pain from the beating. I knew I wouldn't have been able to run very far, even if I had the chance.

Surrender was the only option.

"Okay, point proven," I yelled. "Just stop, Sammy. You're freaking me out."

I shuddered. Saying her cute hamster name was just wrong, even if I was on the verge of being turned into one by magic.

But Slurpy was on a different planet. She totally ignored me, as her milky white eyes remained firmly in place. The ball of blue fire started to twist and stretch in her hands. Wings slowly unfurled from its centre, and a spiked tail snaked from one end, as Slurpy manipulated the shape with her fingers.

The blue flame dragon then opened its mouth and yawned.

"Sammy, stop," I yelled again. "Think of Arthur. Think of home."

"I am home," she replied, in a voice that was at least five registers lower than her normal one.

Unable to move, I waited, sweating as my bonds magically tightened of their own accord. The fire-breathing dragon that had been moulded between her fingers started to twitch, as its wings slowly moved up and down in time with her fingers. Slurpy was like a puppet master, carefully manipulating a magical marionette with invisible strings.

"Sammy…"

She clicked her fingers and uttered a single word.

"Alathincidere."

It was the size of a small bat, but I was unprepared for how quickly it moved. The blue dragon disappeared from Slurpy's hands, and then just as quickly reappeared inches from my face. I screamed in terror as it flapped around my face. There was no escape from it. Even after I buried my face into the dirt, the razor-sharp wings beat against my hair and ears. With every flap that connected, I felt a sharp sting, like a paper cut.

"Enough, Morgana."

The slashing immediately stopped, but the pain remained. My eyes were filled with grit from the ground, and the tiny cuts that now criss-crossed my face stung, as if someone had poured nail polish remover over them.

Two blurred figures were in front of me, but I couldn't see more than their outline. The curvy one was clearly Slurpy, but the other was taller and broader. A male.

"Aqualente."

I gasped with relief as cold water was poured over my face.

"Don't look so concerned, Mordred," purred Slurpy. The normal voice was back. "She isn't hurt, and I've been desperate to practice that little charm ever since you showed it to me. Or would you prefer it if I practised on one of the others?"

"You are still in the realm of transition, Morgana. If you are going to conjure the flame, then at least do it in the open. I am rather partial to this tent. The dragon took an age to slay."

They both laughed, and then the man strode

forward. Through my blurred vision I saw the glint of a curved silver blade. It reminded me of the unhappy moon from the night before. Cold steel was placed against my throat.

"If you want to stay alive, Lady Natasha, then heed my command. I will unbind your hands and feet, and treat you like a maiden of the court of Arthur, but if you try to escape, then my Lady Morgana will not be so forgiving. Do you yield?"

I nodded. I was too terrified to speak.

I was released from the bonds and the pain swamped me. My nose throbbed continuously, while my tongue was drawn like a magnet to a back tooth that had been knocked loose by the blow to my face. As the circulation returned to my left side, I saw that my knuckles were split and bleeding. As for my ribs and stomach, I felt like I had been used as a block of wood in one of Arthur's Taekwondo lessons.

A rough wet cloth was then scraped over my face. I yelped as it connected with my sore nose.

"My apologies, Lady Natasha," said the man. "I do not have the gentle gift of healing."

I could focus on him now as the water had removed most of the dirt from my swollen eyes. He was very tall, with muscular legs and arms. His trousers were the colour of charcoal, and his tight fitting tunic reminded me of a jar of mustard. Long blonde hair fell around his face in straight panels, and his head was crowned with a circular silver piece of jewellery. His large eyes were like blue-green marbles, and his features were razor-sharp; his cheekbones alone could have sliced though metal. For a homicidal maniac, he was pretty damn hot.

"Leave her with me, Mordred," said Morgana sullenly. "You have more important things to plan, like how to get us to Camelot before those idiot knights realise what we now have in our possession."

Mordred glowered at Slurpy.

"Watch your tongue, Morgana. The Knights of the Round Table are not to be insulted in such a manner."

She looked at me and scowled. Despite the pain in my mouth, I grinned. I was more than happy to watch Her Slurpyness dragged down a peg or two. Her humiliation was worth the pain that was probably coming my way.

And it did. Slurpy threw back her head again and her eyes rolled. I cringed. It was like watching a horror movie. She snapped her fingers, and spoke aloud in that freaky deep voice.

"Punctumlispa."

Several tiny black shapes materialised at the top of the tepee. I didn't need eyes to tell me what they were, because the rapid buzzing in my ears was clue enough.

"What the hell are you doing?" I screamed, as the wasps dive-bombed like a squadron of acrobatic airplanes.

"Melasubsisto," barked Mordred. The wasps disappeared in a puff of lazy black and yellow smoke.

"You are draining the fun out of my life, Mordred." Slurpy fluttered her eyelashes, and for one horrific moment I thought she was going to snog him. Thankfully Mordred didn't seem that interested. After cancelling out Slurpy's bit of hocus-pocus, he snapped his fingers. The flap to the entrance pulled back and a dwarf appeared. He was about three and a half feet tall, with thick brown hair that looked like a badly made wig, and he had the biggest nose I had ever seen in my life.

"Food for our guest, Byron," instructed Mordred.

Byron didn't say a word, he just scowled. His forehead creased in thick folds of skin like a pug dog. He had a sack with him that was nearly as big as he was. The dwarf rummaged inside it, and threw me a chunk of bread, and some watery-looking cheese that fell apart in mid-flight.

"Yonder way lies the great castle of Camelot, Lady

Natasha," said Mordred, kneeling at my side. "You will accompany us now."

"The second Bedivere, Tristram and the others see you, you know you're a dead man, don't you."

Byron barked a sarcastic laugh. It seemed to please Mordred, who looked at the dwarf fondly, like he was a child.

"Balvidore and the Saxon scullions will smote down all in their path, and will glory in their destruction," said Mordred, with a thin, twisted smile. "Well, those that endured the battle at the abbey of course."

I stopped eating and threw the tasteless chunk onto the ground. A cold shot of adrenaline raced through my veins once more. I had seen bodies lying amongst the fiery rubble of the Solsbury Hill monastery, but for some reason it had never occurred to me that any of *my* knights were among the dead.

But what about David? What had happened to the young fifteen-year-old apprentice knight? He had been with me on the stairs, but then I had pushed past the white maidens and had run on. The wall had collapsed. It had blocked my way back down. I hadn't given it a second thought at the time, but what if he had remained on the steps when the enormous slabs fell down?

And what of Gareth and Gawain? The gentle knight would never have left his younger brother. Did they get out too, or would the choking magical fumes have proved too much? My over-active imagination pictured the scene with horrific realism. Two twitching bodies sprawled across the floor as they fought for air.

Then there was Talan, who had disappeared with the singing monks. What had happened to him? And Tristram?

The name that I couldn't even consider pushed past all of the others.

Bedivere. Not Bedivere.

In the end he had chosen me. When the walls were

under attack, Bedivere didn't rush to Lady Fleur's side. He came to find me. He tried to save me.

"I see I have given you much to think about, Lady Natasha," said Mordred softly.

I looked into his eyes, and made a silent vow to myself to cause him as much pain as he was now causing me. He bowed to me, then to Slurpy, and slid from the tent like a snake. He was quickly followed by Byron, who cast one last scowl at me before he waddled away, dragging the sack behind him.

"What are you doing with these people?"

"I met Mordred on the outskirts of that castle, the one they called Caerleon," she replied. "I stole a horse, although I had no idea where I was going. I just wanted to get away from you and the other two ginger freaks. And I really can't believe my luck. Mordred has been quite the teacher."

She moved closer towards me; her movements were dance-like.

"You've completely forgotten about Arthur, haven't you?"

"Your brother is the only thing that matters to me," she hissed back, "but if I have to play in this bizarre show, then I'm going to do it on my own terms."

"Meaning?"

Slurpy crouched down beside me; I caught a mouthful of her long dark hair as she flicked it over her shoulder. Why was her hair not greasy? Mine felt dirty enough to fry chips in.

"Mordred has shown me things that would make even your freaky piggy eyes spin in their sockets, little girl," she crowed. "He thinks I'm special. He says I've been here before, and he's right. It wasn't some stupid school trip or a book. This is all too easy for it to be new. I'm special."

"You know Mordred was the one who cut down King Arthur in the tales, don't you? You're ganging up with someone who wants my brother dead. Even when they realise he isn't who they think he is, do you think these gory druids will just let us go when this is over?"

"There is one thing that I am sure of," said Slurpy slowly. "Once we get to Arthur, I won't need you, and neither will Mordred. I think it's called collateral damage."

"Arthur will kill you if you hurt me."

"But how will he know?"

Slurpy started to laugh as she arched her head back. Her eyes were already rolling.

21 THE FALLS OF MERLIN

I wasn't sure if I slept because I couldn't remember dreaming.

I was still in the tepee, sprawled across the damp ground. My riding clothes were torn and bloodied. I didn't need Eve and a copper plate to show me that I was battered, bruised and probably puffed up like a reality television star who had overdosed on plastic surgery.

My thoughts stayed with Eve as I slowly pulled my aching body up from the dirt. I exhaled guilt. She wouldn't have been there if not for me. I hoped she hadn't suffered, and that when the end came, it had been quick. My mind wandered back to the castle of Caerleon and the maid who had seen to Slurpy on that first night. My first impression was that she and Eve had been related. Sisters probably.

Would the maid know that Eve had been amongst those killed in the first attack? I didn't even know the sister's name, but she would certainly be added to the growing list of people who hated my guts.

Once the swaying and nausea had stopped playing

with my mind, I made a quick note of my injuries. Discounting my face, the worst pain was just above my stomach. I pulled up my tunic and looked at my skin. Pale and not very interesting had turned into black tinged with purple. As I gingerly felt around each separate rib bone, I counted two that were painful enough to be counted as broken, or at best, fractured.

The physician, Robert of Dawes, would have pain-killers. I needed him as much as he needed me now.

Did Mordred know about Sir Percivale and the travelling court of Caerleon? They were armed, and in far greater number than the splinter group of knights that had gone to Solsbury Hill. The thought unexpectedly cheered me up. We weren't doomed yet. The battle for Camelot was quickly approaching from all sides, and could prove the perfect distraction while I searched for Arthur.

I peeked out through a gap in the tepee and counted at least seven more tents, although the others were made from a thick cotton-like fabric, and not dragon hide. The druids had made camp next to a towering cliff. The dark craggy rocks rose like jagged skyscrapers into the sky.

I stuck my head further out of the flap. Without the thick scales acting as a barrier, I found I could hear water. It was not the gentle sound of waves lapping against a beach, but the torrential gushing of millions of gallons falling into an open space. A waterfall.

I scanned the perimeter of the camp again. No Mordred, no hooded druids, and best of all, no psychotic Slurpy. Just a few tethered goats that looked thoroughly bored.

There was nothing sharp and silver to arm myself with, but I picked up a long thick stick from a burnt-out fire, just in case. Slowly and very quietly, I stepped out into the daylight. My throat was dry and as coarse as sandpaper. I desperately needed to find water, and if I could take a shower at the same time, then even better.

The ease with which I walked out of the druid camp was unsettling. Anticipation brings with it a unique sense of dread as your body reacts to every sound, magnifying it a thousand fold into the spectre of something dangerous. My eyes were constantly searching the lush green landscape for the colour blue, and the inevitability of pain that came with it.

I followed the rock face and the deafening sound, and found my waterfall. Judging by the noise, I had been expecting something grandiose of Niagara-type proportions, but it was much smaller and elegant.

A jutting lip in the cliff was the starting line. A narrow span of water splashed down at least ten metres into a frothing, bubbling pool. The water was clear, but it sparkled with a green sheen as it reflected the colour of the overhanging bushes, that clung to the dark rock like fluffy clown wigs.

Pockets of tall reeds lined the pool, which was the same size as a public swimming bath. As I nervously stepped over the slippery rocks, a bushy-tailed squirrel suddenly popped out in front of me. It was grey, with inquisitive black eyes. I had never thought of squirrels as being particularly hairy before, but this little fellow had a long collection of fur under its mouth, just like a beard. It rose up on its back legs with its paws resting on its pale grey belly. It wasn't scared of me in the slightest.

The squirrel turned tail and bounded up the nearest tree trunk in a circular motion, but I sensed it continued to watch me as I pulled off my tattered trousers and slowly lowered my legs into the freezing water. Scooping up mouthfuls of water with my hands, I drank until my thirst was gone. Then I washed my lower body, taking care not to fall in.

The sun was still too weak to dry clothes, and so I decided against washing mine. My long tunic covered my thighs, and I left my legs bare. I was in no rush to put my filthy trousers back on and contaminate the only part of me that was now clean.

Lulled into a false sense of security by the hypnotic cycle of the waterfall, I soon forgot about my kidnappers. I was back in the middle of nowhere. Alone and in pain. It was routine now.

Then the echo of a wind chime rustled through the reeds.

"Not all in Logres get to see the sacred Falls of Merlin."

Taken by surprise, I lurched forward. My arms flailed like windmill sails, but it wasn't enough to stop my body from toppling headfirst into the pool. I somersaulted several times as a strong undercurrent dragged me further down into its depths. My lungs burned as I swallowed freezing water. Slimy weeds groped at my legs like tentacles as I struggled in the invisible tide. As I continued to battle with gravity, my bare feet connected with a smooth rock, and I propelled myself back up to the surface. Spluttering and coughing, I broke through to fresh air, and with a weak pain-filled breaststroke, I kicked and dragged myself to the edge of the pool.

"WHAT IS YOUR PROBLEM?" I yelled, as I hauled my body out onto a rock formation that was shaped like stacked pancakes. "Why can't you give me a warning when you're about to appear? Ring a bell or something?"

Nimue laughed, and stepped out from behind the same tree the squirrel had clambered up. My fear had amused her.

"There is only one bell of note in Logres, Natasha, and you have already rung it."

"Yeah, thanks for mentioning that it would collapse our way back," I replied sarcastically, wringing my hair like a towel. "I can now add Robert of Dawes to the long list of people who will want to kill me before this ends."

"This will never end, Natasha," said Nimue. "Not for you or Arthur – not now." Her wavy golden hair glowed like fire. I was hit by the thought that if I got too close, I would end up burnt.

"I found Bedivere," I replied, shivering. "I did what you asked, but I'm no closer to finding my brother."

Nimue waved her hand over a large boulder, and a pile of clothes materialised.

"You are closer than you think, Natasha."

"Are they for me?"

Nimue nodded and I bounded forward, throwing off my tunic in the process.

"Look into the pool, Natasha," ordered Nimue, as I dressed in the clothes she had magically provided: tight black trousers, and a moss green tunic that was like a warm fleecy sweater. Underneath that was a long downy strapping, which brought immediate relief to my aching ribs.

"Why should I look in the water?" I replied, knowing that with my coordination and luck I was liable to end up back in it again. I was clean and dry, and intended to stay that way for at least an hour before Armageddon erupted around me once more.

"Look into the pool, Natasha," instructed Nimue again. Her voice was harsher. "I want to show you how close you are to Arthur."

She had provided me with clothes and so I felt obligated. I peered over a rock and gazed down. The craggy rock face reflected back at me, then, as I inched closer, my own unrecognisable face came into view. Slurpy was right, I looked hideous. While it was my nose that was still aching, my eyes had taken the brunt of the bruising. Long streaks of purple swelling covered my skin. Another black shadow marked the spot where I had been punched by one of the druids at the monastery.

There was no Arthur. I pulled away from the nightmare in front of me.

"You aren't trying hard enough. Look again, Natasha."

Intimidated, I leant over again, but this time I closed my eyes. In my head I willed all my thoughts towards my brother. There were no images, just words. Written in Times New Roman and printed across the black screen of my eyelids.

ARTHUR. ARTHUR. ARTHUR. ARTHUR…

I opened one eye, and then the other. The sight that greeted me made me cry out with happiness and relief. I wanted to touch the pool, to grab him, pull him out and back to me where he belonged.

My brother, with his scruffy blonde hair even longer and stragglier than I remembered, gazed back at me with tired eyes. He knew I was looking at him. He smiled without showing any teeth. It was his knowing smirk. A way to show he was still on top of things. I couldn't see whether he was chained or hurt in any way. The image beaming back at me was just a profile.

"Can I see more of him? Can you show me where he is?"

Her hand rippled through the air, and the image in the pool retracted back. Now I could see the dungeon in its entirety. Arthur was sitting on a straw-strewn floor. He didn't appear to be chained. I quickly checked him for blood or swellings that could be hidden bandages, but saw none. He had been missing for a week, and yet the lucky bastard was in better shape than I was.

And he wasn't alone. There was another guy with him. He was wearing a tunic with a red dragon on the chest, and his face was scarred just above the left eyebrow.

"Who's that with Arthur?"

"Sir Gaheris of Orkney," replied Nimue softly. "A

knight and kin to one you already know."

"Gareth's brother."

"Camelot is less than two moons away, Natasha," said Nimue, "and help is coming. Stay strong and hold fast. The most important part of your quest will soon be upon you. Remember, Arthur is all that matters."

"When you say help is coming, do you mean the knights?" I asked, breathing heavily. I said the plural, but what I was really asking involved just the one.

Nimue started to step back away from the waterfall; her bare feet were silent on the ground.

"Mordred is coming, Natasha. Do not tell him of what you saw. He knows not of the power of this sacred place, and one day that will be his downfall. Morgana's too, if she fails to release that which is not hers before the end."

I looked back into the pool. Arthur was slipping away from me. I bit my bottom lip as tears started to fill my eyes, then laughed as Arthur winked at me. He definitely knew I was watching him.

My fingertips reached out and touched the water where Arthur's hand was. A ripple broke out where I broke the surface. Arthur was gone. I looked back, and saw that Nimue had disappeared too. In her place was the bearded squirrel. He had wound back down the tree and was nibbling on an acorn nut. He looked straight at me, dropped the nut and disappeared into the long undergrowth.

I wiped my eyes, got to my feet and pocketed the acorn. It would be a reminder that this hadn't been a dream.

Seconds later there was a crashing through the undergrowth. Two hooded men, Byron, and a furious-looking Mordred broke through the trees. I didn't try to run. There was no point. They had magic at their fingertips that I couldn't comprehend.

"You were wise to forsake escape, Lady Natasha,"

said Mordred knowingly, striding towards me as I leant back against a boulder. "You would not have gone far."

"I wanted to have a bath, Mordred. Where I come from, people wash occasionally. You should try it."

"Ow."

Byron had kicked a rock - I presumed in anger at my rudeness to his master. He wanted to say something, but was holding his tongue. He was hopping with a constipated look on his squirming face.

"I see you changed your cloth," said Mordred, narrowing his eyes. "Pray, where did you get such garments?"

"On that rock there," I replied, pointing. I held his gaze, proud at the way I was handling the situation without deliberately lying. If Arthur could be held captive and still keep the upper hand, then so would I.

"Check the glade," ordered Mordred to his two henchmen, "but make haste. Something ominous sleeps here. I can feel it."

Scowling, the two druids parted and drifted off in opposite directions. I noticed that neither was keen on getting too close to the waterfall.

"M'lady," said Mordred, offering his arm.

I walked past him and Byron without taking it. If I had had a sword, I would have chopped his arm off.

"Where have you been?" snapped Slurpy, as Mordred and I entered the druid camp. The tepees had been packed away on carts, and the hooded Gorians were gliding away on the morning mist.

"Can you ride?" asked Mordred, ignoring my brother's witch girlfriend.

"On what?" I replied. "A goat?"

Mordred laughed and put his arm around me.

"My steed is strong and can bear the two of us today," he murmured into my ear.

"I'm perfectly capable of riding by myself." I pulled

away from his mouth, which was way too close to my earlobe.

"Lady Natasha, you ride with me, or you ride with Morgana. Count your blessings I have given you the choice. Others would not be so accommodating."

Brilliant, I thought. Other seventeen-year-old girls get to choose what car they want mummy and daddy to buy them for Christmas. I fall into a tomb, go back in time, and get to choose my very own psycho.

Ten minutes later I was being manhandled onto Mordred's glossy black horse. I chose to ride behind him; I didn't want his hands to go wandering. Before we left, I dropped one of my diamond earrings onto the ground.

I knew the odds were against Bedivere finding it, but I had to do something.

I'm coming, Arthur. I'm coming.

22 LOOK AFTER YOUR BROTHER

Guilt is an emotion that breeds with time. It slowly inches its way through your soul, devouring every scrap of conscience, until - eventually - there's nothing left.

You become hollow. A shell.

Nine years ago, my brother Patrick drowned on a camping holiday. In many ways I can say that's when my life started, but not in a good way. I can't remember anything before that day anymore. Guilt ate the happy stuff away. And yet I can't forget anything that has happened since.

I was eight years old when it happened. Arthur was a year older, and Patrick was in second grade. We were living in America – Washington to be exact, although that wasn't where Patrick died.

My dad had taken us on a weekend camping holiday with our cousins and my uncle. My mother hadn't wanted to go. She isn't an outdoors type of person. She has phobias about snakes and spiders and heights and men with beards - although thinking about it, she was always okay about things that flap.

Anyway, mum stayed behind.

My earliest memory is of her and the words she said to me as we were packing up the car.

"Look after your brother."

Six hours later, Patrick was dead.

And it was my fault.

Me, Arthur and Patrick had been playing hide and seek with our cousins. We were hiding and Amy and Robert were seeking. It was competitive in the way blood rivalry always is between relations. Patrick was giggling and whispering and I thought he would give away our hiding place. I got really angry with him and put my hand over his mouth, so the little terror bit me.

Baby teeth aren't soft. They are hard and sharp like fangs.

That isn't an excuse for what I did, but it's the reason.

I pushed him away from me. My baby brother. The one I was supposed to be looking after.

Our hiding place was behind a shield of rocks on the edge of a fast-flowing river. Patrick stumbled back and fell. In my nightmares I still see the splash, as his little body fell in; he didn't have time to scream. Out of the corner of my eye, in that blurry crevice between reality and imagination, I still see his electric blue t-shirt bubbling under the water.

Blue has *always* been the colour of pain.

My world froze, and so Arthur was the first to react. He ran screaming for our father and uncle, who both dived into the river fully clothed. Several others at the camp site threw themselves into the water as well. They were like salmon, jumping about in the river in a frenzy of panic.

It was my uncle who dragged Patrick out apparently, but I never saw it. Two women had herded me, Arthur and my cousins into their tent. I heard the sirens, and I remember five-year-old Robert throwing a tantrum because he wanted to ride in the emergency vehicle with Patrick, but the medics wouldn't even let my father travel in it.

That was the day my life started, and it began with a lie. I told everyone that Patrick had slipped and fallen, and Arthur - the only witness still breathing - backed me up.

People knew though. Perhaps not my father, who was too consumed by his own guilt to notice mine, but my mother certainly did. She was never the same around me after that.

Look after your brother, she said to me, but instead I pushed him away.

I've never been a deluded person. I've always understood my own limitations, and I know I was only eight when it happened. I may live in my own little bubble and have conversations with a voice in my head, but that doesn't make me crazy. Slurpy Morgana can bounce up and down on her horse and jiggle her bits at every druid that passes all she likes, but I'm still a better person than she is. I don't care if she thinks I'm a freak. I defy anyone to live with the guilt that has been eating me for nine years, and not turn out a little strange.

So I'll never, ever make it up to Patrick, but I could sure as hell try with Arthur because, if I was honest, when I tried to dissect the insanity that has shadowed my every move since I fell in that grave, it wasn't even Arthur I was trying to help.

I had been trying to help the ghost of the brother who never leaves me, because while Patrick's headstone reads *Rest in Peace*, he doesn't.

He can't. I won't let him.

The family never talk about Patrick, and we don't have photographs of him in whatever house we are supposed to call home. Guilt whitewashed him away. My father was drinking beer with his brother when it happened. He wasn't drunk or anything, but he has never touched a drop since. Working all hours was his self-imposed punishment. Must keep busy, then I don't remember. That verse is tattooed onto his hollow heart.

My mother flagellates by depriving herself of food. Her stomach must be the size of a walnut now. Her guilt was spread around more evenly. She blamed me, Arthur and dad of course, as well as the medics who got there too late, my uncle for distracting my father, the emergency doctors for not trying to restart my brother's heart for longer…

But I think she moved to the middle of nowhere to try and run away from her own guilt for not being there. Her guilt is tattooed into her very existence.

Guilt was beached on my shoulders as I sat behind Mordred. I was in awe of its colossal power. Guilt was able to shame me because of the past, but it also had the unique gift of forcing me to be frightened of what was still to come. I felt guilty about things that hadn't even happened yet, because - somehow - I knew I would be the cause of more pain.

Mordred and Slurpy Morgana wouldn't understand guilt if it sat on their faces. I couldn't comprehend how either of them could sit on a horse and ride along, all the while knowing what they had done to others back at the Solsbury Hill monastery. I wasn't even certain that Slurpy had even been there, but I decided to lay guilt on her by association. She had abandoned me, and run off into the arms of the first madman that had shown her a flicker of interest. The fact we hated each other's guts was irrelevant. I had still shown her a sliver of loyalty when questioned by Percivale in the hall of Caerleon.

All she had shown me were the whites of her eyes.

I wouldn't feel guilty if something bad happened to her now. Not anymore. She had crossed a line, gone over to the dark side as they say in sci-fi movies. You don't pull that kind of crap and expect to carry on as normal.

Guilt now had another power over me. It was hardening me up. I really was a shell and little more. Bedivere had been the first person to really make me feel special. Unique. Then Lady Puke arrived on the scene and ruined it all.

So, as we rode on towards Camelot, I retreated into my own little world. It was the only place where I was really safe. Mordred attempted to engage me in passive aggressive conversation about Arthur, while Slurpy Morgana threw nasty little comments in my direction, but I blocked them both out. This infuriated Slurpy who didn't like being ignored by anyone, but it made my resolve even stronger. Riding behind Mordred for hours had given me the one luxury that was in heavy supply here.

Time.

Time to think, time to plan. People and places crisscrossed in my mind as I mentally plotted a way to save Arthur. I wanted to get the upper hand on Slurpy. She was so busy trying to impress those around her that I knew she would be reacting once we got to Camelot, instead of being pro-active when it mattered. The travelling court of Caerleon, Mordred and the Gorians, and even Bedivere and his friends, would all be in for the fight. It's what boys and men do. I would use the one skill I really did have: I was a runner. While everyone else was fighting, I would just run. Straight into the castle, down to its dungeons and I would find Arthur.

Perhaps I was finally ready to look after my brother? Then again, the reality was it was just another situation I could totally screw up by just existing.

After a full day of riding, and way too much thinking, we settled down for the night in a blackened forest, which had barely survived a fire at some point. Many of the larger trees were scorched and bare, although there were green saplings rising up along the forest floor. I looked at my watch, but it had finally stopped working. I made a quick calculation that this was my sixth night away from my parents and my own time. I knew it would not be the last.

A chill quickly fell over the druid camp as the sun set. The sky turned a pretty shade of indigo. It reminded me of a camisole top I had bought the day before I fell into the tomb. It was still in a shopping bag with the tags on. Would I ever get the chance to wear it? Did I care?

Mordred and Slurpy went for a walk and left me with Byron. The dwarf didn't say a word, he just scowled, but he made a funny little growl when he wanted my attention. I wasn't even sure he was capable of coherent speech. Byron skewered shrivelled root vegetables on a stick, and once cooked on a normal fire, he would bark at me to take them. I didn't want to offend him, figuring his lack of height probably made him feel inadequate enough, and so I ate every root he poked at me. Some of them could have been fossilised horse crap for all I knew. They certainly tasted like it.

Once fed, he shooed me into a tent, flapping his arms and yapping at me to – presumably – move quicker. I had no idea where M&M were. I didn't want to be near either of them, but I was also annoyed that they had left me in the protective custody of a demented walking teddy bear with OCD. Byron did nothing but fuss, scowl, and fuss some more. He rearranged the fur pelts on the hard ground at least twenty times before he was happy for me to lie on them; he arranged the sticks on the fire in neat vertical rows before he would let the flames get anywhere near them; and then he poured tiny crystals into his hand and coordinated the stones into colour groups. Once he knew he had my attention, Byron would throw the crystals onto the fire. I think he wanted to amuse me with the rainbow smoke display, but I didn't know whether to smile at him, thank him, or watch out in case he bit my kneecaps.

And just when I thought we may have a connection, Byron would make a grumpy little *humph* noise in the back of his throat, scowl, cross his arms and look thoroughly miserable at being in my company.

As the hours passed, strange smells like sweet, stewed fruit started to waft through the tent, accompanied by laughter and small explosions outside. Mordred and the druids were getting high on their own weaponry. Instead of inspiring dread, it encouraged my excitement.

Tomorrow I would see Arthur again, I was sure of it.

Mordred popped his head into the tent at one point. I pretended to be asleep. Byron didn't reveal my true state of consciousness; he just growled at Mordred like a guard dog. Eventually, the druids stopped playing with their toys, and silence fell outside, except for a couple of chattering birds that called to each other from deep within the forest.

Byron wasn't sleeping. He was sat up with his arms and legs crossed, like a school child on the reading carpet. The flap to our tent was closed, but every so often Byron would take a peek outside.

It wasn't long before I realised that every time he

looked out, it coincided with the call of the birds. They appeared to be getting nearer and greater in number as the minutes passed.

I sat up, and Byron scowled at me. Then another bird call sounded, and his stubby little fingers reached for the flap.

"What's going on?"

Byron placed a finger to his lips and motioned to me to be quiet. Sensing danger, I crawled across the ground on all fours and sat down beside him. Bryon flinched back, as if I stank of body odour, which I definitely didn't because I had long become obsessed with checking my armpits for smells.

"Help me, Byron."

He scowled, and then pulled out a knife from inside his fur skin waistcoat. I flinched back, thinking he was going to stab me.

Then I gasped. The knife was the one Talan had given me. The same dagger I had plunged into the leg of my attacker at the Solsbury Hill monastery, and Byron was offering it to me.

Two more bird calls echoed in the evening air, and then for the first time, Byron spoke to me in a cackling deep voice.

"When I give the sign, you are to run, m'lady."

"What? Run where?" I whispered, closing my fingers around the hilt of my knife as it lay flat on Byron's hand.

Three more bird calls, even closer than before. The druid camp was being stalked on all sides now. Deep in my chest, my heartbeat quickened. It was the most delicious feeling. Like being in love, without the pain that comes with it.

Five calls sang out. The numbers were increasing, as was my anxiety, but still Byron sat cross-legged on the ground. I rose to my feet, and Byron nodded his approval.

"Where do I run, Byron?" I asked again.

"To the one who would die to protect you, m'lady."

Bedivere. He was here. Happiness burst from my heart. I was so excited I wanted to jump into the air, but I was afraid Byron would think I was a bit stupid, so I didn't.

"I don't understand. Are you not on Mordred's side then?"

Byron didn't answer. He had just peered out of the tent on the sound of six bird calls. Concentration was carved onto his face, as the deep folds of skin on his forehead threatened to drown his big bushy eyebrows. He opened the flap to the tent so I could see outside. There was nothing but darkness.

Then Byron jumped to his feet and ran at me.

I heard the sound of slicing flesh before comprehension caught up with my senses. Byron had thrown himself onto the sharp point of my dagger. I screamed in shock as hell suddenly broke loose outside the tent.

Male voices cried out in the darkness, as blazing arrows flew through the air, igniting the other tents in a *whoosh* of flames. Hooded figures threw themselves out of the burning structures. Several Gorians were ablaze. Their sacrificial screams magnified through the night air as they threw themselves onto the ground. Bodies rolled around in a vain attempt to put out the flames. Animals bleated and neighed with fear as a firestorm rained down on the camp, quickly followed by the clanking rush of men clad in chain mail. They sliced through those fleeing.

I fell down beside Byron. The dagger had gone through his shoulder blade, but when I attempted to help he pushed and flapped me away.

"Run."

"NOW?"

He pointed to his bloody shoulder and the dagger,

which I was still holding in my sweaty palm.

"That was the sign."

"Stabbing yourself was a sign? Couldn't you have just said *run*?"

"I like to be dramatic," groaned Byron. "Now run, before they have time to summon the blue flame."

I bent down and kissed Byron on his crinkled pug dog face.

"I won't ever forget this, Byron."

"Alas, neither will I," he replied, with a grimace so deep, his face was in danger of imploding.

I ran.

23 THE DAY WITH NO DATE

Terror and confusion swept through the druid camp as the knights surged forward. Every tepee was now ablaze, with the exception of the dragon hide tent that I had been held in. Burning arrows were falling down on it like comets from the sky, but the flames were extinguished before they got to within ten inches of the skin. An invisible, fire retardant force-field was covering it, and by accident – because he still remained bleeding inside – Byron the Dwarf.

I stopped running once I reached the perimeter of the camp. I needed to think. The blood-smeared knife was still in my hand, and so I started hacking away at the bonds that tied the terrified goats. I had to do something useful and that was a start. The animals stampeded away, trampling down one Gorian as he tried to stop their escape.

The fighting in the camp was now at a ferocious level. The knights were outnumbered five to one, but their anger was an army in itself.

The first knight I recognised was Talan. His round grey eyes were alight with hatred as he battled three Gorians, two of whom were armed with long spears topped with blue blades. A third was standing back, but I could see that his eyes had gone white.

"Oh no you don't," I screamed, and I charged at the magician. My head and shoulder collided with his chest and sent him flying back into a wooden cart filled with potatoes. Flames were licking at its enormous wheels, and the druid fell straight into their wooden spokes.

"Lady Natasha," cried Talan, as another druid screamed with pain as the Irishman's sword cut off his hand. The hooded figure slumped to the ground, cradling the stump which was pulsing bloody waves through his long-nailed fingers. The other druid in the trio, sensibly realising he was now outnumbered by Talan and myself, ran for his life.

I threw my arms around Talan's neck and hugged him tightly.

"You're safe. I was so worried."

Talan pulled me away and grinned broadly. His cheek was still seared and swollen from the attack by the Ddraig, and he now had a bloody scab on his forehead.

"Trouble seems to follow you like the plague, Lady Natasha."

"Tell me about it."

"Are you hurt?"

I shook my head.

"No, I'm fine, but there's a little man, a dwarf I think, called Byron, he…"

Talan put his hand over my mouth, cutting me off in mid-sentence.

"Ssh," whispered Talan in my ear. "Sir Mordred must continue to believe Byron is one of his. The dwarf will be safe."

Another knight then ran over to us – it was Tristram. Sweat had glued his curly blonde hair to his face and neck.

"We must make for the horses before the Gorians have time to regroup," he yelled. "Make the call, Sir

Talan."

"Knights of the Round Table," boomed the Irishman. "The folly of the Gorians has been their shame. We have our quarry. Ride on, ride on."

The silver figures stopped fighting and charged for the perimeter. I counted seven, including Talan and Tristram. But which one was Bedivere? I couldn't tell, as Tristram grabbed my hand and dragged me from the burning camp for the dark protection of the wood.

Suddenly a pair of arms was around my waist, and I was lifted off the forest floor.

"Are you hurt?" said an anxious gruff voice. "I swear if they have harmed you I will go back and kill them all."

I squealed and buried my mouth into Bedivere's neck.

"You came for me," I sobbed, twisting my fingers into his straggly long hair.

"Always," choked Bedivere, and he threw his sword onto the ground and took my face in his hands.

"Sir Bedivere," cried a male voice, and I recognised it as belonging to Archibald, the man in black who had embraced Bedivere as a brother on the steps of the monastery. I looked around, and saw the furious expression on Archibald's face. A blue sheen had covered him.

"Get down," I screamed, and I pulled Bedivere to the ground.

Just in time. Two seconds later, a blue ball of flame shot through the air, skimming the top of our heads.

"Make for the horses," yelled Bedivere.

Gareth and Talan were supporting Gawain between them; his feet barely touched the ground as the knights charged further into the darkness. Their sense of direction was astonishing. All seemed to know exactly where to run and what to avoid. Tree stumps appeared out of nowhere, but the knights dodged them with ease, despite the fact that they were weighed down with armour and chain mail.

As we ran on, the outline of seven large objects came into view. I strained my eyes, and realised we had reached the horses. The knights had kept them well back from the fight, trusting in their own fitness in order to protect them.

Tristram, David and Archibald reached the horses first, and quickly set about loosening the reins that had been tied to a low-lying branch. Gareth and Talan, with the barely conscious Gawain, were next, quickly followed by Bedivere and myself.

"My brother cannot ride alone, Sir Bedivere," said Gareth anxiously. "The fight has taken what little strength he had regained."

"You take him, Gareth," I replied before Bedivere had a chance to speak. "I'll take his horse."

"I want you with me," argued Bedivere.

"We don't have time to discuss this," I said, placing my foot into the stirrup strap. Another eerie blue glow was approaching.

Bedivere gritted his back teeth but turned and helped Gareth with his brother. The others were already riding away.

"Stay at my side," said Bedivere, as he became the last to mount his horse. It reared as a blue spinning ball of flame erupted over our heads, spraying us with sparks and intense heat.

"Where are we going?" I gasped, as the fireball sucked in the air around us, leaving Bedivere and I trapped in a vacuum.

"Camelot."

We spurred our horses at the same time and galloped away into the darkness. It was only when I felt the cold night air on my face once more, that I realised I had not seen or heard either Mordred or Slurpy Morgana at any point during the rescue.

Adrenaline is an amazing motivator. It cancels out exhaustion and helps you to forget hunger, thirst or pain. Only when I thought we were safely away from the druids and Mordred, did I start to register the aching weariness that was pumping through my body. I now understood why people could fight with such bravery. When you are in the midst of a battle, you don't have time to acknowledge fear.

Dawn had not broken when we stopped, although a pink haze was starting to spread across the horizon. Tristram had taken the lead, and had shown us to a long thatched building. Chickens flapped and squawked as our horses followed a path to the wooden doors. I walked through mud and cow manure to avoid them.

Tristram, David and Archibald dismounted first and led the horses into the building. Talan and Gareth helped Gawain down and carried him in. Bedivere and I didn't make it inside. The second we were off our horses we fell into each other, quickly making use of a conveniently placed stack of hay.

We came up for air. Our heads had to be placed at an awkward angle for kissing because of my tender nose, but once we stopped, I could gaze into Bedivere's lime-green eyes and forget myself, just for a moment.

"I'll need to apologise to Tristram," I whispered, stroking Bedivere's lips with my fingers.

"May I ask why?"

"He warned me about Morgana, and I didn't believe him."

"Did the witch hurt you?"

"She had a good try."

Bedivere's fingers were on my face, gently tracing the cuts sliced into my skin by her magical miniature Ddraig.

"I need to apologise to you too, Bedivere. For what I did to you at Solsbury Hill."

"I should have told you, my love," he whispered, as

he teased my bottom lip with his mouth. "I feared losing you. I was a fool."

"David said you...you were to marry Fleur." The words were large and dry and became lodged in my throat as I tried to say them.

"Lady Fleur and I are no longer matched," said Bedivere gravely. "Sir Archibald rides with us to avenge his kin once Arthur is free to reign once more."

I sat up with a start.

"Are you telling me that Archibald has challenged you to a fight because you've dumped his sister?"

"It is customary for the brother of a forsaken maiden to challenge the one who has dishonoured her."

"But you haven't dishonoured her."

"It is different here, Natasha."

"So exactly how are you supposed to fight?" I asked, squeezing his hand.

"Joust or duel," replied Bedivere. "Sir Archibald will decide."

"It won't be to the death though?" I cried. I wouldn't lose him, not this way. I would give Bedivere up if it meant keeping him alive.

Bedivere shrugged, and placed both hands behind his head as he stretched back. His tunic had risen up, displaying a gap of pale white skin across his taut stomach. My lungs contracted sharply. I wanted to kiss his skin so badly.

"Did you not wish for my death, Natasha? Back in the gardens of the monastery?"

"I didn't mean it literally."

"Your words were truer than any ever spoken to me, m'lady. Your knee is a formidable enemy for sure. Such pain I have never known."

"And I've said I'm sorry," I replied testily, "but I had just found out that you were engaged to some other girl, and then my brother sends me a letter saying to trust you. If Arthur had been there I would have kicked him in the balls as well."

Bedivere's hand reached out and lingered along my bruised chin.

"Your words are a constant mystery to me," he said softly, "but I am willing to spend the rest of my days discovering their meaning."

I bent down, angled my head and kissed him again. My hands went exploring across his stomach. He moaned and my mouth reacted, pressing down harder as his fingers threaded through my hair. My words were a mystery but his were like poetry. I knew at some point I would start to lose track of the days spent in this land, but I felt like I had known Bedivere for a lifetime and more. Something was connecting us. I *had* been here before. I had been with Bedivere before. We were soul mates. Something time, life or death couldn't destroy – not now, not ever.

"I love you, Bedivere," I whispered, my lips still touching his.

"And I love you, my Natasha," he murmured back. "With the breath of my body and every beat of my heart, I will love you until the end of days."

There are some dates in our history that remain inked into a person's memory: birthdays, deathdays, events that are tragic, and some that mean everything.

I knew that this day would become one of mine.

Bedivere was gentle, and yet it still hurt. Not in a bad way, definitely not, but I wanted it to finish quickly. I had read the leaflets in the horrible sex education classes and so I was prepared – kind of.

But this was still a big deal for me, and I wanted to remember the date. Time had become confused, though, and had blurred into one mass. I was starting to forget *my* place in time. So this day that meant everything, had no date. It was just another dawn, competing in time with a million more. When I explained this to Bedivere, he smiled.

"I have seen nineteen harsh winters, Natasha. I do not need to know the date of the first frost, or the date of the final thaw, to know they were cold. The same can be said for my heart. It is yours now, truly and wholly. The date of ownership is of little relevance."

I briefly thought back to Arthur's letter. My brother had criminally awful taste in girls, but his choice in men was world class.

What a damn shame Arthur wasn't gay.

24 CAMELOT

I had pictured Camelot in my mind from the very beginning. I had imagined a grand castle adorned with turrets, set on a grassy hill and surrounded by a murky-looking moat. Colourful flags would flap in the breeze, as the sound of song and laughter filtered through the wind. A medieval Disney-meets-Glee mash-up.

The reality was more beautiful and terrible than anything my overactive imagination had concocted.

Camelot was set on a hill, but the sides of the towering mound had been excavated away and lined with stone, so it looked like a giant rock dais rising out of the earth. I had also been expecting the castle to be made from the same pale stonework that had been used to build Caerleon and the other buildings we had passed on our journey from Wales. Yet Camelot was black and glossy, like every piece of stone had been coated in thick tar after being laid. It made it look magical, but not in a fluffy rabbit-out-of-the-hat kind of way. This was dark and dangerous. The kind of magic that would gouge the eyes out of your baby rabbit. There were no flags on poles either. Instead, the towering walls were lined with spikes. Several were topped with what looked to be deflating balloons. The whole structure was colossal in size, with towers on top of towers, like layers of a wedding cake that had been covered in glistening black icing. I shuddered as goose pimples appeared all over my body.

The knights and I dismounted. The horses, sweating and panting, trotted off. No one bothered tying them up.

"It is a sight to behold isn't it," sighed Talan, and he started to softly sing an ode to the great who had walked in Camelot's shadow.

"It certainly isn't what I was expecting," I replied, taking Bedivere's hand in mine. He kissed my forehead.

"I see Balvidore is flying his standard," said Tristram, looking at Bedivere.

"Where?" I asked. I couldn't see any flags at all.

"The heads of his enemies," replied Tristram darkly, and he nodded to the deflating balloons.

If I had eaten breakfast, I would have puked it up. The knights crossed themselves, and Talan stopped singing and went pale.

"Please tell me Arthur isn't one of them," I choked. I couldn't look.

"Arthur is alive, my love," replied Bedivere, stroking my back. "He is the bait to summon the knights to Camelot."

"But there are so few of you."

The knights – with the exception of Archibald who was glaring daggers at Bedivere – scoffed.

"Lady Natasha, there are one hundred and fifty seats at the Round Table," answered Talan. "Right now, over one hundred of the strongest, bravest, most victorious knights this realm has ever seen, have woken and are riding to aid their returned king. Balvidore and the Saxon traitors will cower before the moon when we avenge the dishonour that has been done to this glorious land."

I forced my eyes to look once more upon the terrible beauty of Camelot. Instead of concentrating on the upper battlements, they were instinctively dragged to the lower sections. Arthur was in there, somewhere. My mind drifted back to the image in the pool below the Falls of Merlin, and I remembered that I hadn't told Gareth about his brother, held prisoner with my own.

"I've seen Gaheris," I cried, clapping my hands to my mouth. "Nimue appeared to me when I was being held by Mordred and the Gorians. She showed me Arthur and your brother. They are together, in one of the dungeons in Camelot."

Gareth and Gawain grasped for each other.

"He is still alive," exclaimed Gawain with relief. His voice was weak, but a pinkish tinge was now present in his face, which just two days ago had been white and bloodless.

Gareth fell onto his knee and kissed my hand.

"That is wondrous news, Lady Natasha. Our greatest fear had been Sir Gawain's escape would cost Sir Gaheris his life."

"We require a plan, Sir Bedivere," said Tristram, clapping Gareth on the back. "Sir Percivale and the travelling court from Caerleon could be leagues away from here. Do we wait?"

"No," replied Bedivere. "We cannot tarry. Once Balvidore is aware the knights have rallied here, he has no reason to keep Arthur alive. We alone must act with the element of surprise on our side."

And suddenly my own plan to use the battle as a diversion while I ran to Arthur wasn't looking so hot. The knights immediately formed a circle on the damp grass.

"We will split into two camps. Brothers, you are with me. We will enter Camelot via one of the tunnels to the west." Bedivere then spoke to Tristram. "Sir Tristram, you will create a diversion to the east. Take Sir

Archibald and Sir Talan with you."

"And what of me, Sir Bedivere?" asked David.

"If I may be so bold," interrupted Gawain, coughing. I noticed a thin streak of silvery blood on his hand as he pulled it away. "I can find the way to Arthur and my brother, but the tunnels are narrow. I am not of stout build like my older kin and I was able to slip through the bars that block the way. My noble Sir Bedivere, we will need the nimble and slight with us if we are to succeed. I believe Sir David would be most able in our camp."

David beamed, and my heart panged again; he looked so excited to be given such an important role in the rescue of Arthur. The young knight was bouncing on the balls of his feet with anticipation.

"Then it is decided," announced Bedivere. "Sirs Gareth, Gawain, David and I will take the tunnel beneath the west battlement. Sirs Tristram, Talan and Archibald will divert the Saxon scullions to the eastern drawbridge."

I coughed quite deliberately. I knew this was coming. The damsel in distress would stay behind and look after the horses, or prepare their supper, or knit some socks with two sticks and the hair from their chests.

Bedivere grinned.

"Are you ailing, my love?"

"And what do you propose I do, *my love*," I said sarcastically. I wanted to kiss him and kick him at the same time.

"You are with me, naturally," replied Bedivere. "I know from experience what a fearsome warrior lies within."

And with one sentence, all was right with the world again. I really was falling hopelessly in love. Now if I could just get Bedivere a razor.

The knights separated into their respective camps. I was overjoyed to be going with Bedivere, but I was afraid for Tristram and Talan. I didn't trust Archibald as far as I could throw him. His sunken sallow features had taken on a new level of malcontent. His black hair hung limply in greasy segments as he glowered at Bedivere. If Archibald had known the dark arts, I had no doubt he would use them to his own advantage. It went deeper than just avenging his sister. He even smelt bitter, toxic. It bounced off him like sound waves.

I confided to Gareth about my fears.

"You can't trust Archibald."

"Sir Bedivere knows what he is doing, Lady Natasha. Place your faith in him."

"It's not my faith in Bedivere that needs checking, Gareth. It's my fear that Archibald is going to slit Bedivere's throat when he least expects it."

"Then Sir Bedivere had better not turn his back to me, as he turned his back to my sister," said a cold voice behind me.

My insides turned to stone as I turned around to see the leering face of Archibald.

"You touch him and I'll kill you."

Archibald threw his greasy head back and spat out a short, sarcastic laugh.

"And to think my brother-in-arms threw aside the delicacy of Lady Fleur for *this*," he said with a sneer. "They may call you Lady Natasha, but you are no lady. You are a sorcerer's snake, no more than a bitch in heat, and I will see you burned at the stake once I have avenged my sister's honour."

Gareth placed his body in front of mine.

"Your quarrel is with Sir Bedivere and him alone, Sir Archibald," said Gareth quietly. "You will do well to remember the tenets of the Round Table. Your life is forfeit if you touch Lady Natasha, for she is a lady and kin to Arthur."

He stepped closer to Archibald.

"And she is also the true love of Sir Bedivere, and I

will kill you myself if you speak to her in that manner again."

Archibald's front teeth were clamped together and his top lip was quivering. He sidestepped Gareth and spat at my feet.

"Whore."

I saw the sudden movement and the glint of silver as Bedivere appeared from nowhere. He pulled out his dagger and held it to Archibald's throat; his other arm was wrapped around Archibald's neck, holding him in a lock.

"Then let us end this, Sir Archibald," said Bedivere angrily. "You have dishonoured my Natasha more grievously than with any pain I have dealt to Lady Fleur. You want to avenge your lady sister? Then let us be done with this now."

Bedivere threw Archibald forward. Both knights now faced each other, and only Gareth and I were present to stop them.

"I hope her lips were worth it, Sir Bedivere," sneered Archibald, wiping his hands on his tunic. He sniffed and pushed his greasy hair back from his flushed face. "Make the most of them, for now is not *your* time to die."

With his head held high, Archibald strutted away.

"Do something now," I begged. "You can't take him with you."

Bedivere closed his eyes and wrapped his arms around me. I thought he was shaking, but it was just the vibrations of my terror bouncing off of his body. He said nothing.

But in that moment I knew I would never stop watching Archibald, and I would be waiting.

"I have something that belongs to you," whispered Bedivere, and he pulled out the diamond stud earring I had deliberately dropped on the ground by the Falls of Merlin.

"You found it," I gasped, as Bedivere placed it in my open palm. "I wanted to leave a trail, and it was the only thing I had."

"I'll always find you, my Natasha," replied Bedivere.

I threw my arms around his neck and pressed my mouth against his; he tasted salty, like potato chips. It was delicious.

"Don't give up on me or Arthur will you?" I said quietly, fastening the earring to his tunic. "Even if things turn out differently to how you imagined."

Never before had I placed so many hopes and dreams into one fragile outcome.

It was time.

The men clasped hands and saluted each other in a ritual farewell. Bedivere and Gareth shared a few sombre words in private which I couldn't hear. Before the two camps divided for good, I whispered to Talan to take care and to watch out for Archibald.

"Be ready to teach me a new song, Lady Natasha," he said enthusiastically. "One to celebrate the rescue of our king. I am quite enamoured with your Lady Gaga. Tell me, does she have a suitor?"

The sky had darkened with a deep purple veil, and spots of rain were starting to fall. As we crawled through the undergrowth below the towering rock dais, Camelot appeared to stretch upwards and forwards like a yawning black mouth. There was a strange distortion around the castle's perimeter, like the haze that appears on scorching tarmac on a hot summer's day.

Bedivere led Gareth, Gawain, David and I to a small opening at the base of the rock. He placed his finger to his lips and drew his sword. We were all armed: the knights had swords, bows and quivers of arrows strapped to their backs; I had my curved knife and another shorter dagger with a white handle. It had belonged to Tristram, but he had made me take it.

The rock opening was a tight squeeze on all sides, but after a hundred metres or so it widened out. Bedivere and Gareth still had to stoop to stop their heads from skimming the roughly hewn roof, but the rest of us could walk upright without banging our heads. Gawain was now leading the way; his bow held tightly with a feather-tipped arrow already placed in the string. Bedivere and Gareth followed, while David brought up the rear. We heard nothing, except the squeaking of rapidly-moving rats, which brazenly criss-crossed our feet as we made our way along the damp, foul-smelling tunnel.

Gawain led us to a set of stairs. A single torch blazed in a wrought iron bracket on the wall. Next to that were several chains and manacles. Cloth, blood and bone were still strapped to one. I bit into my bottom lip, reminding myself that every foul step took me closer to Arthur.

As we climbed the steps, my stress levels started to increase. I was still convinced that my brother was not the Arthur the knights were looking for. We had come so far, but *what if* was now the prelude to a thousand questions racing through my head.

At the top of the steps, we encountered voices for the first time: deep and rasping.

Wait, mouthed Bedivere, but he pointed to Gareth and indicated that he should follow him onward. Gareth did so without hesitation. He would follow Bedivere into the pits of hell if asked. Moments later there was the sound of a scuffle. Something solid, like heavy metal, rattled onto the floor, as two attempts to cry out were muffled. What echoed instead was a brief gurgle.

Gawain, David and I stepped over the slumped

figures. Both men were dressed in baggy shorts made of thick wool that stopped at the knee. Their red tunics were now soaking up the blood spilling from their slit throats.

"Should we move the bodies, Sir Bedivere?" asked David. Bedivere nodded once, and Gareth and David immediately grabbed hold of two thick hairy ankles, and dragged the men back down the steps we had just climbed up. I stuck my fingers in my ears as the sound of their heads smashed up and down on the stone. Each thud was sickening to hear, as the skulls of the two Saxon guards pulverised into their brains.

In single file we continued onwards. The lower floors of Camelot were like a labyrinth, but all of the knights, with the exception of David, were confident in their direction. Twice we came to a tiny circular opening, like a barred storm drain, and Gawain, David and I would squeeze through as it was the shorter route. Gawain would then double back another way, and would appear in what seemed like an age later with Bedivere and Gareth, who were too tall and broad with their weapons to fit through.

Above our heads we could hear the pounding of feet against the floor. People were running. Had Tristram and Talan begun their diversion? I'm not a religious person, but I started to pray anyway. It seemed like the right thing – the only thing – to do.

"Not far now," whispered Gawain, smiling at me with encouragement. The tension around the five of us was palpable. Every muscle I possessed was tensed to breaking point. The smell from the warren of tunnels was obscene. My eyes streamed and itched, and even though I tried my best to not breathe in the stench through my nose, it found a way in anyway. It was hard to believe that anything human could make such a poisonous smell.

We curved around another corner, and the cause of

the stench was revealed. A rotting corpse, covered in buzzing flies and tiny wriggling maggots, was propped up against a wet stone wall. The jaw bone was exposed, and an eyeball hung from a bloody ligament. I lurched forward and gagged.

Two hoarse cries bellowed behind us.

Bedivere and Gareth reacted immediately, and charged forward with their swords raised. Gawain placed an arrow through the neck of one of the Saxon guards, before David plunged his sword into the man's chest. The other turned about and fled, with Bedivere and Gareth in pursuit.

"Quickly," cried Gawain, taking my arm. "Arthur and Sir Gaheris are close."

Frantically looking over my shoulder for Bedivere and Gareth, I ran on. David pulled a large ring of iron keys from a wall, as Gawain led us down another short flight of stained steps.

There were two doors in an airless chamber. Filthy blackened straw lined the floor. It was empty, except for a small table, which had two wooden goblets on it and a chunk of furry green bread.

"Which door, Sir Gawain?" asked David urgently.

"That one," replied the knight, pointing to the one furthest away from the steps. He was shivering, despite the hot airless conditions.

David was fumbling over the keys and so I snatched them away. I wanted to scream out Arthur's name, but caution had me in a vice-like grip. If this was a trap, then we would all die if more Saxons arrived.

I found the key that slotted into the lock, but it would not budge in any direction. David and I wrapped both of our hands around it and heaved it to the left. An imprint of a sleeping dragon was left embedded in the white skin of my palm.

Gawain and David pushed the door open. It squealed with resistance. A belching blast of hot air gushed out of the dungeon as I ran through it.

Straight into Arthur's open arms.

A torrent of emotion flooded out of me. I started screaming. Then my body went into spasms of violent shaking. I was having a fit; I couldn't control anything. Moments later, Arthur was yelping in pain. I had bitten him on the shoulder.

He pushed me away, but his hands still gripped my upper arms.

"You look bloody terrible, Titch."

I punched him several times. I had travelled through time to find him and the first thing he did was insult me.

"Don't you ever, ever, ever, do that to me again," I cried, pummelling his chest and biceps with balled-up fists. "Don't you ever, ever leave me again, do you hear me?"

Arthur held me until the terror evaporated and I had fallen limply into his arms. Then he turned to Gawain, who had finished unshackling his brother, Gaheris, and was now helping him stand.

"Thank you for finding her, Gawain," he said quietly, with a nod of his blonde head.

"It was an honour to serve my king."

My mouth dropped open. My jaw quite possibly scraped the floor. Gawain, Gaheris and David had all gone down on bended knee in front of my brother.

Arthur. Arthur Paul Roth. My brother. An eighteen-year-old math student with appalling taste in girls, a car that is a chugging death trap, and who – on a good day – looks like he had been dragged through a hedge backwards by a rampaging herd of cows on steroids.

King Arthur? No way.

"We must flee, my lord," said Gawain, rising first.

"Sirs Tristram, Talan and Archibald are making a diversion at the east gate. We are expecting Sir Percivale and the travelling court of Caerleon to arrive soon. Your life will be forfeit once Balvidore realises he is trapped like a fox."

"You said Bedivere would be here. Where is he?" asked Arthur.

"Here, sire," replied a gruff voice from the doorway.

I turned around and saw Bedivere and Gareth, framed like a portrait in the doorway. Something tickled the inside of my stomach. Even sweaty, dirty and covered in a fine mist of blood, Bedivere was hotter than every boy at school. Every boy I had ever met.

Ignoring me, Arthur and Bedivere collapsed into one another, and my jaw definitely skimmed the ground. I had been expecting them to be strangers to one another, not the best of friends, despite the letter.

I must have made a noise because they both looked at me. Arthur seemed fairly amused, despite the fact he had been locked up for days.

"Speed, sire," interrupted Gawain. "The Saxons will be upon us soon."

Arthur nodded with a blaze of fierce intensity across his sun-bleached face. I had never seen him so pumped up, and he can get quite hysterical before a Taekwondo tournament. Bedivere and Gareth took the lead as we ran for our lives. The castle was shaking. Its foundations sprinkled us with hard black icing, as explosions rocked the battlements above. Screams and jeers joined in one continuous stereo of noise.

On through the tunnels we ran. Up and down, left and right. A circle of daylight expanded rapidly as we approached the exit. Bedivere and Gareth charged out; their swords firmly held between their hands. I was the last to leave the tunnel, and the cool fresh air swept over me as I exited. It was instant relief.

The explosions over Camelot were grinding into the

stone. It sounded like a screaming animal. Camelot was alive and in pain. I turned to the eastern wall and saw blue flames devouring the castle.

Mordred and the druids of Gore had arrived.

25 THE INQUISITION

All eyes turned to Arthur. It suddenly occurred to me that this incredible group of knights, who had battled time itself to rescue Arthur and keep me alive, were now expecting him to take charge.

And the thought filled me with dread.

This is where it would all turn upside down. This was the moment when my brother would be revealed as a fraud. Back in the light of day, Bedivere and the others would realise they had come all this way for an eighteen-year-old math student and his sister.

As my stomach churned and perspiration started to soak my neckline, my only instinct was to grab Arthur's hand and run for it.

"Who else came with you?" asked Arthur quietly. His words did little to break the tension. I wasn't sure whether he was talking to me or the boys.

"Sirs Tristram, Talan, and Archibald are at the eastern drawbridge," replied Bedivere, assuming Arthur had addressed him. "They were to create a diversion whilst we entered from the western tunnels. Sir Percivale and Sir Ronan ride with the court of Caerleon. More are travelling from the shores of Brittany and down from the north. Mordred and the Gorians are low in number, Arthur. Their magic is formidable, but we cut many of them down when we rescued Natasha. We can take them and the Saxons."

"They had to rescue you?" asked Arthur, although he didn't look at me as he spoke. He had not moved his eyes from the battlements of Camelot.

"Sir Gareth, Sir David and I will go and find the others," said Bedivere, and he turned to leave.

"Bedivere," called Arthur.

"Sire?"

Arthur walked over to Bedivere. He was still wearing his jeans and t-shirt: the same clothes he had disappeared in. The colours had faded, and the cloth had been torn in several places, revealing tanned freckled flesh that was bruised and scraped. He didn't look like royalty. He looked like someone in need of disinfecting.

"Thank you," said Arthur, and even with his back to me, the emotion in his words was clear. His voice cracked.

"You told me you would come again," replied Bedivere, taking Arthur's arm in his hand. "I never wavered in my loyalty to you, or the court of Camelot."

"I'm not thanking you for that, Bedivere," said Arthur, and he turned to look at me. "I'm thanking you for keeping my sister alive."

Now all eyes were on me. I could feel the burning that was spreading like a pink pox across my cheeks and down my neck. Being the centre of attention was something I dreaded in any circumstance. It was like a teacher calling on you in assembly when you didn't know the answer.

"I will never render a greater deed than the oath I swore to protect her," replied Bedivere, and he smiled at me in a way that made my chest and stomach swap places. "We will return with Sirs Tristram, Talan and

Archibald. Come, Sir David, Sir Gareth. Our fellow knights are in need of our assistance."

"Close your eyes, Arthur."

"What?"

"Close your eyes. You owe me a few seconds."

"Titch, why do I need to close my eyes?"

"Because I don't want you to see this." I threw myself into Bedivere's arms and spread my mouth across his warm lips. He held me tightly, as his stubble scraped my face. I could hear Arthur spluttering and choking behind me, but I didn't care. My fingers wound into Bedivere's hair. Was it normal to want someone this much? To be blissfully happy and yet terrified out of your wits at the same time?

"Find Talan and Tristram, but don't stop for Archibald. Just come back to me, okay."

Bedivere stroked my face; he was tracing my freckles. Memorising them. My cheek was brushed one last time with his lips, and then he turned and ran. Gareth and David followed in a bird-like formation, faithfully flanking Bedivere on either side with their swords drawn.

My heart had never felt more alive, and yet my brain knew how vulnerable it now was. It needed distracting.

"Gaheris, Gawain, are you able to move further to the eastern side?" I asked, deliberately ignoring my brother, who appeared to be having a seizure.

"Yes, m'lady," replied Gaheris. The rescued knight seemed to be in much better health than his younger brother, although I noticed several of the nails were missing from his bloodied fingers.

"We have food and water with the horses. We'll head back there first."

I turned to my brother, who was doing a great impression of the Edvard Munch painting, *The Scream*. His mouth was open, his eyes wide, and his hands were on either side of his face.

"For heavens sake, Arthur, pull yourself together. You're supposed to be their king."

Arthur opened and shut his mouth like a goldfish.

"You…and Bedivere?" he stuttered. "You…and…Bedivere?"

"Yes, me and Bedivere. You told me to trust him, and so I did."

The colour returned to Arthur's face – and didn't stop. He started to turn purple.

"I told you to trust him, not shove your tongue down his throat."

"Well, that is rich coming from you. Do you see this mark on my face," I jabbed at my left cheek, "and this one, and how about this one on my forehead? Do you know how I got them? Your batshit crazy girlfriend, that's how."

"What?"

"Your girlfriend, Samantha - who wouldn't know loyalty if it paid her in cash and condoms - has joined forces with Mordred, and do you know how she celebrated? By kidnapping and then torturing me with a magical, blue flappy thing that she conjured in her hands, that's how."

Arthur turned to Gawain.

"Has she hit her head again?"

I thumped him.

"My head has been hit several more times, no thanks to you," I yelled. "In the past week I've been attacked by humpbacked dwarves on wolves, my nose is barely attached to my face anymore, and I've seen a girl who could have been my first real friend carried off by a dragon and then eaten for breakfast. And don't get me started on Mordred and the druids of Gore. I've been a punchbag, the bullseye for a swarm of wasps, and my arse is still red raw from all the horseback riding."

"And yet you still managed to find time to roll in the hay with Bedivere," shouted Arthur, tugging several rogue strands of straw from my hair. He wasn't gentle.

"What is your problem?" I screamed back, inches from Arthur's face. "And do you mind telling me how you even know him? We all know you like to lord it over the rest of us minions, but pretending to be King Arthur is taking it to the extreme, don't you think?"

But just when I thought he was going to yell another insult, Arthur closed his eyes to the world, scrunched up his face and exhaled a long exhausted sigh. The tension between us suddenly deflated like the air from a balloon. It was very unsatisfying. Fighting was the distraction I needed, and I was starting to crave it.

It was then, as I watched Arthur's face start to crumple, that I realised he wasn't angry about me and Bedivere, and I wasn't cross because of Slurpy. We were furious with each other because we had been so scared. Past, present and future no longer held any meaning. The death of our little Patrick had left such an enormous void. If Arthur and I lost each other now, that hole would become a chasm. I felt the presence of another Roth. A little, giggling figure, running away in blue. We both felt him. Suddenly there were three people in this picture. Yet all three of us were still one thousand years away from existing.

To the eastern walls, the battle continued. Now the earth was vibrating like a taut drum skin. In the distance the cavalry had arrived to take on the druids and Saxons. Yet Arthur and I were still on the periphery – safe – with just our thoughts consumed by pain.

"I know I've been here before, Titch," said Arthur, quietly confirming my own suspicions. "I can see it all. The smell of this place reminds me of home. Not *Avalon Cottage*," he quickly added as I made to interrupt him, "but somewhere else. An island in the mist."

"This is insane, Arthur."

"Doesn't mean it's not real though."

"You aren't King Arthur."

"But I could be."

"How did you even get here? We searched for hours after you disappeared."

"I followed the rabbit. It led me to the tomb you fell in, but when I got there it was empty. I was about to climb out when I was attacked. I couldn't see who or what was in there with me, but something placed a rag over my mouth. It was soaked in a drug because I knew I was going to pass out before it happened. I thought this is it. This was how I was going to die."

"It must have been the Saxons. It's scary to think of them so close to our house. What if they had come through the opening?"

"That's the weird thing though," said Arthur quietly. "It didn't feel like a man who had his hands around my neck and mouth. They were too small, too thin. I know it sounds crazy, but I thought it was a woman. A bloody strong one."

Arthur and I stood in silence. There was only one woman who could hold that much power.

Nimue.

I thought back to the image I saw at my bedroom window as Slurpy and I were leaving *Avalon Cottage*.

Someone who didn't belong there.

"So what do we do now?"

"Sammy is with Mordred, you say?"

"I just hope she stays alive long enough for you to chuck her first."

"So what did you say to Sammy to make her run off and leave you?" asked Arthur wearily.

"Excuse me?" I spluttered.

"You must have done something to upset her."

"I didn't do anything. I didn't even want her to help look for you in the first place, but she insisted on coming anyway, and a right pain in the neck she's been since the beginning. Only now she can roll her eyes into the back of her head, and she has become fluent in mumbo-jumbo."

Now it was my turn to appeal to Gawain, who along with his brother, was scarring tracks into the terracotta dirt with a knife. They were attempting to be as inconspicuous as possible.

"Can you help me out here?" I asked. "Can you tell your beloved King Arthur exactly what Mordred and the Gorians did to the Solsbury Hill monastery? Oh, and by the way," I added, jabbing my brother in the stomach with my finger, "you'll have to get used to calling her another name from now on, because the moron is now calling herself Morgana."

I kicked Gawain's boot as a sign of encouragement.

"I'm not sure I understood all of Lady Natasha's words, sire," said Gawain, "but it is a terrible truth that the sanctuary of Solsbury Hill was besieged by dark magic, not two nights ago."

"And did you see Sammy there?"

"Not...technically."

"Then you can't prove Sammy did anything."

I cried out with frustration. I may have stamped my foot like a child. How could Arthur look at my bruised and battered face and still defend that witch?

"You're such a hypocrite."

"And yet again you're calling dogs with your voice, Titch."

"I hate you."

"No you don't."

"Yes I do. I should have left you here to rot. You have the nerve to question me and Bedivere, and yet you're quite happy to take the side of a mental nutcase over me."

Tears were pricking my eyelids. I had seen this coming, hadn't I? I was the stupid little sister, coming along for the ride, while the big-boobed gazelle in hot pants could do no wrong.

"I just want to talk to my girlfriend and hear her side of the story," replied Arthur. He placed a placatory hand on my elbow, but I shrugged him away. I had come all this way, through time and death, and yet my brother refused to see what was in front of his face. I tried so hard not to cry. I attempted to fill my mind with boring images, like men playing cricket and chemistry symbols, but it was no good. Within moments, my shoulders were heaving and tears, dirt and snot merged into one gloopy waterfall down my face.

Arthur wisely left me alone. Instead he went to talk with Gawain and Gaheris. Camelot continued to scream and groan as the blue flames crackled over the walls, while the bellowing cries of Saxons brandishing spears and swords, gusted through the air. It had become a three-way battle: Saxons, Gorians and the knights led by Sir Percivale. Somewhere in the heaving mass of bodies were Bedivere, Tristram, Gareth, Talan and David: five strangers who had become my friends and so much more.

A hungry sense of sickness that had nothing to do with food started to swell in my stomach. It was longing. I needed Bedivere. I wasn't complete without him. There must be no more standing on the edge. We – I – had to help them all.

In the corner of my eye I saw the blue vision again. I knew if I turned my head for a better look, it would disappear, so I strained my tear-filled eyes to the right in an attempt to see him better.

A little boy was pointing to the distant battle.

I knew what had to happen next. I pulled myself away from the ghost of Patrick and turned to Arthur, who looked older and more serious than I had ever seen him. We weren't safe at all, and we both knew it.

"It is time to reclaim your sword, Arthur."

I hic-cupped as a wind-chime voice sang through the

trees. There was no rigor mortis of fear, no flapping of arms, or screaming with shock.

Because this time I was expecting her.

26 THE SWORD IN THE STONE TABLE

Nimue floated towards us. Her pale blue dress rippled around her body, as the ends of her long hair danced around her face. She looked like a silk flag playing in the wind.

Gawain and Gaheris fell to their knees; their heads bowed towards the ground. I glanced at Arthur, wondering what his reaction would be to this beautiful vision.

Yet again, the surprise would be mine.

"We meet once more, Arthur," said Nimue, with a beguiling smile. "It has been too long."

My brother bowed his head and then grinned; Nimue got the expensive-teeth smile that was reserved for pretty girls.

"Hello, Nimue."

"You know her?"

Arthur nodded, and those pearly white teeth of his did not fade away. From the look on his face, my brother knew Nimue well. Very well indeed.

"For crying out loud," I cried, "are you telling me Nimue is another one of your girlfriends? You know, if you were a girl, people would call you a slut."

"It's not like that, Titch."

He walked over to Nimue, knelt on one knee and kissed a large diamond ring on her slim middle finger. At least I thought it was a diamond. It was big, oval and sparkled like glitter.

"Your sword is waiting for you, Arthur," said Nimue softly. "It has been waiting for a very long time."

"It was you that brought me here, wasn't it?" asked Arthur. He had risen to his feet and was now inches away from Nimue. Their heads were so close that the merest tremor in the earth would have brought them together, in a way that would make Slurpy Morgana very unhappy. Starlight twinkled around them. A disgusting, painful image stabbed into my head. Was Nimue responsible for what happened to Mr. Rochester? Was that how she managed to get Arthur back into *her* world?

"I did not hand you over to Balvidore lightly, Arthur. Sacrifices must be made for the greater good, and it was the only way to unite the Great Halls of Logres and beyond," said Nimue, and her flirtatious attitude towards my brother suddenly changed. Even the buttermilk shading of her skin appeared to tan. My anger with her increased as she continued to speak.

"Return to the Round Table and reclaim what is yours, what is ours. Balvidore will be waiting, and the others who are intent on wickedness will also stake your trail. There are many who are prepared to die to stop glory returning to Logres. Now you must make a sacrifice, Arthur."

"Hang on a second," I interrupted, stepping forward. "What do you mean he has to make a sacrifice? He never asked for any of this, and if I find out you were the one who murdered my rabbit..."

But Nimue ignored me. Her deep blue eyes didn't even register my existence. They were reserved for Arthur alone.

"What about my sister?" asked Arthur. "I can't risk taking her with me."

"Natasha's future is now linked to that of another, Arthur," replied Nimue. She stretched out her hand and caressed my brother's face. The facets of her diamond ring shone, and I blinked as the brightness forced my eyes away. Gawain and Gaheris were still kneeling, but their faces were stunned. I wasn't sure they were hearing any of this. They looked drugged.

Arthur leant forward and kissed Nimue gently on the lips. As they parted, Nimue dissolved into the air. The leaves on the ground rapidly twisted up, trapped in a wind funnel, like a mini tornado. When they fell back to the earth, they were ripped apart with just the veined skeleton remaining.

What did she mean about my future and Arthur's sacrifice? I didn't like the way she was so quick to deal out judgment and punishment on others. We knew she had trapped the kingdom of Logres in an ageing sleep, and she had just confirmed it was her that had given Arthur over to the Saxons. I also suspected she was the one who had killed my baby rabbit.

Nimue wasn't helpful. She was downright dangerous. A wolf in sheep's clothing.

A crescendo of screaming voices slammed into my ears. The earth shuddered with the boom of rocks being hurled against the black walls of Camelot. How long had it been raining? I didn't know. I felt jetlagged. Exhausted. Every inch of me was tingling, but not in a good way. Not in the way Bedivere made me feel.

I gasped. I had temporarily forgotten Bedivere and the others who were now in the thick of the fighting.

Exhaustion turned to fear.

"Gaheris, Gawain," commanded Arthur in a loud voice. He was looking to the walls of Camelot, which looked like they were bleeding torrents of black blood.

"Sire," replied the brothers together; their swords were drawn.

Arthur took my hand.

"Ready to run, little sis?"

"Am I ever."

We didn't belong here, and yet it felt more like home than any other place I had ever lived in. I had never cared this much before. Never been forced to think or worry like this before.

"Take one of these," I said to my brother, offering him the choice of my two daggers. My hands were trembling so much I dropped the blade Tristram had given me. Arthur picked it up from the dirt and wiped it on his filthy jeans.

"Stay with me," said Arthur, squeezing my hand. The four of us started to run back towards the western tunnel. Arthur led the way, flanked by Gawain and Gaheris. I took up the rear point in the diamond formation. Dust and rocks were falling from the tunnel roof. Arthur knew exactly where to go, and soon my aching ribs were burning with pain as I tried to keep up with him. Cries, and deep voices barking commands, whipped around us like ghosts, but we saw no one until we had reached the top of a fourth set of black stone stairs.

Gawain and Gaheris leapt into action. The skirmish was brief, but bloody. Two Saxons, who appeared to be drunk, lost their heads. Another fell down the stairs, and landed with his shocked face staring in the wrong direction. It was the bony bulge in his neck that made me heave, and not the sight of two headless corpses spurting blood onto the tiled floor.

I grabbed Arthur.

"Don't kill anyone," I begged, wiping saliva away from my mouth with my sleeve. "It's different for the others, they're used to it."

Arthur's blue eyes blazed.

"So am I."

We stopped briefly at a narrow slit set high in the wall. It offered a view of the battle raging outside.

"Can you see?"

Arthur shook his head, then turned and ruffled my hair with his hand.

"He'll be okay, Titch."

We ran on. Towering black sculptures lined the corridors. It was like journeying into one black hole after another. All candles had been extinguished and so there was no light to guide us, but Arthur and I somehow knew where to go.

Arthur stopped by a huge set of arched doors. Crude markings of naked bodies had been daubed onto the wood.

"They dare defile the Great Hall of Camelot," snarled Gaheris angrily.

Arthur and Gawain pushed the thick oak panels inwards. They parted without a creak to reveal an enormous hexagonal room. Unlike the rest of the dark and dingy castle, this chamber was filled with light, which streamed in through tall arched windows on all six sides. If I had had the time, I would have taken a moment to take in the beauty of the stained windows, but my eyes were drawn to one colossal object, centred in the room.

A stone table.

I swore. So did Arthur.

The table was gigantic and made from one huge chunk of dark grey stone. The four of us approached it cautiously. Arthur, Gawain and Gaheris whipped their heads from left to right, back to front, keeping a constant eye for trouble. I could not. My eyes were drawn like magnets to a silver sword, plunged up to its hilt, in the dead centre of the stone.

It was only when I trod on a hand that I realised dead bodies littered the paved floor. Most were dressed in rags. Servants. Male, female, and even several children. There were no obvious markings on their pale bodies, but all had a stretched expression of deep pain frozen onto their faces.

"What happened here?"

"Balvidore sacrificed them," replied Gawain. He made the sign of the cross on his chest.

"Why?"

"Only those anointed by Arthur may claim a right to the table," explained Gaheris, as he became the first to touch it. His fingertips swept over the dull stone as he started to circle the perimeter. "If anyone else were to take a place that had not been afforded to them, then the blood of knights long lost would smote them where they sat. Balvidore is too cowardly to attempt to take the table and Excalibur by himself."

"Don't touch anything, Titch," yelled Arthur, as I moved closer. "You aren't a knight."

Gaheris had stopped walking around the edge of the stone table. Both of his hands now rested on some deep carvings. He turned and smiled at his brother.

"Sir Gawain. Come quickly. We are still here. The four brothers, side by side once more."

Now it was my turn to keep lookout, as the three boys arched themselves over the table, grinning like Cheshire Cats.

"So you three can touch it without dying," I said quickly, as a sound like a stifled cough echoed in the corridor we had just left. "Awesome. Now what the hell do we do? Your friends are being slaughtered out there."

"It is time to reclaim what has always been yours, Arthur," said Gawain excitedly.

In one bounding leap, Arthur's long limbs sprang him skywards and onto the table. With his right hand, he pulled the silver sword from the centre of the stone.

The sword itself was quite unremarkable. There were no rubies studded into the hilt like Percivale's sword, and it was shorter than Bedivere's. What was incredible was the reaction of the table itself. Like molten lava flowing from the centre, a thin gold river started to weave its way through the deep carvings. Scores of names and images were revealed, as the glistening ink poured from the heart of the table and stretched out like a spider's web: Sir Tristram, Sir Gareth, Sir Baldulf, Sir Nudd…

"The siege is revealed once more," said Gawain.

There was a heavy whistling sound, and Gaheris collapsed forward with a groan.

Arthur jumped from the table with a cry; his new sword raised high. I stumbled forward and pulled Gaheris from the table without touching it. We collapsed onto the stone floor. A small, triple-bladed axe was lodged in his neck. Gaheris gurgled as blood throbbed out in pulsating waves.

I pressed down on the wound in a bid to stem the bleeding, but it was no use. Any pressure I applied blocked what little space Gaheris had left in his windpipe. His hazel eyes rolled in his head and he died without a word.

I was frozen with shock. It had happened so quickly. One minute Gaheris was smiling, the next he was drowning in his own blood.

Gawain towered above me; his face contorted with raw grief. His fist went to his mouth, and I saw him bite down hard on his skin. I started to rock Gaheris in my arms, willing him to wake up. Choking sobs started to spasm in my chest.

"My aim has become poor," boomed a deep male voice. "The axe was meant for you, Arthur. Now, if you will hand me that sword, I may let the wench live."

I tore my eyes away from the river of blood that was soaking the body of Gaheris. It had been a trap.

Blocking the oak doors were at least ten Saxon warriors, axes clenched in their filthy hands. Bloodlust mingled with the saliva that drooled from their sneering mouths.

And in the centre, with an arrow aimed directly at my head, stood a man mountain draped in fur.

Balvidore.

27 BALVIDORE THE BEAR

His name had been mentioned a thousand times on this journey, and yet I had never really pictured him. I hadn't given him time. He was the mythical bad guy; the bogey-man under the bed. Balvidore had become a figure to be mocked. I thought back to one of Talan's songs: "Balvidore the Bald." A freak of nature that was small and weak.

The man that stood twenty metres in front of me was anything *but* small and weak. He was enormous, at least twice the size of Robert of Dawes. Bear-like, draped in black furs. His hair was thick and the colour of coal. It framed his head like a visor-less helmet. The hair didn't seem to end and it covered his face and neck. His bulging stomach stuck out over the waistband of his magenta coloured pants; a wide expanse of hairy white flesh rippled with every panting breath. I could smell the odour seeping from him and his warriors. It was a vile mixture of sweat and stale wine.

Arthur and Gawain had positioned themselves in front of me. I knew it was hopeless. We were outnumbered. Gaheris was dead, and Gawain was still weak. Arthur knew how to handle a sword from his

Taekwondo lessons, but it was all for show. I was sure his fifth degree black belt master never thought for a moment that the form Arthur religiously practised in the safety of a village hall would ever be put to actual use. Arthur may have wanted to be a king; he may have actually believed that he *could* be their king, but I wasn't delusional. I knew the truth, and I would not lie to myself.

The enormity of what I had woken on that day in the forest finally hit me. Why had I argued with my mother? It was a stupid dance. I should have just locked myself in my room like Arthur did after an *exchange of words*. Instead, I had charged off into the forest, and straight into the path of the unknown terror that had been hidden beneath it for a thousand years.

Why me?

Will you stop your whining. Now think. What is that monstrous stinking oaf expecting you to do?

Panic, I thought to myself. Cry. Faint. I could do all of those things.

Stop being so pathetic. Do you want to live?

Stupid question. Of course I did. Nothing was worse than death.

Then concentrate and keep calm. Now if Balvidore is as stupid as he is fat, then the three of you can still get out of this alive.

Gaheris was still in my arms and I could feel the heat leaving him. The blood loss from the gaping neck wound was now a trickle. But I clutched my arms around him, drawing comfort from his corpse.

I thought back to what the brothers had said of the table: about the blood of past knights. Then an idea sprang into my head as I watched Gaheris' blood run into the gold lettering on the Round Table. The two colours didn't mix together to become one dark sludgy colour. They retained their own identity, running side by side into the deep grooves.

Balvidore would be expecting Arthur to give in, and in such an archaic age as this, the idea that a girl like myself would fight back would not even enter that thick skull of his. I didn't understand American Football, but the words *offensive* and *defensive* kept jumping around in my brain.

Two entities, side by side, were always better than one. We were still a team, even with one man down.

I kissed Gaheris on the forehead, and gently placed him on the ground. My hands and clothes were soaked with blood. A metallic aroma wafted into my nostrils. It was the smell of death.

"Stay behind us, Titch," hissed Arthur, as I squeezed my body into the narrow gap between him and Gawain.

"You have to knight me," I whispered.

"What?"

"Knight me – now. Balvidore won't be expecting that."

"Are you insane?" replied my brother, as the Saxons started to sway. Their movements were ritualistic. Their shoulders hung loose; bodies bent forward at the knees. They looked like a line-up of gorillas, preparing to attack. A grunting moan was coming from every one of them, with the loudest belonging to Balvidore. They thought this was going to be easy, and they were going to enjoy it. It was like watching the New Zealand rugby team perform the Haka before they slaughtered the opposition.

"Knight me. They won't be able to touch us if we're all on the table. It will poison them the second they lay a finger on it. It'll give us more time."

My brother gasped.

"You're brilliant."

"I have my moments."

Arthur swung Excalibur and let momentum carry it onto my shoulders. It was far heavier than it looked, and my knees buckled under the weight.

"Consider yourself knighted, Titch," yelled Arthur. "Now get on the Round Table, both of you."

Before Balvidore and his Saxon warriors had had time to register what was happening, I had clambered onto the table. It was warm to the touch. The golden spidery writing that had inked so many names was still fluid, but it left no trace on my hands. Arthur and Gawain followed, the body of Gaheris held tightly between them. They would not leave him to be the spoils of war.

"Titch, take this," yelled Arthur. He thrust the sword into my hands, as he manoeuvred the legs of Gaheris onto the stone.

The Saxons rushed forward, but their axes were swinging at thin air. One hopeful Neanderthal threw his blade at us, but it bounced back off the perimeter. An invisible force field was in place to repel everything and anything that meant us harm. The short, crude axe rebounded back and hit its owner in the forehead, lodging between his eyes. He slumped down onto the body of a young woman. A putrid blast of gas blasted out of her frozen, wide mouth.

Gawain was now silently crying with Gaheris floppy in his arms. Arthur grabbed me tightly and kissed the top of my head. I could feel the grief shuddering through his body. We both knew the pain that came with losing a brother.

"How long do you think we have up here?"

"No idea," replied Arthur quickly, wiping his eyes. "Now be quiet. I need to think."

He still held me fast, which was uncomfortable. For someone skinny who was all arms and legs, Arthur was a lot stronger than he looked. His neck was arched back and he was gazing at the beamed ceiling. I knew it was no use. We were trapped. There was no way out.

Balvidore was shaking with rage. His sonorous voice was screaming at his men to attack, but all were unwilling to try. Balvidore took to slapping several of them around the head. Motivation, Saxon style.

I was watching him kick a Saxon in the stomach when I registered an increase in the noise from outside the chamber. The clank of metal against metal echoed around the hexagonal hall. The fighting from the grounds was coming closer.

"The walls have been breached, Arthur," choked Gawain.

"Yeah," replied Arthur, "but I think it's our lot that has taken them. Listen."

We could hear voices now. Unmistakable cries and orders that were bellowing out from the corridors of Camelot. I scrunched up my face and strained my ears, willing one particular gruff voice to identify itself in the midst of the near riot that was taking place, not far from where we stood.

Chaos broke out among Balvidore and the remaining Saxons. They had been so busy fighting among themselves, that they had failed to realise that they were now the ones who were trapped. Balvidore fired an arrow in anger. It lodged in the oak door with a violent *twang.*

Bodies surged through the doors. The arrow snapped and was swallowed in the sea of swords and shields that followed through. Percivale and Ronan were leading the charge, and for a moment, I thought we were saved, but in the swell of bodies that had forced their way into the hall, the Saxon ranks also multiplied. Several were hooded. The Gorians were also in the thick of it.

Gawain jumped down from the table brandishing his brother's sword. It was immediately plunged into the back of a small Saxon, perhaps only sixteen years old. He fell to his knees and cried out, stretching his right arm out for help. The Saxon caught my eye and mouthed two words that I didn't understand. He didn't look like a fighter, he looked like a frightened little boy. I had a sickening feeling that he had just called for his mother. His body smashed to the ground, and was immediately kicked and smothered by the fighting. His glassy brown eyes stayed with me, imprinted in my mind, long after his face was kicked in by boots.

"Give me the sword, Titch," cried Arthur, making to snatch the plain but heavy Excalibur from my hands. I pushed him away.

"You'll be killed," I shouted back.

Arthur slid his foot against my heel and tripped me backwards across his bent knee. I fell flat on my backside. I remained the only person protected by the power of the Round Table as Arthur – Excalibur in his hand – jumped onto the back of a Saxon, who was waving a studded club around his head.

Screaming for my brother, I frantically searched the rapidly-moving heads for Bedivere. I couldn't see him. Then a familiar voice caught my attention. A thick Scouse accent that stood out amongst the cries and shouts: Robert of Dawes, the Caerleon court physician, who had also stumbled into this world and was now desperate to escape. He had a sword in his hand, but it was his fist that was connecting with every Saxon nose it could find.

There was nothing left for it. I picked up Gawain's blade and threw myself to the side of the hall. A mace, the size of my head, smashed into the stone wall, just inches from my ear. It wasn't aimed at me, but the brute who was swinging it had just been cut down by a Caerleon knight, and had fallen backwards with part of his skull dripping brains onto the floor.

Sense and sensibility had left me. What had I done? I should have stayed on the table. Despite my true intentions after the Ddraig attack, I'm no fighter. No killer. Then two hairy thick arms grappled me from behind.

"Where do you think you're going, wench?"

Something cold and wet pressed against my throat. Balvidore had placed a bloody knife beneath my right ear.

"Arthur," roared the Saxon king. "I have your wench. Your knights are dying. Give me the sword and I will let her go."

He had to shout his ultimatum another three times before the fighting ceased enough for him to be heard. As the crowd parted, bodies slumped to the floor.

My top teeth were biting down hard onto my bottom lip. I knew I was shaking violently. I was trying so hard to be brave, but I knew Balvidore would slit my throat without hesitation. For the first time, I realised what it was like to be on the true edge of death. This was genuine fear. Everything experienced so far was just the prelude.

Arthur, a bloodstained sword in his hand, moved slowly and quietly to the front of the knights. A long streak of blood was smeared across his chin; his face was puffy and blotchy. On either side he was flanked: Percivale and Gawain. In complete contrast to my brother, Gawain was ghostly white, his eyes dead. He was only fifteen years old. He reminded me of a boy – another outcast – at my last school in America. One bullet later, he was just another suicide statistic. In reality, it isn't difficult to pinpoint those who have lost the will to live.

Don't move, mouthed Arthur, as Balvidore backed into a wall, dragging me with him.

"The sword, Arthur," snarled Balvidore. "I won't ask again."

I screamed in pain as the knife pierced my neck. Arthur cried out.

"Don't hurt her. You can have the sword, just let her go."

"Now just wait, Arthur," interrupted a cool,

measured voice. All eyes swept to the doorway where the handsome Mordred stood, lazily leaning against a beam with a smirk spread across his face. How long had he been there? Watching, waiting for his moment in time. Happy to watch others die.

A murmur of discontent rumbled through half of the crowd. It was clear the knights of Camelot and Caerleon did not see the arrival of Mordred as a welcome intervention.

"I thank you all," said Mordred sarcastically. "I see the halls of Logres remain glorious in their welcome."

"Who is this?" spat Balvidore. "Strike him down."

Mordred suddenly lurched to his left, and dragged a bound and gagged figure to his side. Arthur cried out again. This time it was a captive Slurpy who had his attention.

"As you will see from Arthur's reaction, Lord Balvidore," said Mordred, "this maiden is just as important to him as the one you hold captive."

My mind was racing. What was Mordred playing at? Was this a trap for Balvidore?

"What do you want?" pleaded Arthur, as Balvidore continued to snort, snarl and spit down the side of my face. Arthur appeared panic-stricken at the sight of his girlfriend.

"It is Lord Balvidore I came to speak to," drawled Mordred, flicking his blonde hair out of his eyes, "because I propose a trading of possessions."

Balvidore grunted as the knife pressed further into my skin. My knees gave way to the pain and rose up towards my stomach. The only thing stopping me from collapsing to the ground was Balvidore's arm around my crushed ribs. I was going to pass out with the agony of it all. Hooded Gorians shifted amongst the swell. Unlike the other druids I had seen, these sorcerers did not have the henna tattoos on their skin, and their nails were not painted black.

"What kind of trade?" asked Arthur.

"I was talking to Balvidore, Arthur," snapped Mordred. "Why does everything have to be about you?"

"What kind of trade?" barked my captor.

"I want the maiden, Lady Natasha. You want the sword, Excalibur, and the wealth of Camelot that comes with it," replied Mordred.

"And?"

"Arthur will not give you the gift of Nimue in exchange for Lady Natasha. He does not value her highly enough, especially as she has been despoiled by one of his own knights. Arthur's words are treacherous lies."

Furious protests broke out amongst the ranks of the knights. Several lunged forward with their swords raised. Only another scream from me stopped them from resuming the attack. I noticed several of the hooded figures were starting to group around the Saxons. They looked as if they were getting ready to attack again. My eyes were still fixed on their hands; I was waiting for the blue flame.

"Lady Samantha," continued Mordred, stroking her dark hair with his fingers, "is far more sacred, and she alone has Arthur's heart. Trade maidens with me, and you will have your sword."

Even bound and gagged, Slurpy was a beautiful sight. Her hair remained glossy and dark as the midnight sky. Her body was on show in yet another plunging satin gown – this time sapphire blue in colour – and there wasn't a mark on her pale face. I, on the other hand, was broken, bruised, and dressed in bloody, dirty clothes that boil washing wouldn't clean. On looks alone, it was no contest. Yet I remained confident that I had something Slurpy Morgana would never truly have.

Arthur.

Never in a million years would my own brother betray me and choose that salivating tongue on legs over his own flesh and blood. So when he spoke, I expected him to unleash hell on both Balvidore and Mordred.

Instead he signed my death warrant with three little words.

"Make the trade."

28 MAKE THE TRADE

I must have hit my head again. I was daydreaming. Unconscious. Dead? My brother, the one I had travelled through time and fire and death to find, had just betrayed me to the legend that had once tried to kill the king he wanted to be.

The triumphant gleam on Slurpy's face was enough. Her mouth may have been gagged, but her eyes were wide and glorious.

She had won.

Arthur couldn't bear to look as Balvidore threw me towards Mordred. I landed by his feet, which were long and flat. In the corner of my eye I saw five hooded figures shifting position. They were moving closer to Arthur. Positioning themselves to strike him down and take his sword by force. He had noticed them too. His body had tensed into one of attack. I had seen this during his martial arts displays.

Slurpy had glided over to Balvidore. No rough handling for the witch.

"Arthur…"

Was this his revenge for Patrick? Arthur had lied for me all those years ago – but he alone knew the truth.

Did I deserve this?

Mordred pulled me to my feet and then clamped an arm across my ribs. His mouth was close to my earlobe; his hot breath blew down my neck.

"So gallant of Sir Bedivere to warm you up for me, m'lady. Tonight I will have my own quest to enjoy."

"NOW," cried Arthur.

Five hooded men threw off their cloaks. A knife span through the air like a Catherine Wheel firework, glistening and sparking. It struck Balvidore in the throat, right in the core of his bulging Adam's apple. Slurpy screamed and fainted, landing in an elegant coil on the ground. Balvidore gasped and pulled the blade from his gullet, spraying a thick mist of blood from his throat as he exhaled. He grabbed at a set of long blue drapes. They collapsed from their hangings as he slid down the wall.

Bedivere, Tristram, Talan and David immediately started fighting once more. The fifth hooded man was Gareth. With hatred in his eyes, he ran forward and plunged his sword into Balvidore's stomach.

"My brother is avenged."

I screamed Bedivere's name. As soon as the hooded men had revealed themselves, I saw his eyes before anything else, but while he hadn't taken them away from mine, there were still countless Saxons baying for blood between us.

And Mordred and I were already at the huge double doors.

"There is no dishonour in retreat, Lady Natasha," puffed Mordred, as he started to drag me away.

I started to kick and pummel him with my elbows. My nails were nowhere near as long as Slurpy's, but with a bit of force, I could gouge out a fair bit of skin if required.

Suddenly I felt Mordred stiffen into my back. I was about to slap him hard when he yelped like a dog that had been kicked.

"Run, m'lady."

I looked down and saw Byron the Dwarf, standing just metres away from the door. A small bow, like a child's toy, was clutched between his stubby fingers. Sweat pooled in the deep folds of skin on his forehead. He looked like he had run a marathon.

"You traitorous little scullion," roared Mordred, yanking an arrow head from his backside. "My hands will choke the breath from your worthless carcass."

It had worked once and so I decided to let my knee do the talking. Resting my hands on Mordred's broad shoulders, I kicked him between the legs.

There were still five hulking Saxons between me and Bedivere. He was cutting through them like he was hacking down trees, but it wasn't enough. A one-eyed thug already had me in his Cyclops-like vision, and he was thundering across the floor with a razor-sharp axe clenched in his hands. Arthur had disappeared completely. Corpses and limbs continued to fall like dominoes. The noise that screamed around the cavernous room was deafening as the windows shattered. The stone table became another warrior as it poisoned every Saxon who touched it. The hulks didn't get the chance to scream; they died where they stood.

"Run, m'lady, run," growled Byron. He had jumped over the groaning figure of Mordred, and was now tugging at my tunic. "I will keep them at bay."

"I won't leave Arthur or Bedivere."

A figure slumped to the floor in front of me. His chain mail had been torn away, and his hands were cradling a hole in his chest. Blood oozed from an open wound that looked like raw liver.

It was Talan.

"No," I screamed, falling to the ground.

"We will be...victorious...Lady...Natasha," he

groaned.

"Stay with me, Talan," I sobbed, frantically searching the cluttered floor for something to stem the flow of blood.

Byron landed beside me; he had hurdled Mordred.

"Help me, Byron."

The dwarf plunged his hands into Talan's chest in an attempt to plug the wound.

"Find the yellow seeds in my waistcoat, m'lady."

He wriggled and squirmed as I rummaged around in his leather pockets. The depths of one were wet and slimy. Inside another I found a dead mouse.

In the third I pulled out a handful of long pieces of grain: yellow with blackened tips.

"Chew on them, m'lady. They must be moistened."

David had thrown himself down beside me. His sword, which was twisted and bent at the hilt, clattered to the ground.

"Let me help," he begged.

My mouth had run dry. I couldn't get enough spit into the seeds. They were sticking to my mouth. I spat several out and sprinkled them into David's hand. He was shaking more than I was.

It's hard to describe the sound of medieval warfare. In my time it was all guns and bombs. You see it on the television, you can even hear it. The loud *boom, boom, boom* of rapid fire. You know people die because you see the returning coffins draped in flags. Car bombs explode, but the sound is gone in seconds. The tuneless wail of an emergency vehicle is the sound of Death on his chariot.

But that was nothing to this, a totally different kind of death. It was like being in a butcher's shop with the continual thudding of blades against meat. The difference being the pigs and cows don't make a noise that haunts your soul.

I was always under the impression that boys and men couldn't scream - I was wrong. It gets under your skin. You can feel it in your veins. Scratching, pulling, tugging, trying to get out. The sound slams through your entire body, and you wait, wait to hear your own voice join the chorus, because even the bravest scream. The sonic aftermath of the Ddraig attack had deafened me to the sound of death, and so I never heard Eve. But the sound now bleeding into the black walls of Camelot would stay with me for a lifetime and more. And it was worse than a nightmare, because this was real.

David and I mixed the grains into a chewy pulp, which was the colour of wet sand. Bryon kept one hand plugged into Talan's chest, the other he used to spread the paste into the wound.

"Have you seen my brother, or Bedivere?"

David was white beneath a film of swollen bruises, smoke and dark blood. He nodded.

"Arthur is magnificent. He and Sir Bedivere are back to back. I have never witnessed such bravery."

But I didn't want my brother or Bedivere to be magnificent or brave. I wanted them alive.

A couple of Saxons bolted out through the doors, like a couple of lumbering cows, sensing their chance of survival was now greater outside the walls of Camelot than in them. What started as a trickle of deserters turned into a stampede. Leaderless and broken, the Saxons fled.

A roar went out from the knights still standing. They knew Camelot was theirs once more. Many of them took part in the chase that followed. It became a sport, disgusting and violent. It was like watching a barbaric television show. Three points for a sword to the stomach; five points if you came back with a head. There was no honour in my eyes. It was difficult to see any when everything was swimming in blood.

Talan's breathing was becoming shallower. His lungs were collapsing. Robert of Dawes fell in a heap, nearly crushing Byron in the process. Silent tears were streaming down my face. My lungs simply didn't have the energy to sob anymore.

"Make him live," I begged Robert.

"I can do no more than has already been done, Natasha," gasped the physician, pulling off thick, elbow-length gloves. The sweat was dripping down him in a stream.

I felt fingers in my hair.

"Let him go, Natasha," whispered Bedivere.

Grief welled up in my chest. Not Talan. I started to play God in my head. Take someone else I thought. Let's make a trade. Take two knights I didn't know, but spare this one. It's amazing the silent bargaining that can go on when you're dealing with life and death. I would willingly sacrifice Percivale – he was a lord, worth extra points surely – or what about Ronan? Heir to Caerleon. He was a handsome prize for Death to claim. The skeleton with the scythe was not going to steal Talan away from those who loved him.

Bedivere, Tristram, Gareth and David each prised a limb from my arms, and just as the knights had carefully carried David away after the attack by the dwarf-riders, so they placed Talan down on a stained cloak and carried him off. Gawain followed behind, Talan's broken sword in his hand.

Arthur knelt down beside me and wrapped his arms around my shoulders.

"You weren't really going to trade me, were you, Arthur?"

"Not even for an Aston Martin."

"So this is Arthur?" exclaimed Robert of Dawes, who was now lying flat on his back, panting heavily. He extended his right hand. "Glad to meet you. I'm Robert of Dawes, although back in our time it's just plain old

Robert Dawes."

"You're one of us?"

"I am indeed. I was out rambling a couple of months ago. Longest and hardest holiday I've ever had. Found that tomb and went hunting for treasure. I'm a newly qualified doctor and up to my eyeballs in debt. Figured I could make a bit of cash on the sly before the historians got in there for a poke. I ended up at Caerleon, near death myself. Then everyone woke up and I've been looking for a way back ever since. I had given up hope to be honest, and then young Natasha here rides in. What a girl. She's going to save both of us, Arthur."

The perfect moment had presented itself. I could finally tell Robert of Dawes that the way back was closed to us all. Arthur too. He could hear it at the same time and I wouldn't need to repeat myself. Let them deal with it. I was too exhausted to do anything anymore. I thought back to the place that Arthur called home. In the blurred recesses of my mind, I knew our parents would be frantic. My mother would probably be comatose with the knowledge that all of her children were now gone. It would be a grief so consuming I wouldn't be able to understand it. It would probably annoy me if I was there to witness it. I knew that sounded awful and selfish, but I couldn't deal with other people's problems at the best of times. Perhaps that was why I had so few friends. Woes over boyfriends and spots and "am I fat?" – get lost. I didn't care. I can't handle the serious stuff – what did I care for trivial whining? My little brother was dead. My older brother and I were now trapped in a time that wouldn't rest until we were dead. I had seen a friend ripped to pieces before my eyes, and a gorgeous happy knight carried away by his friends to die. You want to go home, Robert of Dawes? Then go home. Find your own way. What did he expect me to do? I couldn't help him. I was hopeless – useless.

None of this I said aloud, of course. I can be confrontational in my head, but it usually gets lost on the way to my mouth. Let Robert think there was still hope, even if I had lost all myself.

"I think *it* is coming round."

I nudged Arthur in the ribs, pointing to Slurpy who was groaning on the ground. She was making only slightly less noise than Mordred, who was pinned to the ground by Byron. The dwarf was sitting on Mordred's chest, with an arrow pointing to what was left of Mordred's man bits.

"Will you be alright if I go and see her?" asked Arthur.

"Just make sure you don't hold back when you finish with her."

Arthur said nothing. Boys are hopeless at multi-tasking. They have the brain cells for one thing at a time, and with the fighting finished, Arthur's grey matter was now consumed by his hideous, slurpy girlfriend.

He wouldn't trade me, but he wouldn't trade her either.

"I'm going to find Bedivere."

I needed arms around me. Arms that loved me totally and unconditionally. Not brotherly arms, but arms that wanted me because of who I was, not for who I am.

I pushed past fallen boys and men. Their clothing identified them, but to me they were all of one class: the dead. The knights who had survived were carrying their fallen friends out gently and with respect. The Saxons that had been left by those who ran were dragged out by their legs and hair.

I found Bedivere, Tristram, Gareth and David in a freezing chamber just off the corridor that led from the hall. Gareth was beyond distressed. He had been forced to stay hidden beneath a Gorian cloak, even though he must have seen Gaheris' body when the surge of fighting broke into the hall. Revenge had been taken on Balvidore, but now Gareth had to stand and watch as Camelot's physicians battled to keep one of his closest friends alive.

David was trying to sing to Talan, but the words and tune kept choking in his throat. The Irish knight was covered in a sheen of perspiration; his skin unnaturally white and threaded with visible grey veins. He looked like one of those carved marble figures that lie on top of tombs in ancient abbeys.

Make the trade, Death. Just make the trade.

29 AND THE WINNER IS…

Without a working watch, minutes, hours and days disappeared. Time was gauged by sunrise and sunset, with an unhealthy dose of fighting in the middle to starve away the boredom.

When I woke up on the cold, damp floor of the chamber, I was alone and it was dark. Late evening or early morning? I had no idea. Someone – I willingly assumed it was Bedivere – had placed a thick tapestry over my body. It smelt musty and old. My mother would have thrown it in a skip. I pulled it up to my ears.

Voices were echoing along the corridors. Low, slow-moving voices. Words spoken deliberately and with meaning.

Did people in this time gossip? I always meant to try it out with Eve, but never got the chance.

I was surprised to find myself alone. It was almost as if I had been forgotten. I guessed Arthur would be with *that* creature (I didn't know what name to call her now), and Bedivere and the others were with Talan. The only way Robert of Dawes would have let me out of his sight was if he was needed by Sir Percivale and the travelling Caerleon court…

I started ticking off names in my head, trying to account for their whereabouts.

Frustration soon got the better of me as I went through each face: strangers who had become my friends.

Something wasn't right. Someone was missing.

Rising, I almost collapsed as my knees buckled under the weight of pain I was in. This is what it must feel like to be stretched out on a rack, I thought, staggering to the door. My limbs felt wooden and too long for my body. Blood had congealed on the scrapes and cuts that criss-crossed where my flesh had been bared and unprotected. Every movement dislodged the healing, causing the open wounds to start weeping and bleeding again. Worse was the Balvidore-inflicted gash to my neck, which stung with the slightest movement. As I groped my way down the corridor, feeling the stone with my fingertips, I felt the trickle of warm blood inching down to my collar bone. The green fleecy tunic that Nimue had given me by the Falls of Merlin was now stained and ripped. Tie-dyed by warfare.

Camelot was heaving with bodies, but at least they were live ones. Women and children scuttled along the corridors, lighting the few torches that hadn't been pulled from the walls. Where had they been hiding? Water was being slopped onto every surface. If they scrubbed hard enough, they might forget what had happened here.

Arthur found me staring out of a thin slit in the wall. Outside, a huge pyre was burning, spitting bright amber sparks into the inky sky. The smell was hideous.

"They're cremating the Saxons," explained Arthur.

"What happens to the dead knights?"

"Buried. There's a place reserved within the walls of Camelot for them."

And I knew where it was without seeing it. Deep in a memory, I had been there before.

"Bedivere and Tristram have taken charge of everything."

"How are we going to get back, Arthur?"

Arthur sighed.

"I don't know, Titch."

"The way through the tunnel is blocked. It collapsed."

"We'll find a way."

"But Robert Dawes…"

"Don't worry. We'll find a way."

The thing was, I wasn't worried. Not in an aching, I miss home, kind of way. I wasn't like Dorothy. I couldn't click my heels together and say there was no place like home, because where was home? *Avalon Cottage* wasn't home. It was a house I slept in. I loved my parents because I had to – they were my parents. But I didn't like them. Friends? I had none – not in my own time.

They say home is where the heart is. My heart was now here. Bedivere had it, although I wasn't sure where he kept it. He was the first person I had ever given it to, and I didn't want it back. I thought back to his terrified face in the Solsbury Hill monastery. It was me and only me in his thoughts. Bedivere had found my earring by the Falls of Merlin, and had tracked me in the darkness with the calling of birdsong. I remembered the previous perfect night with no date. It seemed like forever ago.

And I wanted more just like it.

I could make a home here, I thought to myself. Well away from castles and knights and death. We could keep horses, or even a few rabbits. No chickens though. Nothing that flapped. Home isn't a structure, it's a feeling. A warm fuzzy feeling that roots in your stomach and spreads to every part of your body. It's knowing that you can gaze into someone's eyes and not feel self-conscious doing it. Home is the anticipation of a long kiss, the wanting, the needing. Stealing Bedivere's breath, and knowing he was taking mine right back because he needed it as much as I needed his.

"What are you thinking about?" asked Arthur, ruining my moment. "You have that look of concentration on your face. The one that makes people think you have trapped gas."

"Bite me, Arthur."

He laughed. It was good to hear. Almost normal.

"Do you think Bedivere would mind if I went to him?" I asked, finally dragging my eyes away from the burning. "I don't want him to think I'm clingy."

Arthur did that annoying older brother thing by ruffling my stinking, greasy hair with his hand.

"He won't think you're clingy. For some unknown reason, Bedivere appears to be madly in love with you," he teased. "I told him you are a neurotic little freak who talks to herself, snores, and wets herself whenever a bird comes within a five mile radius, but it still didn't put him off."

Clenching my fists was agony to my split knuckles. Punching my brother would hurt even more, but I could cope.

"It was a joke, Titch," said Arthur, quickly backing away, hands up in surrender. He knew me better than anyone, and pain was no barrier to wrath. The spaghetti vein in my forehead was disintegrating with stress.

"This is hardly the place to practice stand-up, Arthur."

"Actually, I think it's exactly the place," he replied, stepping forward and slipping an arm around my aching shoulders. "Otherwise we're going to go insane, Titch."

"I went mad years ago."

"I was being polite."

"Is Talan still alive?"

"He was not long ago. Byron and Robert Dawes are vying to be chief healer. He's a funny little chap."

"Robert?"

"Nah – that Byron. I like him. Anyone who can fire an arrow into Mordred's ass with such precision deserves a bit of respect."

"Where is Mordred?"

"Ran for it apparently. Once he had found his testicles and could walk again – you're pretty lethal with that knee, you know. Everyone was so preoccupied with Talan and Gaheris that they didn't notice Mordred had gone, until it was too late. I have no doubt we'll see him again. The druids of Gore were waiting with horses by the front gates; the cowards never even entered the castle. They just used that blue flame and waited for the Saxons to implode."

I had to ask the question.

"And where is your vile ex-girlfriend?" Heavy on the pronouncement of the X.

"Don't start, Titch."

"You *have* dumped her? She attacked me with magic, Arthur."

Arthur let out a long groan.

"Can we discuss this later?"

"Oh my God. You're still with her aren't you?"

"You've been through a tough time, Titch. Let's go find Bedivere and the others. Get you some food while we're at it."

The patronising tosser. I didn't want to eat; I wouldn't have been able to get it past my throat, let alone into my churning stomach. I shoved Arthur into a wall.

"What did she tell you? She denied it all, didn't she? The magic – the rolling eyes – the blue flames in her hands. Ask the others. Ask Tristram. He told me that Sammy went through some re-birthing ceremony. She joined Mordred, Arthur. She tried to kill me."

"That's enough, Titch," yelled Arthur, raising his voice as he pushed me back. "I know all about the things she went through when she was with Mordred. She did it to stay alive, Titch. She was frightened out of her wits."

"SHE ATTACKED ME."

"Will you listen to yourself, Titch? Now I don't know what you *think* you saw after Mordred kidnapped you, but Sammy is as capable of creating that blue flame as I am."

"I'm not lying," I sobbed.

"I'm not saying you are. But you've been through a hell of an ordeal, and have banged your head countless times since this started. You're confused. They probably drugged you."

Arguing was hopeless. I could barely get the words out between the hiccupping gulps that had trapped in my chest and throat.

"She set...wasps on me...Arthur."

"This is hopeless," snapped Arthur angrily. "I'm taking you to Bedivere. Maybe he can talk some sense into you."

The fool. The stupid fool. How could these people believe he was their king when he was so blind? Tristram's words about the real threat to boys and men repeated in my head.

The subtle craft of a maiden. One who ensnares the heart and renders a man as helpless as a baby. Love is a powerful ally, but it is also the most dangerous foe there is.

Samantha Scholes-Morgan, Slurpy Morgana, was going to be the most dangerous foe there was, and my brother was walking right to her.

I stormed off, determined to find Talan. David was the only knight keeping a bedside vigil. Byron was there as well. He must have won the battle with Robert of Dawes.

"I've stopped the bleeding," was the blunt reply from the dwarf when I asked how Talan was.

"They are burying Sir Gaheris," whispered David. He was clenching Talan's sword between his knees. "I wanted to be there, to pay my respects, but what if Sir Talan was to die alone? I would never forgive myself."

"You did the right thing, David," I said quietly, and I kissed the top of his head. "You're an amazing knight, and an even better friend."

"I should probably go find them," replied Arthur. He had followed me to Talan's makeshift hospital bed, but we hadn't spoken. I was still too angry.

"They are also burying Sir Ronan," added Byron. He was pulling apart strips of white cloth.

Sickening shame engulfed me. I could feel it from my toes to my fingers and it was burning hot. I had willed Ronan's death. Made a pact with the Grim Reaper. Let us keep Talan and take a lord of Caerleon in his place. Yet another death was now on my conscience.

"Are you ailing?" barked Byron, tugging at my tunic. "You look too pale, Lady Natasha."

"I need Bedivere," I gasped. "Find him, Arthur. Find him now."

Several figures swept into the large room, just as my legs betrayed me. A mop of long, straggly chestnut hair flew through the air and caught me, just as I was about to slip away. Two green starlights pulled me back.

"You need to sleep, my love."

Words started tumbling out of my mouth. Incoherent and twisted. I wasn't making sense to myself, let alone those around me. Bedivere and Arthur combined to prop me against a wall. Tristram poured warm oily water into my mouth, but it went the wrong way and got trapped in my nose.

I once had a panic attack on the New York subway. Power failure. I was trapped. I couldn't get out. The same was happening now. The black, wet walls of Camelot were closing in around me. I was never going to leave. I wanted to go home, but I didn't know where home was. I was floating into space: airless and lost. Making stupid pacts with Death, only to find Death was a willing player.

"Breathe slower, Titch," prompted Arthur, massaging my bent knees. "In and out, in and out."

"Is she asthmatic, Arthur?" asked a Scouse accent.

"No," replied my brother, who was still attempting CPR via my knee-caps. "Just prone to the hysterical."

"Like most women," said Robert.

They laughed, and then abruptly stopped when I swore at them.

My breathing steadied, but something still wasn't right. There was the threat of unfinished business hanging in the air. A black cloud. Lightning was waiting to strike. Then, as I saw the fork of brilliant white blaze from the heavens in my head, it changed shape. The sharp angles became softer, curved. It morphed into a scythe.

Death. He wasn't finished with me yet.

My eyes sprang open. The knights I had come to know and love were standing in an arc around Talan and me. No one was watching the door.

Not one person was staring in the direction of the figure in black, who had slipped into the room unnoticed. They couldn't sense the treacherous intent, because their lives were bound by honour.

Not one person saw the glint of silver, a moonbeam, reflected from the long blade that was raised into the air.

Except me.

"NO."

I've always been good at running. I had the legs for the sport, and they didn't fail me. The wall was my starting block as I heard the gun shot in my head. I knew I would win. I had the quickest instincts for the fight.

The blade slashed down, but I was through the tape first. It broke across my stomach. I heard the roar of the crowd.

I had won.

I lay on the cold ground, trying to catch my breath. It wouldn't come. I saw Tristram bundle Archibald out of the room. He still had the knife in his hand: the blade that was to avenge his sister, Lady Fleur. It had been meant for Bedivere, but I had come first.

Dark shadows started to play with my eyes. Amorphous blobs swam across my vision. I had a stitch in my side from the running. I had become very unfit because it was hurting.

And then I was in Bedivere's arms. Finally. I wanted to go to sleep in them, but Arthur and Robert of Dawes were screaming at me to keep my eyes open.

Bedivere was crying. I couldn't understand why was he doing that? It made his eyes red and swollen. Blue was the colour of pain, but green would always be my favourite.

I was so tired. I just wanted to sleep – just for a few minutes.

The world had become very bumpy. Didn't they know I was trying to sleep? And it was hot. So very hot and wet. I was drowning in my own perspiration. I hated being sweaty because my clothes would cling to my skin and make me feel fat.

I wanted to sleep in Bedivere's arms.

Bedivere kissed my face continuously. His stubble was back. I couldn't remember what year razors were invented. My legs and underarms needed one desperately. The stitch in my side was still there. It was hurting even more, even though I had stopped running hours ago. *Bump, bump, bump.*

I just wanted to sleep.

I heard Arthur arguing with someone. It was definitely a female. I thought he was breaking up with Slurpy - at last. Hope didn't make the pain go away, or the sweat. My gums felt swollen. My throat lined with spikes. The white fluffy clouds above me looked like blankets. Warm and inviting. I couldn't hear Camelot screaming anymore, but there was crying.

And still Bedivere held me in his arms. I was home.

A haze of blue. I was scared. I wanted the green of home. Where was Bedivere? Where was my brother? Hands started to lift me, and then Bedivere arrived.

"It has to be me."

His voice was breaking. Wind chimes in the breeze. The gentle lapping of water on the shore. *Bump, bump, bump.* I was rocked from side to side. The pain had spread from my stomach. It was everywhere. It wasn't just a stitch anymore, although I was still out of breath. This was a fire. I was Joan of Arc, martyred in flame.

"We aren't all going to fit."

Slurpy. She was haunting my sleep.

"We have to. I'll keep her alive."

Robert of Dawes. Desperate.

"I swore an oath to protect her."

My Bedivere. I felt his calloused hands on my face. His tears mingled with mine as he kissed me. Why was he saying goodbye?

"The Vale of Avalon is the only place that can save Natasha now."

They were taking me away. Pulling me from Bedivere. No, I wouldn't let them.

"She's rocking the boat."

It worked. I felt Bedivere's breath on my face. He smelt of warm bread. Delicious.

"I will find you, Natasha. If I have to travel through the boughs of time itself, I will find you."

I opened my eyes and saw starlight. It was my earring: the small diamond stud I had fixed to Bedivere's cloak before the battle of Camelot.

"I love you."

"I will love you until the end of all things."

"Please don't let them take me away."

Bedivere started to pull away. I tried to grab him, but I couldn't raise my body. I was in Hell. Death was taking me. I was in Charon's boat, crossing the water to the Underworld.

"Stay with me, Titch. Stay with me. Squeeze my hand. No. Don't close your eyes. Keep them open – keep them open. We're going home, back to mum and dad. Just hang in there, just hang on. For me."

The figures on the shoreline raised their hands. I heard their voices, but one by one they fell away. My eyes stayed on that little glint of starlight, until the clouds closed in around us.

I saw Eve, smiling shyly; her beautiful red hair floated around her head, like she was suspended in water. Maidens with covered faces, and monks in sacks;

they were counting glistening gold coins. Sir Gaheris, a dragon roaring on his tunic, saluted us as we passed through. Then Sir Ronan, red-faced, eating a chicken leg and laughing.

Finally, a little blonde-haired boy in a blue t-shirt.

"You have to let me go," he called.

The mist and cloud became thicker and darker. It whispered like the wind. It gave me permission to sleep, and finally, I closed my eyes.

30 ON THE MOVE AGAIN

I could feel hands on my ankles. I yelped in fear of the ghosts, and threw myself forward towards the blurred figure in my peripheral vision.

"Titch, Titch, it's alright," cried a familiar voice. "You're safe now."

A thin beam of light shone directly overhead. I became aware of the burning smell of bleach and antiseptic in my nostrils.

No. Not again.

I forced my eyes to remain shut. Strange, zigzagged shapes floated across the darkness. Blankets were tucked in around my body, but I still managed to click my bare heels together.

There's no place like home, there's no place like home.

"Natasha, open your eyes sweetheart. You're safe now."

It was my mother's voice. My father was there too; I could hear him breathing – snorting – through his nose. I was used to people telling me I had inherited it. That was why I snored.

Snoring and running – such gifts to bestow.

Arthur had told Bedivere I snored.

The tears forced my eyes to open. I was going to drown in them if they remained shut.

Arthur was there. My tall, gangly brother. He was standing at the end of the bed. It had been his cold hands on my ankles. He was wearing faded ripped jeans and a white t-shirt. A few bruises and cuts had joined the freckles, but he was clean, even if his hair was still all over the place.

"Go tell them she's awake, Arthur," ordered my mother. Her pale blue eyes were glistening.

Arthur didn't move, and so she snapped the request again.

"Let him stay, Iraine," said my father, placing a hand on my mother's bony shoulder. "I'll go find the doctor."

My father's smile was warm with relief as he left the small box-like hospital room. The ends of his dark brown moustache flared outwards as his muscles stretched. I knew I was in a private hospital room because I was the only patient in it. Health insurance was essential in the middle of nowhere.

"Do you know where you are?" asked my mother.

I nodded.

"And do you know who we are?"

I looked at Arthur through the tears. Why was my mother treating me like an imbecile? Why was I here? Why had he taken me away from Bedivere?

I could hear voices outside in the corridor. The door opened, and in walked three men: my father, a young male dressed in blue scrubs, and the man with a voice that did belong here.

Robert of Dawes had joined my wake.

"So, you're conscious at last, Natasha," said the young male in blue scrubs. "That's excellent, excellent. Now, I'm going to take a few vitals, and ask you a couple of questions. Nothing too taxing to begin with.

A consultant will be here in a moment, he's just been paged."

He continued to babble on as he checked my pulse, shone a light in my eyes and prodded and poked my stomach.

I still had a painful stitch from the running.

"Do you remember Mr. Dawes?" asked my mother. "He was the one who found you all. He saved your lives."

"It was nothing," replied Robert, gazing down at me. He appeared smaller now than in my dream.

But it wasn't a dream. It was real.

"Stop being so modest, Robert," said my father, slapping him on the shoulder. "Our family will be forever in your debt. If you hadn't found Arthur and Natty when you did, then we can't even begin to think what might have happened."

When did my father start calling me Natty?

"Can I speak to Arthur please?"

My voice sounded like a child's.

Not a ripple of movement. I simply didn't exist. Not in this world, not in this time. Not anymore.

"I want to speak to Arthur – alone please."

But instead of leaving, the crowd around my bed increased as the door was thrown open again. In walked a tall, severe-looking man in a pinstripe suit. His tie, which was thin and knotted tightly against his rash-covered throat, was flung over his shoulder. "And how is our patient this afternoon?" said the man to the doctor in blue scrubs. Clearly I wasn't capable of answering for myself. He snatched away my medical file and ran a pen across the scribbled notes. Then he repeated the prodding and poking, paying particular attention to my stomach. As he pulled down the bed covers, I realised for the first time my stomach was heavily padded. The pain provided me with my first smile.

It hadn't been a dream, and I would have a scar to prove it.

"Does this hurt?"

"Yes."

"And does it hurt here?"

"Yes."

"And here?"

"Where are my clothes?"

"Natty, just answer the specialist," ordered my father.

When the hell did I become Natty? It's Natasha or Titch. I would take *freak* over a name that sounded like an insect. These people didn't know me at all.

"Where are my clothes?" I repeated. "The ones I was wearing."

"Those disgusting strange things have been thrown away," replied my mother impatiently. "Now answer the specialist. Does it hurt where he is pressing?"

"Arthur."

I winced as I pleaded with my brother to help me. He was a king. Couldn't he order these people to obey him?

"I have to go pick up Sammy," mumbled Arthur. My mother and father nodded, giving him permission to leave. He wasn't a protector of kingdoms anymore. He was a child.

"Don't leave me," I begged.

Arthur crossed the bleached floor in a couple of strides. The pinstripe specialist was talking to my mother and father; I was happy for him to ignore me. I had more important things to worry about, like how I was going to get back home to Bedivere and the others. Arthur bent down and kissed my forehead.

"We'll talk later," he whispered, pressing something small and hard into my hand. "Just keep quiet for now, even around Robert."

Robert Dawes – I assumed he had now lost the *of* – must have overheard Arthur, because he started to say his own goodbyes in his thick Scouse accent. My mother hurried across the room to him, knocking my notes off the food trolley as she went. She hugged him awkwardly.

"You must come to dinner. Luther can get a table anywhere in the country with his contacts."

Someone take me away from this, I thought, as my fingers closed tightly around the small hard object that Arthur had passed to me. I knew what it was without looking. It was the only physical reminder I now had of Logres and the people in it.

It hadn't been a dream.

Sleep came for me again, and I willingly ran into its arms.

I had been unconscious for three days, and I was discharged from hospital five days after that. It was almost a month to the hour since I had first been admitted after falling into the grave. The specialist wouldn't let me leave until the IV was removed from my arm. I tried to take it out myself, but that just gave me another bruise to add to the collection. What a macabre hobby I now had.

My father was called away to New York. Something to do with the UN Security Council. I was left alone with my mother, Arthur and *her*.

Most of the time I remained hidden in my bedroom. Having the box room finally paid off as it was too cramped for visitors. The people of nowhere all called on *Avalon Cottage* to see how I was, but I left my mother to deal with them. I didn't want them. I didn't need them.

The stab wound inflicted by the treacherous

Archibald healed. Inflamed red skin turned to pink. It should have been blue. Lives returned to normal and the press - who had devoured the tale of the three missing teenagers that had returned from the dead in the arms of a rambler - gave up, and went back to their desks.

I was given another watch to replace the one that had stopped working after the Solsbury Hill attack. The new one was gold. Swiss. Expensive apparently. I didn't care about time anymore. I gave up caring about anything, as the pain where my heart should have been grew larger every day. Bedivere was the first person I thought about when I woke up, and the last person I remembered before falling into my nightmares. Every moment of time in between was consumed by him as well. I couldn't eat; I could barely breathe. Going to school was out of the question, but after a while even my English teachers stopped sending me coursework to read through. I had become a ghostly imprint. Everyone else was moving forward, but I was stuck in the past.

A thousand years in the past.

Autumn became winter, and a thick layer of white smothered everything. It didn't stop Arthur and me from our daily walks, which were getting longer and longer as my strength returned. We were both looking without saying.

But we couldn't find the hidden grave. The past had closed itself off to us.

It was the not knowing that was slowly killing me. Had another enchanted, ageing sleep been placed over the kingdom of Logres? If I did find Bedivere once more, would he be the green-eyed angel of my dreams, or the crumbling blind warrior of my nightmares?

So we looked for the answers – hour after hour, day after day.

Our parents freaked out, of course. They tried to ban us from the woods, and when that failed, they did the only thing left open to them. The one thing they were good at.

I was in my bedroom. Hailstones the size of acorns were bouncing from the sky. I took out my own acorn and held it in my white palm. My skin was loose and puckered.

What if I plant you? I thought to myself. Would you grow into a beanstalk and take me back to Logres?

Don't you think it is time to give up on the fairy tales? It's been nearly four months.

"I'll never give up," I whispered. "Not on them, not on him."

But everyone is starting to give up on you. The concerned mother act lasted less than a week. Your father has abandoned you again. Even Arthur prefers the company of Slurpy.

"Please leave me alone."

I am the only thing that is with you now, and even that is because I can't get away.

"Leave me alone."

You're pathetic, is it any wonder you don't have any friends? You could die tomorrow and no one would come to your funeral. There would be no Facebook tribute page for a psycho loser like you.

I put my hands over my ears and leant forward. The condensation from the single-glazed window squelched under my forehead. I could smash my head through this window and the pain would be glorious. Anything to remove the agony in my head.

"SHUT UP, SHUT UP, SHUT UP," I cried, smacking my head against the glass.

There was a gasp behind me, but no *exchange of words*. What else was there left for my mother to say?

That moment, though, was the end of *Avalon Cottage*.

My mother was still paranoid about terrorists, but now she assumed the threat was closer to home, because it was the terrorists in my head that were going to be the death of us all. And so it was her perception of my sanity – or lack of – which stopped her and my father from telling us we were running away, yet again.

Arthur and I were out when the removal vans trundled up the snow-covered lane beside *Avalon Cottage*. We were trying to find the tomb, of course. So we never saw five men jump out with packing boxes and bubble wrap. I never saw them dismantle my bedroom.

I was too busy looking for my heart.

Thankfully, the acorn from the Falls of Merlin was in my pocket when my mother cleared out the debris from my room. Otherwise I had no doubt it would have been the first item into the black garbage bag. Arthur had salvaged it from the pocket of my torn and bloodied clothes as we went into the mist. It was my only link to Bedivere. The only proof I had that Logres and he existed outside of the myths and legends.

Any legend will have its foundations in a truth.

Bedivere said those words to me before our first kiss. Our first proper kiss. What happened in the hall of Caerleon didn't really count. My truth remained in my pocket. Magic at my fingertips.

Slurpy became hysterical when she found out we were moving. She ran up the drive as Arthur's brass bed frame was carried into one of the removal trucks. Her begging became threatening when it became obvious my parents were not going to back down. Arthur promised to visit her all the time, but it wasn't enough for the witch. Slurpy turned on me – naturally. It was my fault we were leaving. The freaky little sister that needed locking up.

Her vicious bitching bounced off me, until she got in my face and told me she was going to find the tomb if it killed her. She was going back to Logres, and she would make Bedivere suffer like she was suffering now.

We were eventually pulled apart by several of the removal men, who far from being professional packers, were actually Australian back-packers looking to earn enough money to fly home to the sun and surf. They didn't get paid danger money.

They wouldn't have lasted ten seconds in Logres.

My nineteenth house in seventeen years was a Georgian terrace townhouse in the heart of London. I was given a room on the second floor. The window was locked and barred before we arrived. A new psychiatrist was employed to help rid me of the terrorists in my head. At our first appointment she asked me what I wanted.

"To go home."

No one, other than Arthur, understood that home was a thousand years in the past. I could have unburdened my head and the gaping chasm where my heart once was, but what was the point?

The psychiatrist would have thought I was lying.

31 FIVE FRIENDS

I had nothing left to cling to. Nothing. Other girls split with their boyfriends and they still have letters, cuddly bears, or images on a cell phone to gaze at.

I had zilch, zip, nothing.

I did try to live, I really did. But there's a difference between living and existing, and I was firmly sucked into the latter. Arthur was the only person I could really talk to, but he was facing his own demons, namely a girlfriend who was a constant presence in our house, whether she was physically there or not. If it wasn't the never-ending beeping of text messages, it was the Skyping. If it wasn't the Skyping it was Twitter – 140 characters being all she could coherently manage. Slurpy was on every flat screen in the house and my hatred of her was now at pathological levels. I knew she was trying to recreate the blue flame; I heard her whispering the mumbo-jumbo when she thought she was alone. Perhaps it only worked in Logres, but her emerald eyes stayed the same colour. When I wasn't thinking about Bedivere, I was having waking nightmares about what I would like to do to her. She had everything she wanted and I had nothing.

It wasn't fair.

Arthur came in from his part-time job one Saturday evening with a plastic bag. Mother and I were attempting to eat dinner. There really is nothing more pathetic than two people who cannot eat for grief.

The bag was handed to me.

"Present," announced Arthur. "You like books, and I thought you'd like this one."

"How thoughtful, Arthur," said my mother, rising with her plate of untouched food in her hand. "Now eat up, Natasha," she added.

Natty, and the pretences that came with it, were dropped once we left Wales.

I took the bag from Arthur with one hand, and continued to roll a butter-coated potato around my plate with the other.

"Well look inside, you ungrateful wench."

My mother exclaimed her shock at Arthur's language from the kitchen, but it actually made me grin. The knotted muscles near my earlobes ached, as they were finally put to use after months of inactivity.

"It's been a while since anyone called me that."

"Wench."

"I thought I was a knight."

"Wenchly knight then."

"Supreme knight."

"Still not as cool as king."

"A king who got captured by a girl within ten seconds of going back."

"Look who's talking. And how many times did you get kidnapped?"

"That was different."

"Because you were a wench."

I kicked at him, but this teasing was the most fun I had had since…Logres. It was normal. I longed for *my* kind of normal.

"Well, look inside the bag, Sir Natty of Nutsville."

I peered inside. It was a small book, leather bound, with one of those frayed string bookmarks that no one ever uses.

"This had better not be anything to do with grammar text or the death of the adverb," I said. My enrolment at a new school had not gone well. The batteries in my freak beacon had been well and truly recharged by another stay in hospital. Fitting in is impossible when you're a square peg trying to fit into a round hole, and already I felt the weight of eyes watching me, marking me out as different, without knowing why.

"You are the world's worst recipient of anything," exclaimed Arthur. "Honestly, if you ever won an Oscar, they would take it straight off you again for being so utterly crap at saying thank you. You're like a fatter Kate Winslet."

Ignoring Arthur, I pulled the book out. It was surprisingly heavy for something so small. The smell of thick paper, real stuff like old parchment, wafted up from the plastic.

Arthurian Legends: Magic, Myths and Men.

"No way."

Arthur's voice dropped to a whisper.

"I know we don't talk about it much anymore, but it doesn't mean it wasn't real. I thought you would like reading this and correcting the myths about the gang until we find a way back one day. Beginning with how awesome I am in real life."

My fingers were already sliding down the index, searching for one name. They didn't go far. The contents were in alphabetical order. I went straight to page eight.

"Read it," I instructed, handing the book to Arthur.

"You read it."

"Just tell me he doesn't marry that Lady Puke

creature. Or any girl for that matter."

Arthur took the book from my trembling hands. I watched his blue eyes flick from right to left as he read down the page.

"Bedivere married three times and had fifteen children," announced Arthur, snapping the book shut. A thin plume of dust exploded skywards.

My stomach turned inside out. The plate of food was knocked to the side as my elbows fell onto the kitchen table. My head slumped into my hands. Carefully balanced cutlery crashed onto the white cold tiles with a noisy clatter.

I had lost him.

"And the Oscar goes to…me," said Arthur, throwing the book at my head.

"What did it say?"

"According to this, Bedivere became a hermit," grinned the anti-Christ. "A life of Godliness and penitence. All done completely on his lonesome."

"That doesn't sound like Bedivere," I replied, rubbing my head where the hard cover had hit me.

"Well, read the title," snapped Arthur. "The book is full of myths. Now I've done my good deed for the day, you should eat some food and then go do your homework."

My father was in London, but not at home. Arthur was taking on the surrogate role again. Things were not going well between our parents, and the gulf that existed between them had become oceanic. Secretly I suspected my father of wishing for terrorists. At least it would give him something to talk about, something to do.

My stomach seemed to be clawing for the food on the plate for once. I ate my cold potatoes and then went to my room with the book.

To my horror, Talan and David were not even mentioned in the fancy italic script. Gareth and his brothers were in there, as was Tristram, who was more famous for being in love than anything else.

Arthur was the obvious presence throughout, although I had to smile at his description: old and naïve, the ultimate in cuckolded husbands. I couldn't bring myself to read anything that mentioned Morgana. The bile rose in my throat the second I saw the name.

Fire at her fingertips? I wanted the flame at her feet.

I left Bedivere's entry for last. I wanted him to slip into my dreams. It would make a change from the nightmares.

There was an image of him. A painting, like a king in a pack of playing cards. Mud brown, wavy hair with matching dirt coloured eyes. This wasn't *my* Bedivere.

A piece of paper fell out of the page. A flyer.

"I thought we could go," said a voice from my doorway.

"A medieval enactment of the infamous battle of Breguoin," I read aloud. "Are you insane?"

"It could be fun."

"I don't want to watch a handful of overweight men with no lives, dress up like knights and pretend to kill each other," I replied. "It makes a total mockery of everything we all went through."

"Well, I'm going," said Arthur, shrugging his shoulders, "and Sammy's coming as well."

I levered myself off the bed, crossed the room and slammed the door in his face.

I could hear him, rustling in the trees. Always ahead of me. A flash of brilliant white turned to a glimmer of green. The trees were beckoning me forward, whispering in the leaves. *He has come, he has come.* My eyes were squinting with the pain of straining. Just one glance, anything. I could hear him breathing. Slow, measured. He was waiting. Biding his time. Then a woman in blue appeared. She was holding a long, thin dagger, shaped and coloured like a frozen icicle. I was back in my little room in *Avalon Cottage*. The woman started to stride towards me. I expected her movements to be graceful, like rippling water, but they weren't. She was coming for me. I screamed as a bell started ringing.

The alarm clock belched out its harsh cry. The red pixels blinked at me. I watched them change from 7:01 to 7:07 before I could move away from the night terror that had paralysed me.

I slipped on a pair of faded blue skinny jeans and my black leather boots. There had once been a heel on them, but it had worn down. A rainbow striped hoodie, a knitted green hat that covered my ears, and fingerless black gloves were slowly added, layer by layer.

Why was I doing this? It was going to be torturous in every way imaginable.

Arthur was driving, if that hunk of junk called a car held out for long enough. Forget the seventy miles to Winchester. We would be lucky to make it out of London. Plus, Arthur's threat proved prophetic: Slurpy was also coming. She had arrived the night before. Judging by the sounds that filtered out from Arthur's room, it was unlikely either had caught much sleep.

I climbed into the back of Arthur's rust bucket. It stank of spilt milk. For two hours, I pinched my nose and read my book on Arthurian Legends. I ignored the driver – who became lost twice – and the passenger – who was navigating, and therefore the reason we became lost twice. Thankfully, they were so busy arguing I didn't have to contend with them licking each other's face off. I would hitch-hike back to London if they started that.

We reached Winchester before lunch. The sky was

pale grey and the smell of rain was heavy in the air. The enactment was taking place on a farmer's field, just outside of the city. The grass was thick and green and kept short by fat sheep that lumbered around without a care in the world. Evergreen and deciduous trees mixed side by side in large copses. I thought about trying to climb one, just so I could read my book in peace and quiet.

"Hail, noble warriors," cried a man dressed as a court jester. His pointed face kept slipping out of an orange and red hat that was shaped like a starfish. It even had bells on it.

"We're here to watch the battle," replied Arthur. He was grinning.

"That'll be ten pounds each," replied the jester, sticking out a hand with long dirty fingernails.

Arthur paid. Neither Slurpy nor I bothered to take our hands out of our pockets. Three more flyers were handed to us with the afternoon's events: maypole dancing, a joust, and fighting in the ring. The battle had been cancelled because half of the enemy were stuck on the M4 motorway after their coach broke down.

"This is such a stupid idea," I mumbled, burying my cold face into the neck of my hoodie.

"Stop complaining," replied Arthur. "I'm the one who has paid for this."

"I need coffee," said Slurpy, lighting a cigarette. "Can you get me one, babe?"

I walked over to a group of middle-aged women who were dressed in long dresses. The low scooped necklines showed off their wrinkled cleavages. They beamed broadly at me.

"It's nice to see some young blood here," remarked one. She was turning blue with the cold, although she wasn't shivering. "Is this your first time, love?"

"Not exactly," I replied, wishing to be polite without lying.

The women were sheltering under a large tent. It was royal purple with long, bright yellow tassels. Every time the wind blew they fluttered in the breeze, like strands of fluorescent hair.

Suddenly a tune gripped at my insides. Wind chimes. The sound took my breath away. It was unmistakable. I had it memorised.

"Pretty, aren't they, love?" said one of the women. "Only twenty pounds each, thirty if you buy two."

My excitement was extinguished. Hanging from the roof of the tent, on a thick piece of nylon wire, were scores of wind chimes. Their long, thin metal flutes gently knocked against each other as the tassels fluttered.

"They're lovely," I replied. There would be no sale.

Men dressed in glinting golden armour mingled with the crowds, happily posing for photos with children who had been thrust towards them by over-zealous parents, determined to have a good time. I couldn't see Arthur or Slurpy, and so I bought a hot chocolate and went to sit in one of the tiered stands that had been erected for the spectators. My book was tucked safely into the large front pocket of my hoodie. Along with the acorn, the book was turning into my favourite possession.

The maypole dancing had thankfully finished and the joust was about to start when I heard the wind chimes again, this time matched by a deep baritone bell. They seemed to be battling to be the loudest. At that very same moment, my scar, now a faded seven inch curve across my stomach, started to tingle.

I pulled the book out of my pouch, just as a large bottomed woman pushed past me. Balancing myself, the scalding hot chocolate, and the book took too much coordination, as the tiered seats wobbled precariously. The book fell between the gaps, onto the muddy grass below.

"Move over," wheezed the enormous arse - all I could see above me was dimpled flesh squeezed into pale pink leggings. It wasn't pleasant.

A voice crackled over the loud speaker. The knights were being introduced for the joust. My ears pricked up as I heard the name David, but it was just a person called David Barnes from Rochester. As I made my way to the steps leading down, I saw a black horse rearing in the foreground. David of Barnes was having trouble keeping hold of his balsa wood lance and the reins. It seemed obvious to all that his horse would unseat the rider without the need for a challenger.

I clambered over slippery steel construction rods and headed underneath the stand towards my book. It had fallen open at the page describing Merlin.

Then I heard the wind chimes for a third time. They were distant, muffled. A bell rang out. It had one tone, but it echoed into the country air with a musicality I had never heard from a church bell before. Something started to surge into my bloodstream. It was uncomfortable. A feeling of nervousness tempered by the threat of disappointment. The kind of anxiety I used to get before a race.

"Nimue, are you here?" I whispered, crouching down low under the stand.

"Talking to yourself again, freak?"

The tingle in my stomach was swamped by the fire of hatred ignited by that Welsh voice. It was a little scary, feeling so out of control. Knowing that if I could get away with it, I would cause her real harm.

"If I hear you call my sister that again..." said Arthur angrily.

"It was a joke," whined Slurpy.

"No it wasn't," snapped Arthur, "and I'm telling you both now, I'm sick to death of being in the middle of your constant fighting."

"She started it," we cried.

"And I'm ending it," yelled Arthur. "If you two actually made the effort, the pair of you could be friends, you know."

"Hell will freeze over first."

The joust had started. Feet were drumming the metal stands, and every few minutes a roar would rise up into the grey sky, as a would-be knight was sent crashing to the ground. Yet the three of us continued to argue like children.

It was Arthur who heard the ringing of the bell next. He stopped snapping like a piranha, and looked around the steel structure we were all sheltering under. I had seen the expression on his face before. He had starlight in his eyes.

"You can hear it too, can't you?"

"Hear what?" asked Slurpy; she was looking slightly fatter in the face. She was the only person in the world who could put on weight and still look gorgeous.

"A bell," replied Arthur softly. He stared at me, and then levered himself out through the poles.

"Don't you dare run off again, Arthur," I called, following closely.

A huge groan surged out from the crowd. The tannoy announced a draw. They hadn't paid ten pounds each for that. They were baying for fallen warriors, dented armour and splintered wood.

"Titch."

There was urgency in Arthur's voice.

"What is it?"

I drew level with him. He was staring in the direction of a copse of trees. Grouped together were five figures. Two had their hands on their hips and appeared to be deep in serious conversation. Another was gesticulating wildly as he watched the unfolding joust. Another two were lazing back against the thick, sturdy trunks of a couple of trees.

There was a rush of blood to my head. If my skull hadn't been there to stop it, my brain would have exploded into a million pieces with the force. I felt pressure behind my eyes, in the tubes of my ears and nose. I think my stomach was in my mouth and it was the consistency of custard.

Arthur and I took several paces forward. A cheer from the crowd. The figure who had been gesticulating wildly was now on his knees, pounding the ground with his fists. A tall male with curly blonde hair was laughing at him.

Another of the figures caught sight of Arthur and me. His face, which was round and plump, broke into a huge friendly smile. He motioned to one of the males leaning back against a tree. I couldn't hear what the other person was saying, but from the way his mouth was moving, it was clear he was singing.

Why were my cruel eyes playing tricks on me? And why was Arthur complicit? This wasn't real – it was a mirage. A happening when your desperate senses combine to betray your brain.

The fifth figure was now separating from the group of friends. My eyes were not drawn to the deep green windows that fizzed in the grey conditions. Instead, they were drawn to a sparkling pinprick attached to his olive coloured tunic.

An earring. Lost over a thousand years ago.

The figure was racing towards me. The cracked edges of his thin mouth started to rise. It would have been optimistic to call it a smile, but it was an attempt.

I started running.
I've always been good at running.

ABOUT THE AUTHOR

Donna Hosie is an English writer currently living in
Australia. She blogs at Musings of a Penniless Writer
and has written extensively for the Harry Potter
fandom. *Searching for Arthur* is her first novel.

TITLES IN THE RETURN TO
CAMELOT TRILOGY

5058275R00166

Printed in Great Britain
by Amazon.co.uk, Ltd.,
Marston Gate.